Readers love Faith Ma

'A must read for all crime fiction fans'

'Have become an addict of Faith Martin – love her novels'

'Cracking good read'

'Plenty of action and drama to keep the reader gripped through to the end'

'I would recommend this to anyone who enjoys crime fiction'

'Compelling murder mystery'

'Fabulous police procedural'

FAITH MARTIN has been writing for nearly thirty years, under four different pen names, and is about to have her fiftieth novel published. She began writing romantic thrillers as Maxine Barry, but quickly turned to crime! As Joyce Cato she wrote classic-style whodunits, since she's always admired the golden-age crime novelists. But it was when she created her fictional DI, Hillary Greene, and began writing under the name of Faith Martin, that she finally began to become more widely known. Her latest literary characters, WPC Trudy Loveday and city coroner Dr Clement Ryder, take readers back to the 1960s, and the city of Oxford. Having lived within a few miles of the city's dreaming spires all her life (she worked for six years as a secretary at Somerville College), both the city and the countryside/wildlife often feature in her novels. Although she has never lived on a narrowboat (unlike DI Hillary Greene!), the Oxford canal, the River Cherwell, and the flora and fauna of a farming landscape have always played a big part in her life – and often sneak their way onto the pages of her books.

Also by Faith Martin

A Fatal Mistake

FAITH MARTIN

ONE PLACE. MANY STORIES

This novel is entirely a work of fiction. The names, characters and incidents portrayed in it are the work of the author's imagination. Any resemblance to actual persons, living or dead, events or localities is entirely coincidental.

HQ
An imprint of HarperCollins*Publishers* Ltd
1 London Bridge Street
London SE1 9GF

HarperCollins*Publishers*
1st Floor, Watermarque Building, Ringsend Road
Dublin 4, Ireland

This paperback edition 2022

13
First published in Great Britain by
HQ, an imprint of HarperCollins*Publishers* Ltd 2018

ISBN: 9780008321086

MIX
Paper from
responsible sources
FSC
www.fsc.org   **FSC˚ C007454**

This book is produced from independently certified FSC™ paper
to ensure responsible forest management.

For more information visit: www.harpercollins.co.uk/green

Printed and bound in Great Britain by
CPI Group (UK) Ltd, Melksham, SN12 6TR

For all my new Ryder and Loveday readers

Chapter 1

Summer 1960

Jimmy Roper stopped to let Tyke, his ageing but still inquisitive black-and-white mongrel, cock his leg against the wall overlooking Port Meadow. It was a glorious morning in mid-June and, overhead, the sun shone with an intensity that warned him the temperature would skyrocket come noon.

It was not the sort of day, you'd have thought, when anything bad could possibly happen.

The village of Wolvercote lay mostly behind him now, but from someone's open window a wireless was playing the latest pop tune that all the youngsters nowadays seemed to find so enthralling. An obliging DJ told him he'd been listening to the Everly Brothers' April hit, 'Cathy's Clown'.

As he approached the large expanse of Port Meadow, he paused to observe a really fine view of the legendary 'dreaming spires' of Oxford. In front of him, the river wound its way through the water meadow, which was just now ridding itself of its spring blaze of buttercups. Tyke happily sniffed about among the thistles.

As he approached the riverbank, he noticed that two fishermen had set themselves up for a day's sport. One, sitting at the top of

1

the bank with his legs dangling over the side, had on an old, floppy, wide-brimmed hat. This served not only to keep the direct sun off his head, but no doubt helped stop the garish sunlight reflecting off the water and into his eyes. It was festooned with colourful fishing flies. He had his head down and was watching his float intently. After a second or two, Jimmy also spotted it – a red spot making its way gently downstream.

His companion also wore a hat and, for added measure, was wearing a pair of large sunglasses. He'd elected to sit closer to the river's edge, at a spot where the rather steep bank had given way, and the previous tenants (a herd of Friesian cows) had trampled down a path in order to drink. He seemed to be dozing, though, rather than watching his float, for Jimmy noticed it had been allowed to catch in a patch of river weed.

He wished them both a courteous but quiet 'good morning' and, not wanting to disturb the fish, walked with a lighter tread as he passed them.

He hadn't gone much further, following the course of the river absently upstream, when he became aware of a gaggle of voices. Youthful and bantering, they sounded like something you'd hear at a party, and were thus oddly out of place in the peaceful country setting.

Rounding an oxbow in the river, he suddenly noticed a gay crowd congregating on the banks in front of him and had no problem identifying them as students, intent on enjoying the end of their exams.

Some of the young women in the group – at least twenty strong, Jimmy estimated – had already laid down gaily striped beach towels on the grass and were setting out the beginnings of a picnic. At barely eleven o'clock in the morning, Jimmy wondered whether it was supposed to be a late breakfast or a really early lunch. Then he supposed that, to these bright young things, it hardly made much difference. He noticed that strawberries, boxes of chocolates, fruit and bottles of wine featured predominantly.

Which was very nice for some, he thought, a shade enviously.

Clearly no dark thoughts could have been passing through the minds of these happy young things. They were out to enjoy their youth, the sunshine of the day, and the delights of an alfresco party. To them, death was a foreign concept, something that wouldn't have to be considered for many decades yet.

Besides, on a day such as this what could possibly happen?

One young woman, with a mane of silvery fair hair, patted the place beside her on a towel and a young lad, who looked barely eighteen, hastened to join her.

Jimmy was pretty sure the fishermen downstream wouldn't be best pleased by all the noise and frolicking about. Every self-respecting pike, chub, dace, roach and perch within a quarter mile must have heard them thumping about and skedaddled for quieter waters!

One or two of the young men were quickly stripping down to their bathing trunks, obviously intent on cooling off in the water.

He meandered on, smiling as one of the (rather pretty) girls shrieked as a lad scooped water over the side of the bank and splashed her. As he went past the group, however, he noticed a tall, freckle-faced man with a head of shockingly vibrant red hair, standing a little bit away and on the outskirts of the scene, watching with an expression of disdain on his face. This, and the fact that he looked to be in his mid-twenties at least – and thus a few years older than the average student – made him look out of place.

Jimmy was too intent on reaching the shade of some nearby trees to stop and pay any attention to the strangers and their doings. But as he walked on, he suddenly saw, up ahead, a plethora of disembodied heads floating along in what seemed to be the middle of the river. For a moment it brought him up short, but then, as they came better into sight, he realised they were just yet more revellers, arriving via two large punts.

Punts, he noticed with a look of mixed alarm and amusement, that looked vastly overloaded and were lying very low in the water. Surely there shouldn't be *that* many of them crammed onto each craft? What was more, both of the lads who were standing on the rear platforms and wielding long punting sticks looked a little the worse for wear!

And even as he watched, the punting youth on the lead boat called out some request to one of his passengers, who was sprawling dangerously close to the waterline. Thus admonished, the very slender youth, dressed casually in white slacks and shirt, and with a head of hair so fair it was almost white, reached obligingly underneath him and produced what looked suspiciously like an open bottle of champagne, which he handed up to his friend.

The young man accepted it with a cry of triumph and casually stopped work to swig from it, tottering back a step. He would almost certainly have ended up in the river if someone else hadn't reached out just in time to grab his trouser leg and haul him back again.

Naturally, this caused a load of heckling and good-hearted chaffing from the others, and Jimmy shook his head, not sure whether to laugh indulgently at the youthful shenanigans or to self-righteously wonder just what the world was coming to.

He finally reached the welcome shade of a line of trees that skirted the village road, and sat down on an old tree trunk. Tyke, glad to rest his old bones, gave a little grunt of satisfaction as he lay down at his master's feet in the cool, shaded grass.

If some dogs actually did possess such a thing as an intuition for evil, or a sense of impending calamity, Tyke wasn't troubled by such a gift.

And so, for about ten minutes, the retired milkman and his little dog simply sat there, listening to the drone of bees and watching yellow-brimstone and orange-tip butterflies flitting about the meadow. Then a quick glance at his watch told him that his wife would be getting his lunch on soon so, with a small sigh, he got up and began the return journey. If he didn't miss his guess, it would be fish-paste sandwiches and a slice of her Madeira cake – one of his favourites.

As he retraced his route along the river towards the noisy and boisterous student party, he noticed a third punt was following a little way along behind him but paid it little attention. Instead, he gave them all a wide berth, returning to the river only when he was once again beyond the oxbow.

He wasn't surprised, a little later on, to see that neither of the fishermen had remained in their places. He could well imagine how they must have cursed the students for selecting that spot for their revelries.

And so, Jimmy Roper and his dog went back to the village and to their midday meal, neither one of them giving the students so much as another passing thought.

Thus it was left to someone else to stumble upon the tragedy a capricious fate had always had in store for such a bright and beautiful day. Someone, perhaps, who was far less equipped to deal with the consequences of human darkness than an old soldier.

Barely an hour later, Miriam Jenks, a new mother to a rather large and placid baby girl, was pushing her pram down the village street, on her way to the village shop to order in a few necessities. Waiting on the pavement for old Dr Thomas's 'moggy' Morris Minor to pass by, she decided it would be a good idea to get out of the fierce heat. So, she steered the pram onto the hard, flat, grassy path beside the riverbank to take advantage of the shade provided by the willow trees that lined the river course there. As she went along, she started to croon a tune to the baby, who had started to grizzle.

She was still humming the lullaby when something caught her eye, and she looked down to see a human body floating in the water just beside her. Having got caught up in the protruding roots of a particularly large willow, it was being moved gently about in a small eddy, one arm rolling up and down, for all the world as if it was waving at her.

But the young man with dark hair was lying facedown in the water, and she knew at once that he was dead. But even as she thought this, the current moved, and with what seemed to her to be a slow, dreadful and fascinating inevitability, the body turned inexorably onto its back.

Naturally, this made Miriam come over 'all queer', as she was to later tell her best friend. For a moment or two, however, she froze where she was.

But the sight of that face, pale and so pitifully and irrevocably beyond all human help, made her knees fold abruptly beneath her, and she found herself suddenly on the grass. She put out her hands to save herself, but even so, she was now much closer to the edge of the river and the body it cradled.

She noticed his clothes had ballooned, the trapped air helping to keep the boy afloat. She also noticed, fleetingly, that he seemed a good-looking lad and not much above twenty.

So young.

And so dead.

She heard a noise and realised it was coming from her. She was sobbing, softly.

For a second, the body seemed close enough for her to touch, if she reached out, down the bank and across the water – but, of course, she knew that wasn't so. Nevertheless, she saw her hand moving forward, shaking uncontrollably in front of her as if to offer… What? her shocked brain demanded rather scornfully. Succour? Comfort? Help?

A cold voice in the back of her head told her she could provide none of these things.

She began to shiver violently, which made no sense to her. The sun was at the point in the sky when it was almost at its hottest. Even the birds had ceased singing, as if the heat had enervated them.

Feeling sick, she forced herself to her feet and began to run, pushing the pram wildly in front of her and bumping it roughly over the path. Naturally, this delightful motion promptly sent her daughter off to sleep more thoroughly then any lullaby.

She felt absurdly guilty – as if she was abandoning the dead boy when he needed her the most. She almost wanted to turn her head, to make sure he wasn't watching her cowardly retreat with accusing, beseeching eyes.

But she had just enough sense, through the fog of shock, to realise this couldn't possibly be so.

She was still sobbing softly when she emerged once more onto the street proper, frantically stopping the first person she saw, who happened to be an old man wheeling his wheelbarrow to the nearby allotments, and tearfully gasping out what she'd seen.

The old man promptly took her home with him, told his wife to look after her, called the police and then nipped off to the river to see the spectacle for himself.

Obviously, nothing as exciting as this had happened in the village in years!

7

Chapter 2

Nearly one week later, Dr Clement Ryder, a coroner of the City of Oxford, sat at his bench, listening to the court proceedings getting underway at the inquest into the death of Mr Derek Chadworth, aged twenty-one, a former student of St Bede's College, Oxford.

At the age of fifty-seven, the coroner was a tall man, standing at an inch over six foot, with healthy, abundant white hair and somewhat watery grey eyes. And if he was just beginning to have rather more meat on his bones than in his youth, he wore the extra pounds well. The role of coroner was a second career for him after having spent the majority of his adult working life as a renowned surgeon. But not liking to dwell on the reasons for his enforced change of direction, he now watched the courtroom and its denizens with some interest. As was to be expected in a case like this, the public gallery was full, with its fair share of local reporters taking up a jockeying position. The jury, looking both sheepish and self-important, had just taken their places. A police constable waited to give his evidence rather nervously. He looked young and inexperienced, and Dr Ryder hoped he wasn't going to have any trouble keeping him to the point.

Widely known to be a man who didn't suffer fools gladly, he

was in appearance an imposing figure, and many of the members of the public (as well as some of the court officials) watched him warily. He had the look of someone who had no problems whatsoever in juggling such weighty issues as life and death in his obviously capable hands.

He displayed no signs of outward impatience as the proceedings finally got underway. And the first of the court's functions (to assign a name or identity to the deceased) was rapidly disposed of, as Derek's parents had already identified his body.

Having done that, the often much trickier second question – of trying to ascertain exactly how the deceased had come to meet his end – was tackled.

First up was a nervous young mother, who gave her evidence of having seen a body floating in the river near the village of Wolvercote in a rather rushed and whispery voice. Dr Ryder, while handling her kindly, had to demand more than once that she speak up.

Next came the medical man. Dr Ryder knew him, of course – and was most certainly known *by* him! All those who had to give medical evidence in his court understood that no fudging would be tolerated, as it was quite clear he knew as much – if not more – about medicine as those actually giving the evidence! According to Dr Clement Ryder, at least. So it wasn't wholly surprising that police surgeons and pathologists weren't particularly happy when called upon to give evidence while Clement was the presiding coroner. Some of the older brigade, who naturally felt superior to both jury and coroner, and had thus become used to taking it for granted that their word would be taken for law, now refused to set foot in court if he was presiding. Of course, none of them was willing to admit that perhaps they hadn't kept quite as up to date with all the new science and medical practices over the past decade as they should have. And they most certainly weren't willing to concede that his own years as a surgeon gave him the right to show them up in public or drag their mistakes and uncertainties to the attention of the press.

The present medico, however, was of the younger, brasher and more confident generation of men and had no qualms about stating his opinions concerning the medical evidence uncovered in his autopsy. These opinions he proceeded to relate to the jury in no uncertain terms – including the time of death, which he stated as between 8 a.m. and 2 p.m., with a small leeway on either side.

Dr Ryder listened without interruption (a minor miracle in itself, some aficionados of the court might have said) and occasionally even nodded in approval. Mainly because the young man, without condescending or speaking down to the jury in any way, was managing in a clear and concise way to convey the facts.

The cause of death had clearly been drowning. What was more, the water found in the dead man's lungs had been consistent with a second sample taken from the river and it was noted that there was rather a lot of sediment present, suggesting that the water the victim drowned in had been significantly churned up. Furthermore, froth at the mouth and all other signs of death by drowning had been present and meticulously noted. There were no significant signs of anything else untoward – such as a blow to the head of the type so beloved of many penny-dreadful murder-mystery books. Nor were there any scratches on his face or hands, or anything else that might indicate the young man had been in a fight or suffered any other assault upon his person.

Here, the coroner cynically noted that a number of those present seemed vastly disappointed. Evidently they had been hoping for rather more drama – especially the press men.

Unaware of this, however, the young doctor swept blithely on. He had also found alcohol present in the deceased's stomach – not enough to state that he was very drunk, but enough to suggest he perhaps wouldn't have been operating at his best. (Later evidence would prove the young man had been out drinking into the early hours.)

10

When the young doctor finally stepped down, the coroner's brisk thanks ringing as an endorsement in his ears, Clement could see he'd made a good impression on the jury, who were now looking a little more relaxed, if not downright relieved. And it wasn't hard to understand why.

In his two years as a coroner, Clement had come to read juries as clearly as if they were his old medical texts. No matter what the case, he'd learned all juries had certain things in common.

Nearly all of them, for instance, were anxious and aware of the burden being put on them by being called to carry out their civic duty. This was especially apparent in obvious cases of suicide, where none of them wished to add to the burden of bereaved families by labouring the point, and where, nearly always when bringing in this verdict, they included the rider 'while the balance of their mind was disturbed'.

Sometimes they were afraid – if, for instance, the cause of death was particularly harrowing and they knew they would have to listen to horrific evidence, such as some poor farm worker being pulled into a combine harvester or something along those lines.

In the case of a suspicious death – a rare occurrence – there was always the added element of excitement and scandal that gave a particular glow to their cheeks.

Clement had seen all sorts sitting on the jury – working men, housewives, mothers, a smattering of professionals, and the occasional layabout or academic. By and large, though, they were good, honest (if not particularly intelligent), average men and women, who could be relied upon to have common sense and bring in a sound verdict. But if, by any chance, it looked as if they might be about to wander off the straight and narrow and deliver some silly verdict because they'd got a bit above themselves, or had become confused or bamboozled, it was his job to steer them back onto the right path.

Occasionally, a juror would surprise him. But he thought he had the measure of this bunch all right.

The old boy with the rumpled blue suit, for instance, was undoubtedly going to nominate himself as chairman of the committee, and would probably be backed up by the two middle-aged stalwarts from the WI, who were sitting at the far right of the line. A younger woman and two younger men were clearly impatient and wanted only to get it all over with. No doubt they felt they had better things to do. A rather vacant-eyed middle-aged man was actually taking it all in keenly, which was more than could be said for an old woman who was busily knitting something surreptitiously on her lap. As for the rest, they were the usual mix and match to be found anywhere in British society.

After the medical man came one of the boy's tutors, who maintained he'd been a steady, reliable sort of chap, and would almost certainly have passed his exams with a good upper second. As far as he knew, Derek Chadworth had no money worries, or girl trouble, and the last time he'd seen him he had been as bright and breezy as ever. In other words, Clement thought, eyeing the witness indulgently, he was making it clear that the boy had no reason whatsoever to go about chucking himself in the river and thus making such a nuisance of himself.

It went down well with the jury, who could now relax even further, since the nasty little spectre of suicide seemed less likely.

Next up came the boy's parents, his tearful mother making everyone feel sympathetic and uncomfortable in equal measure. She too stated that her son's last letter home had been cheerful, and full of what he intended to do once he'd matriculated. When asked by the coroner, she said her son could swim a bit, after a fashion, but that he wasn't what you'd call 'particularly at home in the water'.

So far, Clement thought, keeping a careful eye on the clock (since one of his remits was to keep the schedule ticking along nicely and make sure things didn't overrun – otherwise his officers tended to get restless), it was all shaping up to be either misadventure or death by accidental drowning.

He expected it to be all over bar the shouting by four o'clock. Which would suit him fine. He was rather looking forward to a round of golf before it got too dark. And he thought if he could find old Maurice Biggleswade at the eighteenth hole, he might win a guinea from him in a bet as to who could get a birdie.

However, as luck would have it, the next few witnesses began to make him sit up and pay closer attention.

First up was the police report. Delivered by a young PC, his evidence was simple enough on the face of it. They had established that, on the day in question, up to fifty or more students had congregated on the banks of the river in Port Meadow to hold an impromptu picnic party in celebration of the end of exams for most of them. This party comprised three separate contingents. First, a group of fifteen or so students had arrived at the banks of the river via bus or motorcar. These had consisted largely of young women and a few young men, who had brought food, towels, bathing dresses and such. A second group had arranged to meet them via punt and had hired two such vessels from nearby Magdalen Bridge, setting off down the river at around 9.30 a.m. However, a third party of students, who had also rented a punt, had just happened to meet up with them and accidentally collided with the other two punts, tipping a large number of students into the river.

A few dry words of query from Clement quickly established that most witnesses, when questioned early on that afternoon (once the body of Derek Chadworth had been pulled out of the river a little downstream), had been clearly rather the worse for drink.

Indeed, the PC admitted with a deadpan face, most of the students had admitted to being a 'bit squiffy' on orange juice and champagne, supplied by Lord Jeremy Littlejohn in his rooms in college, even before setting off to hire the punts. And that, on the journey towards Port Meadow, beer and yet more champagne had been quaffed liberally.

Lord Littlejohn, it became clear, was the sun around whom most of the other students orbited, *the* leading light in student society, and it simply didn't do to disappoint him, or otherwise incur his laconic displeasure. Not if you wanted to be in with the 'in' crowd, anyway!

About half the partygoers had elected to stay 'larking about' on the punts while half had disrobed and swum to shore by the time the third punt arrived and the collision took place.

When asked what the immediate result had been when all three punts collided, tipping the majority of passengers into the river, most students agreed that everyone thought it was 'screamingly funny' and 'a bit of a jape'. Nearly everyone from the original two punts had clambered up and onto the banks, for the river was hardly wide at that point. They then proceeded to strip off all they decently could (and perhaps not so decently in some cases, the constable muttered darkly) in the hope that the hot sun would quickly dry their clothes – and themselves – off.

All those from the third punt, however, had elected to climb back onto their vessel and – amidst much ribald argument over who had caused the accident – head back to Oxford the same way they'd come.

All those questioned were adamant they had heard no calls for help, nor seen anyone in obvious difficulty in the water.

Having given his evidence, the PC left the stand with obvious relief.

Obviously, not every student present at the party had been called to give testimony – only a small cross-section. But it was when these students were called to give more specific evidence that Clement Ryder first began to smell a rat.

First off, one Rt Hon Lady 'Millie' Dreyfuss was called to the stand. A third-year English literature student from Cadwallader College, she stated clearly that, although she hadn't known Derek Chadworth, she was sure he couldn't have been part of the picnic party. She had been in charge of laying on the food and making

14

the travel arrangements, and had delegated some of these chores to three other girls, who'd brought along their boyfriends to help. But they hadn't offered the dead boy a lift in their cars, nor had he been one of the small group of students who'd caught the town bus.

The next witness up was the lad who'd been responsible for the third, 'random' (as Clement had come to think of it) punt. He'd been indignant and hotly insistent that the blame for the dunking hadn't lain with his boating prowess. He claimed the two 'Lord Littlejohn' punts had been meeting end to end across the water when he'd rounded the bend in the river, and that he'd had no chance to avoid a collision.

Since both he and the passengers on his punt were among the most sober of the witnesses questioned – according to the police constable – the coroner could see the jury was inclined to believe him.

He was also quite adamant that the drowned boy had not been a member of his party. As well as having the regulation number of passengers only (and not being vastly overloaded, as everyone freely admitted the other two punts had been), this punt had comprised exclusively engineering students, who were all known to one another.

Clearly, then, Derek Chadworth must have been on one of Lord Jeremy Littlejohn's punts. On the face of it, this seemed by far the most likely explanation, as several witnesses had testified that 'we all poured onto the punts by Magdalen Bridge until there wasn't an inch of space left.' And 'none of us wanted to be left behind, as Lord Jerry gives such great bashes, so we all crammed in.'

However, as the afternoon wore on, it became clear to Dr Ryder that something untoward was afoot. What was more, he wasn't certain the jury had noticed it.

It began simply enough, with one sheepish student after another taking the stand and admitting to being present on a punt, but to having very little real memory of what had happened. 'Had a bit too much champers, I'm afraid' was a familiar litany. As was 'when we all ended up in the drink, I just splashed to the bank as best as I could'. And 'I didn't notice anyone else having any trouble or I'd have helped the poor blighter out'. *But not one of them mentioned seeing or talking to Derek Chadworth before the accident.*

The jury seemed less than impressed with these examples of drunken high jinks, but most of them looked ready to dismiss it as 'one of those things'. The rich upper classes would play. And these things happened.

But Clement wasn't so sure.

Eventually, he decided to take a more active role in order to get some answers, and he chose his victims carefully.

He waited until a theology student by the name of Lionel Gulliver had taken the stand, and – working on the somewhat precarious premise that someone who was training for the church would be less likely to lie under oath – began to question him in earnest.

'So, Mr Gulliver. I take it that, as a potential man of the cloth, you were perhaps… er… a little less the worse for drink than some of your fellow students when you got on the punt at Magdalen Bridge?' he asked, fixing the nervous youth with a flat stare.

Lionel Gulliver, a rather small, neat-looking young man with a quiff of sandy hair and big blue eyes, went a trifle pale. 'Well, I'd had one glass of Lord Littlejohn's Buck's Fizz. To show willing and all that,' he admitted with a gulp.

'But only one?'

'Yes, sir.'

'So you were more aware of your fellow students and surroundings than most of your party?'

'Oh, well, I don't suppose I was quite as… er…' The theology student plucked his collar nervously. 'But, as the good Lord said, let him who is without sin cast the first stone and all that.'

16

Dr Ryder smiled grimly. 'Yes. I fully understand your not wanting to come across as morally superior, Mr Gulliver,' he said sardonically. 'But this is a court of law, and you've taken an oath on the Bible to tell the truth, and these good men and women of the jury need facts if they're to deliver a fair verdict.'

At these steely words, the young man paled even further and visibly stiffened in the witness box.

'Oh, of course.'

'Splendid,' Clement said dryly. 'So, can you tell us… did you know Derek Chadworth by sight?'

'Oh, er… yes, I'd seem him around once or twice.' He went rather red, and then cast a quick, nervous glance towards the public gallery. He then hastily looked away again, his lips firming tightly together.

'And so,' the coroner swept on, 'was Mr Chadworth one of those on the same punt as yourself?'

Again, the young man plucked at his collar and glanced nervously across the courtroom, as if seeking inspiration. But he didn't seem to find any, because he turned a rather miserable-looking face to the coroner and took a deep breath.

'You know, sir, I don't believe he was,' he said reluctantly. Far too reluctantly, in the circumstances, the coroner thought. After all, it should have been a simple enough question to answer – not one that gave the theology student cause for so much angst.

Clement felt a touch of excitement lance up his spine. Yes, he knew it. There was definitely *something* about this case that wasn't quite as cut and dried as it seemed. But what exactly? And why did he have the feeling that all the young men and women who had just testified in his court had been at pains not to speak out of turn about something?

'We understand that both punts were rather overcrowded, Mr Gulliver. Are you quite certain that Derek Chadworth couldn't have got on without your seeing him?' Clement began to probe delicately.

17

'Well, he might have,' the young man said, seizing so gratefully on this olive branch that he positively beamed his relief at the older man. 'Oh, yes, that might have happened, I'm sure.'

Dr Ryder smiled rather grimly to himself. Not so fast, my slippery young fish, he thought, almost fondly. As a doctor, he'd been used to his young interns trying to slip things past him. Not that they'd ever succeeded; if they'd failed to read the notes he'd set them, or had neglected to do the experiments proscribed, he'd always found out about it.

Now he regarded the sweating theology student with a shark-like smile. 'Well, let's see if we can't get to the bottom of this, then,' he said, ignoring his clerk, who was beginning to shift about restlessly. 'Where exactly were you sitting on the punt, Mr Gulliver?'

'Er, right at the back, sir,' the suddenly unhappy student admitted quietly. 'I was going to take over the punting from Bright-Allsopp if he needed relieving, as a matter of fact.'

'So you had all the occupants of the punt in front of you?'

'Er… yes, sir.'

'And did you see Derek Chadworth among them?'

Defeated, the young man was forced to admit he hadn't. With a quick glance at the jury, just to make sure they were paying attention, the coroner dismissed him.

He was then forced to bide his time until he found the next suitable candidate. Of necessity, he now needed a witness from punt number two. Barring a theology student, he finally decided that, of all the witnesses called, one Miss Maria DeMarco, an Italian student of fine art, was his best bet.

As she was called to the stand, he approved her sober and respectful dark-grey skirt and jacket, and her neat little black felt hat. She was not beautiful but had a certain elan. And as he'd expected from someone who looked the epitome of a good Catholic girl, she took her oath in a quiet, serious voice, and looked composed but very uneasy.

He was gentle but firm with her.

'Miss DeMarco, I understand you were on what I shall refer to as the second punt – that is, the punt on which Lord Littlejohn himself was present?'

'That is so, yes.'

'And Lord Littlejohn was the main instigator of the party?'

'Yes, that is so.'

'He invited you?'

'Oh, no. A friend of his did. It wasn't what you would call a very formal affair. Most of those present were good friends of Lord Littlejohn, but his friends had invited some people, and they in turn had brought some people of their own. You see how it was?'

'Yes. This might account for His Lordship having seemingly misjudged just how many punts he would need to convey everyone safely to the picnic site,' Clement said dryly. 'Did you know the deceased?'

Clement had his court officer show her a photograph, provided by the boy's parents, of Derek Chadworth.

'Oh, no,' she said firmly. 'I don't know this man.'

'Would you study his likeness, please, Signorina DeMarco? Fine. Now, tell us. Did you see this man among the party on your punt?'

The Italian girl shrugged graphically. 'I'm not sure. It's hard to say. It was very crowded. Everyone was squished in… like, how you say… sardines in a tin, yes?'

Dr Ryder nodded. 'Yes. But a punt isn't exactly an ocean liner, Miss DeMarco. And the journey from Magdalen Bridge to Port Meadow must have taken you at least twenty minutes.'

'Oh, yes, but most of the time I was talking to my friends – Lucy Cartwright-Jones and Bunny Fleet. I pay no attention to the men. They were rather… er… loud from the beer and wine.'

'I see. When the accident happened, and your punt overturned in the water, you must have been frightened?' He tried another tack craftily.

'Oh, no, I swim like the fishes,' the Italian girl said with magnificent insouciance. 'I was more annoyed to get my lovely clothes wet.'

'I see. Did you notice any of your fellow students struggling to swim to the shore?' he said.

'Oh, no! I would have helped, of course, if I had. But the river was not wide, or deep.'

'No, I see. Well, thank you, Miss DeMarco.'

As he watched the young woman depart, rather impressed by her ability not to let herself be nailed down to a single straight answer, he mentally shook his head.

Why were they all so evasive when it came to talking about the dead boy? To the point that nobody seemed even willing to say whether or not they'd seen him at the party?

'I think we'd better hear now from Lord Jeremy Littlejohn,' Dr Ryder said flatly.

Chapter 3

Probationary WPC Trudy Loveday stifled a yawn and got up from the uncomfortable chair she'd been sitting on for the past four hours. Her posterior felt rather numb, and she was glad to stretch her legs, but as she did so she glanced automatically at the poor man lying in the hospital bed in front of her. He didn't stir. And from what she'd overheard of the doctors' low-voiced consultations with one another earlier that morning, she rather feared he never would.

A car had mounted the pavement and hit Mr Michael Emerson in Little Clarendon Street late last night. The driver had failed to stop, and witnesses hadn't been able to provide a decent description of the vehicle that had knocked him over, breaking his arm and fracturing his skull.

When she'd reported for duty at the station that morning, her superior officer, DI Harry Jennings, had assigned her to sit by his bedside in the event that he regained consciousness and began to speak.

But she hadn't been at the Radcliffe Hospital (ironically, barely a stone's throw from where the poor man had been run down) more than half an hour before she'd begun to suspect the futility of her task. Clearly none of the medical staff believed he would survive, and Trudy felt desperately sorry for the man's wife, who was right now sleeping in the chair on the other side of his bed.

Careful not to wake her, Trudy put down her notebook and pen on the bedside table and walked stiffly to the window to look outside.

The hospital was a large and beautiful pale-stone building, rather Palladian in style, surrounding a central courtyard on three sides, with Cadwallader College on the right-hand side of it, and a stand of old cedars to the left. As she glanced out at the soot-blackened pub on the opposite side of Woodstock Road, she blinked a little in the bright sunlight.

It was another hot summer's day and very warm in the ward, and underneath her black-and-white uniform she was uncomfortably aware that she was perspiring a little. At least she didn't have to wear her policewoman's hat indoors, but her long, curly, dark-brown hair was twisted into a neat, tight knot on top of her head, and her scalp felt distinctly damp and itchy.

The window was open, though, allowing a scant breeze to come in, and she supposed she should be glad it wasn't winter, when the air would be thick with smoke from all the chimneys. But even as she watched, an old Foden lorry trundled past, adding its bit of pollution to the grime that seemed to coat the beautiful city of dreaming spires and left everything looking and feeling slightly grubby.

She was just contemplating returning to her uncomfortable chair when she heard the soft slap-slap of the flat shoes all the nurses wore. She turned around, expecting to see a nursing sister taking her patient's vital signs.

Instead, a young nurse she hadn't seen before was beckoning her over. 'There's a telephone call for you. You can take it at the desk,' she informed her quietly.

'Oh, thank you,' Trudy said.

She smiled an apology at Mrs Emerson, who had awoken at the sound of voices, but the poor woman barely noticed as she once again fixed her gaze intently on her husband. She'd learned from a hurried conversation with the matron that the couple had been married for nearly twenty-five years and had three grown-up children, and Trudy simply couldn't imagine how she must be feeling.

Feeling depressed, she followed the briskly trotting nurse to the desk in the centre of the ward, where a tight-faced sister handed her the receiver before bustling away. Clearly, she was of the opinion that she had better things to do with her time than act as secretary to a lowly policewoman, and Trudy didn't really blame her.

'Hello, WPC Loveday,' she said smartly.

'Constable. Get back to the station sharpish, please. I have another assignment for you.' She recognised DI Jennings's voice at once, and automatically stiffened to attention.

'Yes, sir,' she said. But already she could hear the dialling tone in her ear.

She trotted back to Mr Emerson's bedside and stowed her accoutrements neatly away in her police-issue satchel, only stopping at the nurses' desk on her way past to ask someone to send word to the local police station should their patient say anything.

Then she jogged outside, where she collected her bicycle, mounted it and began to pedal fast towards St Aldate's. Luckily it wasn't far and wouldn't take her long. She knew how DI Jennings felt about being kept waiting.

As she pedalled, careful to dodge the many other cyclists thronging St Giles, she wondered why she'd been called off her duty at the hospital so soon.

At nearly twenty years of age, she was an intelligent young woman, and had quickly realised DI Jennings wasn't at all happy at having one of only a few women PCs assigned to his station. Trudy had quickly become resigned to being given the dregs of police work, keeping her clear of his eyeline and out from under his feet. Thus, she had gloomily been expecting to stay at the hospital for days, hugging her notebook and pen in case of the odd mumbled word, and fighting off boredom and pity in equal measure.

So what on earth could the sudden summons back to the station be all about? She hoped, glumly, that she hadn't done something wrong that she was about to be hauled over the coals for. Any minor misdemeanour of hers was always noted and sarcastically commented on, whereas if PC Rodney Broadstairs, the station house's blue-eyed boy, made the same errors, nobody said a word.

When she got to the station, there was nobody about to give her any clue as to what was in the wind, although Walter Swinburne, the oldest PC at the station, gave her an encouraging smile as she passed his desk.

But the moment she tapped on her DI's door, waiting for his summons before entering the office, her gloom lifted like magic. For there, sitting in the chair in front of DI Jennings's desk and scowling ferociously at him, was Dr Clement Ryder.

And probationary WPC Trudy Loveday was probably the only copper in the city who was ever glad to see him!

DI Jennings watched her come in, noting her flushed cheeks and damp hair – no doubt the girl was feeling the heat and the bike ride had winded her. He bit back a sigh of impatience and the retort that rose to his lips that a man would have been able to take such physical exertion in his stride. And if the picture of some rather overweight male constables flashed through his mind to give lie to this thought, he firmly suppressed them.

Instead, he sighed heavily and indicated the chair next to his unwanted visitor. 'Take a seat, Constable Loveday,' he said flatly.

'Thank you, sir,' Trudy said smartly, and sat upright on the edge of the chair indicated.

'Hello, Constable Loveday,' Clement Ryder said, turning to her and thinking how charming she looked today. A little dishevelled, perhaps, but her dark-brown eyes were dancing with curiosity and interest. Just as he remembered them.

'Dr Ryder,' she said calmly, displaying none of her happiness to see him. This took some effort on her part because she'd already guessed that he'd come into her life to rescue her from the humdrum routine of her usual working days. Just like the last time she'd seen him, when he'd asked for her help on another case. A case, she was very happy to remember, that they'd solved between them.

Harry Jennings sat up a bit straighter in his chair. 'Dr Ryder was just telling me all about the Chadworth case, Constable. Are you familiar with it?'

'No, sir,' Trudy admitted, and promptly wondered if she would be in the doghouse for not knowing. Was it something she should have been studying?

Harry Jennings shrugged his shoulders. 'No reason why you should be, I suppose,' he admitted, a shade reluctantly. 'You weren't called out to take a part in it, as I recall. Perhaps Dr Ryder can give you a brief summary,' he added, thin lips twitching slightly. He'd already had his ear bent for the past quarter of an hour on the subject and didn't feel inclined to repeat it.

'Derek Chadworth, a law student, found dead in the river last week,' Clement obliged him succinctly.

'Oh, yes. I know the case,' Trudy said at once, and with some relief. She hated looking ignorant in front of the coroner. As her DI had said, it wasn't her case, but she *had* overheard some of her colleagues talking about it in the outer office. 'He was one of the drunken students on the punts that overturned, wasn't he? Death by accidental drowning?'

'That's what we all thought the verdict would be.' DI Jennings couldn't help but interrupt, his voice sardonic in the extreme now. 'However, it seems the… *jury*—' and here he laid a rather pointed emphasis on the last word '—in their undoubted wisdom, chose to bring back an open verdict instead.'

The coroner's lips twitched slightly. Trudy caught the tension in the room and forced back a smile. If it came to a battle of

25

wills or wits between these two men, she knew who the winner would be.

'And as I was just telling the Inspector here,' Clement Ryder slipped in smoothly, with an expression as innocent as a newborn babe's, 'an open verdict requires a little more investigation.'

DI Jennings sighed heavily. 'And as *I* was telling *him*,' he said through teeth that, if not exactly gritted, seemed inclined to stick firmly together, 'it's a verdict that will have caused upset to many families.'

'The dead boy's, you mean, sir?' Trudy said, a little puzzled. Only to swallow hard as the DI shot her a furious look.

'Not just the deceased parents, Loveday,' he snapped. 'Although, naturally, they can't have been very happy with such a—' and here he shot the bland-faced coroner a telling look '—meaningless verdict. I was also thinking of the parents of all the other students present on that tragic day.'

'Most of whom are ladies and gentlemen of distinction and means, naturally,' Clement put in, shooting Trudy a twinkle-eyed look.

'Be that as it may,' Jennings snarled, 'you can see their point of view! Nobody wants their son or daughter to have to deal with such a tragic turn of events on what should have been a day of celebration. Having a friend die young can be a very traumatic event in any circumstances. But to have that tragedy drawn out even further by a coroner's jury leaving matters so up in the air… and with nobody quite knowing what to make of it… well!'

He threw his hands out in a gesture of annoyance. 'Naturally, people want answers and to be able to decently draw a line under things. And a verdict of accidental death, or even death by misadventure, would have allowed them to do just that.' He took a deep, steadying breath. 'The Chief Superintendent is of the opinion that the case should be allowed to quietly settle down, allowing the boy's parents to bury him and grieve in peace. And for all the other young men and women involved to get on with their lives.'

Dr Ryder slowly swung one leg over his knee and regarded his ankle socks thoughtfully. He had, of course, as DI Jennings had surmised only too accurately, influenced – some might even have said *instigated* – the verdict that had been handed down.

It had been quite easy for a man like Clement Ryder to arrange, naturally. He'd merely had to fix the foreman of the jury with a gimlet eye as he took them through a summary of the evidence, and stress certain facts. For instance, when telling them that 'if, on consideration, you feel that some questions *remain unanswered* to your satisfaction, then it is only *right and proper* that you return an open verdict'. And, 'if you feel that you are *not* sure exactly how Mr Chadworth came to drown on that day last week, then you *mustn't* allow yourself to *guess*, or be *swayed* by any one theory'. This last had been directed at the WI matrons, who'd taken the hint all right.

Oh, no. He hadn't wanted a cut and dried verdict, but one that would give him time to get to the bottom of what had really been happening in his court, and an open verdict was the only one that would allow him to do so.

Now he smiled benignly at the irate Inspector and spread his hands in a gesture of appeasement. 'Of course, it's an intolerable situation for everyone,' he surprised Jennings by admitting. 'Which is why the case needs investigating a little further,' he reiterated.

'As if we don't have enough on our plates as it is,' the Inspector grumbled. 'We had a hit and run last night, and we've still got that Sussinghurst case dragging on…'

'I'm sure you're very busy, Inspector,' Clement interrupted smoothly. 'Which is why I've asked you to spare just a solitary and humble PC to help me do a little more digging.'

As he spoke, he saw Trudy Loveday's face begin to glow with pleasure as she realised that her hopes about the reason for this call to the DI's office were well-founded. For, once before, the coroner had come to the station to ask for a police officer to help him with a case, and the DI had assigned him Trudy.

And that time, between them, they'd managed to catch a murderer!

Of course, there was little likelihood of that happening again, Trudy knew, but even so! It beat sitting about in a stuffy hospital for hours on end, either waiting for her patient to say something meaningful, or for the poor man to pass away.

Jennings, suddenly tired of being the old so-and-so's cat's paw, shook his head and, like Pontius Pilate, seemingly washed his hands of the whole affair.

'Haven't I said you can have WPC Loveday for a few days?' he said testily. 'And may I remind you, only for a few days! I can't spare her for long, haring about on some open-and-shut case, just because you've a bee in your bonnet about some students being less than candid!'

'Thank you, Inspector. I'll be sure to thank the Chief Constable for your forbearance when next I see him at the club,' Clement said, smiling affably as he rose from his chair.

At this parting shot, Jennings flushed mightily. He rather suspected that 'the club' the coroner was referring to had something to do with the Masons – an institution he was determined to join just as soon as it could be arranged.

Any ambitious officer needed to be a member of that club all right, and this timely reminder that it didn't do to get on the influential Dr Ryder's bad side had him backing off rapidly, albeit with little grace.

'Yes, well, thank you, Dr Ryder,' Jennings muttered. Then, as the medical man began to make for the door, Jennings, too, rose from his seat. 'I'll just have a few words with my officer, sir, before you go,' he added quietly.

'Righty-oh,' Clement said cheerfully, opening the door and passing through it without shutting it behind him. Trudy, seeing the look on the Inspector's face, hastily rectified that and then returned to stand meekly before his desk.

But her heart was racing. She was going to work with Dr Ryder again! She was actually going to watch and listen and be taught things, instead of being given paperwork and ignored. She could have sung with happiness.

'Right then, Constable,' Jennings said heavily. 'You know the drill – same as last time. Just keep the old man happy, and report back to me every day. I want to know everything that man is up to. Understood?'

'Yes, sir,' Trudy said. She knew Dr Ryder was too clever a man not to know she would be forced to do this, so didn't feel at all treacherous in agreeing to the orders.

'Try and reign him back from any real excesses. And watch you don't go about upsetting any VIPs,' he added, all but wagging a finger at her. 'Most of the parents of the young people at that picnic party are members of the aristocracy, or the new money set. And if you go about upsetting them, they'll get on to the top brass, and the top brass will have me roasted. And I won't stand for that! Understood?'

At this, Trudy gulped. She wasn't quite sure just how she was supposed to go about stopping Dr Ryder when he wanted something, and when he could be, well, perhaps a little *straightforward* in his speech and manner.

Seeing her hesitation, and guessing the reason for it, DI Jennings sighed heavily. Even he had to concede that it was hardly fair to ask a young girl of nineteen to handle someone like Ryder. Someone who could blister the paintwork with just a look or an acid phrase, and had been known to best the sharpest of QCs and any number of other dignitaries. 'Oh, just do your best, Constable,' he finished wearily.

'Yes, sir,' Trudy said, and, with a feeling of infinite relief, quickly left the Inspector's office.

*

Once outside the station, it was just a short walk to Dr Ryder's office in the coroner's court and mortuary complex in Floyds Row. His secretary, recognising her from their first case six months before, smiled at her as Clement strode in, ordering 'tea and cake, and plenty of it' as he swept past her.

The older woman shook her head and sighed at his cavalier manner. But Trudy noticed she was smiling.

A few minutes later, Clement Ryder was eating a slice of angel cake and watching his young protégé thoughtfully as she read through the court documents on the seemingly unremarkable case of the drowned law student. He was curious to see what she made of them.

On their last case he'd come to acquire a great deal of respect for this young woman's intelligence and backbone. She was still very green, of course, but she had plenty of potential, if steered right. Which was why, of course, he'd made damned sure Jennings assigned her to him again. Of course it helped that the buffoon of an inspector totally underestimated the girl's qualities. Given the proper mentoring by her older and more experienced colleagues, she could really shine. Not that that was likely to happen, he thought, a shade gloomily.

Still, he'd do all he could to help her hone some skills while she was helping him get to the bottom of his latest project.

It took her half an hour to read every scrap of paper in the file, and when she'd finished she leaned back in the chair, a slight frown pulling her fine, dark brows together over her dark, pansy-brown eyes.

'Well?' he asked sharply.

'On the face of it, sir, it looks rather straightforward, doesn't it? There was a large party of drunken students, and two very overcrowded punts. There was a collision with a third punt and, as a result, a lot of people were pitched into the river. It's quite possible Derek either couldn't get to the surface quickly enough, or perhaps got trampled underneath someone else's feet, expelling all the air from his lungs before he knew what was happening.'

'Oh, yes. All of that is possible.' The coroner surprised her slightly by agreeing at once. 'Mind you, I still think it rather odd that nobody saw him getting into difficulties. There were at least twenty or more students in the water.'

'Who would have been looking to save themselves, most likely,' Trudy put in.

'Oh, almost certainly.'

'Perhaps he couldn't get to the surface because of the sheer weight of numbers? Who knows, maybe somebody flailing about actually stood on him?'

'Again, perhaps. But supposing any of that happened, with so many eyes actually in the water, and so many eyes on the bank watching it all happen, is it very likely that nobody saw the body rise to the surface at some point and float away?'

'Perhaps it didn't rise to the surface?' She played devil's advocate automatically.

'Most bodies do,' the coroner said, then shrugged. 'Then again, who's to say? Perhaps they did see a body float away but agreed among themselves to keep quiet about it.'

'That's rather far-fetched, isn't it?' Trudy said doubtfully. 'Why would they do that?'

The coroner shrugged. 'Who's to say? The thing is, the reason you have an inquest in the first place is to tackle issues like the hows and whys.'

'So you're not convinced the court did get to the bottom of what really happened?' she asked slowly. She'd learned a lot from her last encounter with this sometimes difficult, but always brilliant, man. And if he thought something was 'off', she wasn't going to gainsay him out of hand.

'Forget about the mechanics and facts of it for a moment, Trudy,' Clement advised quietly, leaning back in his chair, and feeling his right leg tremble slightly.

With a scowl, he surreptitiously rubbed it under cover of his

31

desk, quickly checking to make sure she hadn't noticed this sign of weakness, and sighed. 'Just run the testimony of the students over in your mind. What strikes you most about it?'

Trudy again went up a notch in his estimation when she didn't answer straight away, but instead gave the question some thought. 'Well… it does strike me as rather odd that the deceased had been invited to the party at all. I mean, from what I can tell, most of the partygoers were there at the invitation of this Lord Jeremy Littlejohn,' she went on, checking the relevant pages. 'The younger son of a duke, isn't he?'

Clement snorted. 'Indeed he is.'

Trudy shot him a quick look. 'You didn't like him?'

'Irrelevant,' the coroner said briskly. 'Carry on with what you were saying.'

'Well…' Trudy frowned, trying to find a comfortable way of talking about social class with this professional man, while not letting her own, strictly working-class, origins get in the way. 'It seems to me that his sort… I mean, most of his friends were wealthy and, well, upper class. But Derek Chadworth, according to his tutors and parents, was a scholarship boy. His father was merely a country solicitor. And he didn't seem to do anything out of the ordinary to put himself on the map, so to speak, did he? He wasn't a rowing blue, or a rugby star or anything, was he?'

'So?' Clement encouraged.

'Well… he hardly seems a likely candidate to have belonged to their set,' she concluded nervously, and immediately felt relieved when the coroner nodded approvingly.

'No, he doesn't. You're quite right. And yet, when it came time to give *his* evidence—' Clement nodded at the folder resting on her knees '—Lord Jeremy clearly stated, in an offhand manner, that he might have issued the invitation to Derek Chadworth. But that he couldn't be sure whether or not he'd taken him up on it.'

Trudy nodded, rereading His Lordship's evidence. 'Yes. He says... Yes, here it is. "I knew Derek from around – I'd had a few ciders with him at the Eagle and Child and that sort of thing. I told him we were having a bash at Port Meadow and, if he wanted to come, he needed to be at the bridge and on a punt by half nine." Hmm, he goes on to say that, on the day in question, after a couple of glasses of something called... er... Buck's Fizz... at breakfast, he was feeling a big tight and wasn't sure whether or not he'd seen him among the crowd piling into the punts.'

'Buck's Fizz is a mixture of freshly squeezed orange juice and champagne,' Dr Ryder informed her dryly. 'A popular choice for indolent young pups and arrogant lordlings who like to hold breakfast parties in their rooms for their minions.'

Trudy nodded and mentally made a note. Dr Ryder *really* didn't like Lord Littlejohn. He must have done something to ruffle the coroner's feathers. But from what she'd read of his evidence, she couldn't quite see what it might be. True, he had been annoyingly vague about the dead boy – but so had all the other students.

'Anything else strike you as odd?' Clement asked mildly. But his eyes, when he looked at her, were as sharp as flint.

Trudy frowned. There was something nagging at her, something that didn't exactly feel as if it fitted together. But no matter how hard she tried to track down the cause for her unease, she wasn't able to. Eventually she shrugged. 'I'm not sure.'

Clement nodded with a soft sigh. Well, perhaps that was only to be expected. It wasn't as if the young WPC had attended as many coroner's sittings as he had!

'OK – try this. Put yourself in the shoes of one of them,' Clement said with a slight grimace. 'Not that you'd want to, mind. But you've just finished sitting your exams. You have a job in the City, or a job in Daddy's firm or some such, just waiting for you to step into, and your whole life is stretching ahead of you in a golden haze of wealth and comfort. Now, just how much would you want to "come down" from Oxford with your name mixed up in some death-by-drowning scandal?'

Trudy shuddered. 'I wouldn't! Mummy and Daddy wouldn't like it for a start. People like that need their reputations to be spotless, don't they, and… oh!' Suddenly, as light dawned, Trudy began to quickly reread the transcripts again.

'Exactly!' Dr Ryder said sharply, seeing she'd spotted the discrepancy now. 'So why didn't they all simply deny the dead boy had been part of their party? There is nothing, after all, in the physical evidence to say he *had* to have met his death while attending that celebration. He could have got into the river by some other means, at some other time. The time of death itself was given as between 8 a.m. and 2 p.m., after all. Granted, that supposition stretches coincidence quite a bit,' he added with a frown.

Trudy, busily reading over the evidence of the Italian girl again, knitted her brows, only half-listening to him. 'Well, perhaps they couldn't deny it. I mean, if he was there… and there were so many witnesses… they couldn't run the risk of being found out to be lying. Isn't that committing perjury? Unless they all got together and agreed to say the same thing – and that's almost impossible, isn't it? I mean, that many people… a conspiracy on that scale… surely it's not feasible.' She broke off her reading to look at him intently.

The coroner sighed and shrugged. 'I'm not so sure about that, Trudy. People en masse can act very differently from people as individuals. Just look at riots, and mass hysteria and mobs. These students were all of an age, and all friends, and all had their own necks and best interests to look after. So they definitely had good reason to tell the same story. And don't forget that all of them – mark my words – were under the thumb to some degree or other of our Lord Jeremy Littlejohn. A proper little Machiavelli, if ever I saw one! I thought as much the moment the man opened his mouth to give evidence in my court. Then there's such a thing as peer pressure, you know. Nobody likes to be thought of as a snitch. And who among them could have afforded to become an outcast by going against the consensus of opinion? Don't forget, Lord Littlejohn and his family wield a lot of influence in the world these people inhabit,' Ryder warned her. 'One word in a banker's ear, and somebody doesn't get that job in the City he was looking forward to. Or one whisper from the Countess to some society matron or other, and some young girl can find her marriage prospects withering. Oh, yes. I can quite see how they could all be coerced or bribed or bullied into towing the line.'

Trudy went back to reading the files again. And wondered. Was she allowing Dr Ryder's comments to colour her view of things? Or did the testimonies now all seem to have a certain 'sameness' about them?

'So you think they were coached in what to say? By Lord Littlejohn?' she asked uncertainly. 'They all lied to keep him sweet?'

The coroner caught the scepticism in her voice and shook his head with dissatisfaction. 'Not necessarily. I'm just saying there's something that doesn't ring true about the evidence they gave,' Clement said grimly. 'Time and time again, they say the same vague thing. "Derek might have been there, but I didn't see him." Or, "I was so drunk, I couldn't say for sure that he was there. But then I can't say that he wasn't either." Why, if you're going to distance yourself from such a tragic event, and you all get together and agree to put on a united front, don't you just go the whole hog and say, "Derek wasn't there. Nobody saw him." That way, the police would have to take your word for it. Even if they didn't believe it, how could they prove otherwise?'

Trudy shook her head. Put like that… 'But maybe they *were* telling the truth. Maybe they were just all so drunk they didn't remember.'

'Perhaps,' Dr Ryder said, clearly not believing it for a minute and blowing out his breath in an annoyed whoosh. 'But just take it from me, young Trudy,' he said firmly, sitting up straighter in his chair. 'Somebody—' and here he nodded at the folder in her hands '—was trying to pull a fast one at that hearing. And in my court too! *And I'm not having it.* Something, as the Bard said, is rotten in the state of Denmark, and I intend to find out what it is. Of course,' he added, feeling compelled to be honest with her, 'when we do find out what it is, it might be nothing earth-shattering. It might not even be relevant to Mr Chadworth's death. It might just turn out to be some silly stunt or secret the students are keeping to themselves for some reason. But until we find out what it is, we can't know, can we?'

'Do you think it's possible they all collaborated to kill him?' she suddenly asked breathlessly, her eyes glittering, her cheeks flushing in excitement.

And at this outburst of youthful exuberance, Clement grinned widely. 'Whoa! Nobody said anything about *that*!' He reigned her back kindly.

'But is it possible somebody at that party deliberately killed him?' she persisted.

'Well, let's think about it for a minute,' he said, thoroughly enjoying himself now. 'There were more than twenty kids splashing about in the water. How likely is it, do you think, that someone could have grabbed hold of him and held him under without anyone noticing? Given that drowning men tend to splash about a fair bit.'

Her face fell. Then lightened again. 'But if, say, three people *did* see it, and were for some reason keeping quiet about it…? That might explain why you think their evidence was suspect.'

'Perhaps. But if you were going to kill someone, would you risk doing it in front of so many potential witnesses? And don't forget, even if you were willing to take a chance on being able to bribe or threaten your fellow students in some way, that doesn't negate the possibility that someone outside your control – an independent witness on the riverbank, for instance – would see you and spill the beans.'

Trudy sighed heavily, but, not willing to give up just yet, said tentatively, 'Well, perhaps he wasn't drowned at the party. Perhaps someone knew there was going to be a party and took advantage of it.' With growing enthusiasm she sat up straighter. 'The killer lures Derek to the river and drowns him there, knowing the punting party will be blamed.'

'In which case, how did he know there'd be an accident? Unless he had an accomplice on one of the punts?'

Trudy sighed. 'That does seem to be rather overcomplicated. But it's not unheard of, is it? Two people conspiring to commit murder. But perhaps the accident was just a coincidence?' she mused brightly. 'The killer didn't know there was going to be a collision, but at a picnic party, on a hot summer's day by the river, he or she could count on there being a fair amount of swimming and bathing taking place. Perhaps the killer just relied on the fact that a drowned student, found in the river on a day when there'd been so many students mucking about in the water, would naturally be presumed to be one of their number, who had come to grief at the party?'

'Perhaps. But have you considered the difficulty in that scenario?' Clement cautioned her. 'The killer would have to lure Derek to the river. How? On what pretext? He or she would then have had to drown a very fit and able lad, in a large stretch of water. The medical evidence made it clear he hadn't received a blow to the head or been incapacitated by any obvious drug. Even if he was still a bit tipsy and hungover from a night's drinking, you can be sure Derek would have put up a fight. And the chances of him being able to wriggle away are quite high, you know. It's not as easy to drown someone as you might think. For a start, the killer would be certain to get drenched too.'

'But it's still possible,' Trudy persisted stubbornly.

'Perhaps. But again, the medical evidence puts time of death at around eight in the morning at the earliest. So where on the river could the killer feel safe from prying eyes? At that time, a lot of people are out and about, going to work, walking their dogs, fishing and what have you. If you were a killer, would you risk it? How could you be sure of going unseen and unnoticed?'

Trudy reluctantly acknowledged all these problems, and her woebegone expression made the coroner smile.

'I'm not saying anything you've hypothesised *didn't* happen. Just that we don't know! Which means we need to do a lot more digging. So… are you ready to start?'

At this, probationary WPC Loveday grinned widely. Was she ready?

Of course she was ready!

'Do we start at the scene of the accident?' she asked brightly.

'Whatever for?' Clement asked, sounding surprised, but with a small smile playing on his lips. 'I doubt there'd be anything to see after all this time, and the police went over the ground pretty thoroughly anyway. Any clues they might possibly have missed will long since have been trampled over by cattle or washed away in the river. Or do you think we might find a cigarette butt, containing tobacco made only in a small Malay village, and only sold in this country to three Emeritus Fellows and a recluse? Thus leading us straight to our prime suspect?'

Trudy laughed. 'All right, point made! That sort of thing only happens in Sherlock Holmes novels. So, where do we start?'

Chapter 4

Their first port of call was Webster Hall, the college where Lionel Gulliver had been studying theology for the past three years. He was due to 'go down' within the next two weeks, and the coroner was grimly aware they needed to act fast, since most of the witnesses to what had happened to Derek Chadworth would likewise also soon disperse.

The college was quiet, and when they enquired at the porter's lodge after Lionel Gulliver, the guardian of the gate recognised Dr Ryder at once. Trudy knew (mostly from the grumbling comments of her Inspector) that Dr Ryder had many high-ranking friends in the town, and porters of colleges were notorious for knowing – and cultivating – anyone who was anyone. So she wasn't particularly surprised when the bowler-hatted individual greeted the coroner by name.

'Ah, Dr Ryder, sir, pleased to see you again. I take it our Dr Fairweather hasn't managed to beat you at chess yet, sir?'

Clement gave a grunt of laughter. 'No, he hasn't, nor will he. But since he serves the best port in Oxford, I'm happy to let him keep on trying. Can you tell us what house and room number Lionel Gulliver is currently occupying?'

'Of course, sir,' the porter said smoothly, consulting a list and promptly coming up with the goods. He added softly, 'I take it you're here about that poor boy from St Bede's? Tragic event that, sir, if I may say so.'

'Oh, yes, indeed,' Clement said, his face and voice becoming very bland indeed. Trudy, who'd expected him to be anxious to get on with things, suddenly realised he was in no hurry after all, as he leaned nonchalantly against the doorframe and sighed. 'A young life, cut off in its prime... It was a sad day for the university, Barstock. Did you, er, know young Mr Chadworth particularly?' he added casually, making Trudy prick up her ears.

Like nearly all college porters, Barstock seemed to know all and could be persuaded to expound a little if the mood took him.

'Not very well, Dr Ryder, sir. No, I wouldn't say that,' the porter responded carefully. 'But I'd seen him around. He and, er, certain other young gentlemen belonged to one of the clubs that sometimes met here.'

'Ah,' Dr Ryder said with a smile. 'Say no more. Boys do like to set up their clubs, don't they?' He allowed his tone to become indulgent. 'In my day, I belonged to a pudding club. Once a month we met and tried to eat a pudding in every restaurant in Oxford. Couldn't do it nowadays,' he added ruefully, patting his rounding stomach. 'Indigestion for one thing!'

The porter duly laughed. And Trudy, who'd begun to feel impatient with all this chit-chat, suddenly (and rather belatedly) cottoned on to the fact that the coroner was actually working his way up to something specific.

'Of course, nowadays, undergrads have far more, er, esoteric things to form clubs about, I daresay,' Clement mused idly.

'Oh, yes, sir. Take young Mr Gulliver, sir, the young man you're enquiring about,' the porter went on smoothly. 'A nice chap – his uncle was once Bishop of Durham. Hoping to emulate him one day, I daresay. Now, he's a member of several clubs.'

'All harmless, I'm sure.' The coroner played along. 'Being a theology student and all that.'

'Yes, sir. Harmless, mostly. One's a birdwatching outfit, and one is a folklorist society. And, of course, since his uncle on his mother's side is a baron, he's also a member of Lord Littlejohn's club,' the porter tossed in, very casually.

At this, Trudy stiffened like a pointer spotting a falling pheasant. She was very careful now to keep absolutely quiet and still, in case she should attract attention to herself, and her uniform should stop the porter's tongue.

'Ah, yes... Lord Littlejohn,' Ryder said, his voice as bland as milk. 'He had to give evidence at the inquest. An... interesting sort.'

'Yes, sir,' the porter agreed flatly.

'Rather taken with himself and his social ranking, I thought,' Ryder swept on, having accurately guessed that the porter's opinion of His Lordship exactly matched his own. 'In fact, I got the impression that he thought he deserved to be next in line to the throne, as opposed to being the mere son of a duke – and the second son at that.'

But this was a step a little too far for the porter, who made an indistinct murmuring sound, and the coroner quickly backed off.

'Still, I daresay the club he formed is harmless enough. Does it have an official name?' he enquired casually.

'Yes, sir – they call themselves the Marquis Club. I think the title is a reference to their aristocratic credentials.'

Trudy looked nonplussed at this but Ryder caught the reference at once. 'Oh, of course. The fighting men! So Lord Littlejohn regards himself as a man with backbone, does he? Funny. I saw no sign of it in my court.'

The porter's lips didn't actually smile, but managed a twitch. And having decided he'd done his civic duty in a manner that in no way brought his college into disrepute, he brought the conversation smoothly to an end by informing the coroner that he was sure he would find Mr Gulliver in. Clement, accepting he'd got all he was going to, thanked him and moved gracefully away.

As they walked through the grounds to the staircase indicated by the porter, Trudy looked about her with interest. It wasn't often that she had cause to set foot inside one of the city's famous colleges. All was pretty much as she'd expected (golden stone buildings, velvet grass lawns, neatly tended flowerbeds), and she quickly turned her thoughts to the matter in hand.

She refused to show her ignorance by asking Dr Ryder about the origin of the club's name. Besides, she didn't need to – clearly the original Marquis, whoever they were, had been fighters of some kind. And from the porter's comments about Lionel Gulliver having a relative who was a baron, it seemed as though you had to be some sort of 'gentry' in order to become a member.

Instead, she zeroed in on the porter's behaviour.

'He clearly didn't think much of Lord Littlejohn, did he? Or his chosen name for their club.'

'No, and I don't blame him,' Clement said shortly with a little huff. 'A more indolent, lazy and self-indulgent specimen I have yet to meet.'

Trudy was about to say something when, at the bottom of the stone staircase, she saw the coroner stumble slightly as he lifted his foot to mount the first stair. As she automatically reached out to help him, however, the coroner clutched at the wooden rail lining the inner wall and, without a word, began to climb vigorously.

Wisely, she said nothing. She knew that, sometimes, older folk weren't quite as robust as they once had been. And if her old granny was any indication, they didn't like to be reminded of it!

For his part, Dr Ryder mounted the steps with tight lips – he knew the stumble had had nothing whatsoever to do with incipient old age.

A few years ago, he'd noticed a slight tremor in his left hand – and, as a surgeon, it had instantly raised alarm bells. Under an alias, he'd undergone a set of tests, and had been diagnosed with what his medical colleagues were beginning to call Parkinson's disease. The condition had been known about for centuries, of course, and under a variety of different names – the Shaking Palsy in Europe, and under the ancient Indian medical system of Ayurveda as Kampavata.

But whatever name you gave it, it had meant the end of his time wielding a scalpel, and hence his change of career. He'd been very successful, so far, in keeping his condition a secret from both his friends and work colleagues, knowing that, if they found out about it, it would end his working life.

But as the condition slowly progressed and worsened, and his various symptoms became more and more obvious, he reluctantly acknowledged that it could only be a matter of time before he was found out.

Still, he was determined to keep going for as long as possible before that happened. And, so far, he was sure nobody even suspected. He could only hope his young protégé hadn't noticed his uneven gait or had put it down to a simple misstep.

At the top of the staircase they found room eight. With a brisk rap of the iron ring knocker against the centuries-old wooden door, he announced their presence.

The door was opened quickly enough by a small, lean youth, whose face fell the moment he recognised his visitor. He had a short cap of dark-brown hair with a propensity to curl (which was probably the bane of his life), a rather nobbly chin and large hazel eyes. The expression in them, when they slid from that of the coroner and took in Trudy's uniform, became almost panic-stricken.

'Mr Gulliver? You remember me? Dr Clement Ryder, city coroner.'

'Oh, er, yes, of course.'

'I have just one or two more questions concerning the death of Mr Derek Chadworth.'

The young theology student gulped. 'Oh. Really? I, er, rather thought that was all over and done with.'

'No, sir. Not with an open verdict. We're still investigating,' he said with quiet satisfaction. 'May we come in?' he demanded, his tone indicating he didn't know what the youth of today were coming to, keeping their elders and betters standing about on doorsteps.

The young man instantly flushed and hastily stepped to one side. 'Oh, of course. Sorry. Do come in. Excuse the mess. I'm in the process of packing up to "go down".'

Trudy, glancing around the room thoughtfully, didn't think much of the 'mess'. The room looked neat and tidy, if perhaps a little bare.

'We'll try not to keep you long,' Clement assured him mildly. 'There were just a few things that struck me in the evidence you gave in my court that I'd like to have clarified.'

'Oh, er, right. Please, sit down. Can I nab a scout and see if I can lay on some tea or something?' he offered, indicating chairs and glancing half-heartedly out of the window.

For a moment, Trudy was stymied by his use of the word 'scout', then vaguely recalled that college servants were called that, for some arcane reason or other.

'Oh, no, thanks. We're fine,' Clement said.

Trudy took the chair furthest from the student's eyeline and tried to make like she was invisible. Nevertheless, as she slipped her notebook out of her satchel, she noticed his eyes swivel in her direction and then move quickly away again.

He looked unhappily at the coroner as he sat down and rubbed his hands nervously across his trousers at the knees. 'My evidence? I don't know that I was much use, sir. I really didn't know anything, unfortunately.'

'Yes, that was very apparent,' Clement said, so dryly that the younger man actually blushed. 'Let's see if we can't get a little more specific, shall we?'

The young man swallowed hard and made a stab at a smile. 'I'm not sure it'll be much use, sir. I don't really know why I was called at all, if I'm honest.'

The older man waved that sally away as if swatting a fly. 'You say you never actually *saw* Derek Chadworth on the punt you were on?' Dr Ryder began, gently but firmly.

'No, that's right. That's what I said. But, of course, he might have been on the other punt.'

'Hmm.' The coroner made no attempt to hide his reaction to this bit of flummery. Instead, he went off on a different tack. 'Did you know Derek well?' he shot out crisply.

'Oh, no.'

'But wasn't he a member of the Marquis Club?' Clement slipped the knife in smoothly.

Trudy was interested to see the young man actually start in his chair and then go very pale. 'What?' For a moment, his face seemed to fight for some sort of expression. Horror? Surprise? Dismay? Confusion, certainly. Eventually, he swallowed uncomfortably and gave a rather sickly smile. 'No. No, I'm sure he wasn't.'

'Ah. I thought that might have been why Lord Littlejohn invited him,' Clement said, careful to keep his voice conversational.

Lionel Gulliver, perhaps taking heart from this, seemed to gather his wits together with a bit of an effort, and manage a second, more convincing smile. 'Oh, no, I don't think that could have been the case. Er, I mean, you'd have to ask Jeremy that, wouldn't you?' he added, glancing longingly out of the window.

Trudy, her shorthand competently filling her notebook, thought Lionel looked as if he wished he might jump out, so uncomfortable did he seem.

'Yes, we'll be sure to do that when we see him,' Clement said non-committally. 'So, let's have this straight once and for all. Is it your opinion that Derek Chadworth was *not* at the party the day he drowned?'

Again, Lionel seemed to start in his chair. He really was a

nervous sort, Trudy thought, beginning to feel, perhaps for the first time with any confidence, that the coroner really was on the track of something with this case.

'Well, as a matter of fact, no, I don't think I *am* saying that,' Lionel said, a shade confusingly. 'I'm beginning to think that perhaps Derek *was* on one of the punts after all.'

Trudy felt her mouth fall open at this unexpected about-face. She shot a quick, perplexed look at the coroner, who was regarding the theology student with his head cocked a little to one side, rather like a robin regarding an interesting worm.

'So, are you saying you *did* see him that day? At the party?' Clement said slowly.

'No! I mean… I think I might have. But I can't swear to it.'

The coroner regarded the young man steadily for a moment or so and noticed that the unfortunate youth was actually beginning to sweat – not to mention fidget about nervously on his chair.

He also noticed that Gulliver's rather weak mouth had now begun to set in a thin, stubborn line, and that his chin had come up. Clearly, he'd reached the point where he was willing to be stubborn about things. Which meant pushing him further would be pointless.

Thus, Clement sighed and rose to his feet, catching Trudy completely unawares. 'Well, thank you for your time, Mr Gulliver,' he said abruptly. 'I understand you're going to train for the priesthood?'

'The Church of England, yes,' the young man said, getting to his feet with alacrity, a look of utter relief passing across his unremarkable features.

'Hmm. In which case, you'll know what the Bible has to say about bearing false witness?'

Lionel Gulliver gulped audibly. 'Yes, sir, I know that,' he muttered wretchedly.

The coroner nodded, smiled briefly, and then clapped the

young man on the back so hard he had to actually take a step forward to prevent himself from falling flat on his face.

'Well, good luck, Mr Gulliver,' he said jovially, and Trudy, hastily shoving her accoutrements back into her satchel, trotted out after him, very aware of one pale-faced theology student staring miserably after them.

Once again in the sunshine outside, she stood blinking in the bright light for a moment, and then sighed heavily. 'Well, that was a waste of time,' she muttered.

'Do you think so?' Clement asked, and something in his tone had her shooting him a quick, suspicious look.

What had he seen or heard or deduced that she had missed?

'You know, I'd be willing to bet... yes, I'd be willing to bet half a crown that that young man has been "got at",' Clement mused out loud. 'Someone has persuaded him to keep his mouth shut.'

Trudy didn't know if she was willing to go that far, but wisely kept silent, accurately guessing that he wasn't going to elucidate any further.

They set off up the path bordering the quad, and called out a farewell to the porter as they passed through the gates and headed towards the coroner's car. This was a smart-looking Rover 75-1110 P4, which he'd parked (illegally, Trudy noticed with a guilty flush) on some double-yellow lines in a side alley.

Like the gentleman he undoubtedly was, he unlocked and held open the passenger door for her and then shut it once she was safely inside. After getting behind the wheel, however, instead of turning the key in the ignition, he settled in his seat and stared blindly out at the city going about its business outside.

'You know, Trudy, I think it might be time you learned how to work undercover,' he astonished – and thrilled – her by saying.

'What do you mean?' she asked eagerly.

'Well, you're of an age to be a student. Out of uniform, you could easily pass for a college gal. I want you, starting tomorrow, to dress in civvies and start hanging out at the regular student haunts – there's that bookshop café in St Ebbes for a start. And the pub by the river – you know the one. Use your initiative. Start making friends. Chat about Derek and the Marquis Club. Find out what your average student not in Lord Littlejohn's intimate little circle is saying and thinking about it all. But don't be too obvious about it. Think you can do that?'

Trudy, who was feeling a mixture of alarm and excitement at the thought of working while not shackled to her uniform, forced herself to look calm and serious.

'Of course I can, Dr Ryder,' she said calmly. But, inside, her heart was beating like that of a bird caught in a trap. To work like a proper detective, and without having her uniform instantly identify and restrict her, was freedom indeed! Rising to the ranks of the CID was her ultimate (and secret) ambition. She'd be the first woman to…

But then, as reality came back in a dampening rush, she felt her heart fall. 'I'm not sure DI Jennings will agree to it, Dr Ryder,' she said despondently. In fact, if she knew her superior officer (and, alas, she did, only too well), he would worry she'd get in far too much trouble working undercover. He'd be terrified she'd bring the force into disrepute and earn him the ire of his immediate superiors.

'Don't you worry about him. He'll tow the line,' Clement predicted confidently.

Trudy, slightly awed by his easy belief in his own power, blinked. 'Yes, sir,' she said. But she wasn't any too sanguine that even the crusty old coroner would be able to make her DI do something he thought might rebound badly on him.

Seeing that it was getting on, Dr Ryder drove her to the station so she could finish her shift, and then drove back to his office to work on his other cases.

Trudy wasted little time in tapping on her superior officer's door in order to give her report of her day's activities. Jennings surprised her considerably, after listening to her quietly, by agreeing somewhat tersely that she could indeed dispense – temporarily – with her uniform whenever she needed to pose as a student for Dr Ryder.

As she left his office, a little glow of delight warming her insides, she could only conclude that he didn't believe his WPC talking to a bunch of students about a mare's nest of the coroner's own making could get either of them into any trouble.

Which, as things turned out, just went to show how little DI Jennings knew!

Chapter 5

That evening, as she sat down to tea with her mum and dad in their council house kitchen, she found herself excitedly telling them a little about her latest case. On the radio, Anthony Newley was singing 'Do You Mind?' The radio was only on at all because her father didn't want to miss a repeat of *Hancock's Half Hour* that was due to begin soon.

She was careful not to go into any detail, of course, mindful of the rules that stated police work should never be discussed with 'civilians'. But she knew neither of her parents was happy with her career choice, and she wanted to point out to them that she was doing well in her chosen profession – even if she was gilding the lily a bit!

'So you see, in letting me work in plain clothes, DI Jennings must be starting to trust me at last,' she concluded, somewhat less-than-truthfully.

'Well, I don't know, our Trudy,' said her mother, Barbara Loveday, worriedly. 'Them students can get up to some wild things. And a drowned lad ain't very nice.' As she crossed the yellow-and-brown linoleum floor with the dirty plates and deposited them in the deep sink, she cast a concerned glance over her shoulder at her husband.

Frank Loveday had been a bus driver all his life. He was proud of his son, Martin, who worked as a carpenter for a building firm, since he considered him to be an artisan, and therefore a step up from his old man. And although he outwardly backed his wife up whenever she argued that Trudy should be thinking of finding a nice young man and settling down, he was, in fact, secretly even more proud of his daughter.

It took guts to join the police, and for a young slip of a girl… Even so, he wouldn't have been human if he didn't worry about her.

Now he folded his newspaper and looked at her over the top of it. She was a picture, her eyes shining with excitement and her cheeks flushed and happy. And he didn't have the heart to bring her down.

Nevertheless, he felt a slight flutter of alarm in his stomach. When she walked the beat in her uniform, he felt fairly content that she would be safe. People admired and respected the police, and her uniform, he felt, offered her considerable protection.

But if she was going to go around dressed as any other girl, nosing about in something nasty… 'Exactly what are you supposed to be doing for this here coroner chap, then, our Trudy?' he asked gravely.

'Oh, Dad – nothing dangerous! Nothing silly! I'm only going to go to some student hangouts, and chat and gossip! It's not like I'm entering dens of iniquity or anything.'

By the sink, her mother heaved a massive sigh. She was counting out some money and putting it in a biscuit tin – which meant it was being put by for the rent. The money for the electric and water bills, which she took down to the post office and paid whenever they came in, was kept in an old Bisto tin and a canister marked 'ginger' respectively.

'Lucky it's summer and the electric bill won't be so high this time,' she muttered to herself, and Trudy felt a flash of something very close to shame.

51

Although she paid for her 'keep', she knew it wasn't all that much, and probably didn't go very far. The trouble was, her wages weren't exactly generous. But she could always do without, couldn't she? Stockings, for example, weren't needed in the summer either.

'Mum, would you like a little more for my keep each month?' she asked, walking over to her and slipping her hands around her mother's ample waist. 'I can always make do…'

'No, you won't, then, our Trudy,' Barbara Loveday said firmly. 'Brian dropped by earlier. Wanted to know if you wanted to go to some dance or other on Saturday night. It's time you had a pretty new dress to be seen out and about in. Your "best" is looking a bit dated now. You save your money up and treat yourself.'

Trudy, well aware her mother considered Brian Bayliss, a boy she'd known since infant school, as prime husband material, bit back a sigh and forced a quick smile onto her face.

'Oh, I expect I'll see him around,' she agreed peaceably, releasing her arms and walking casually back to the kitchen table.

As usual, the table had a small lace cloth on it that had come down in the family from her namesake, Aunty Gertrude. In the centre was a small vase of Poole pottery (her mother's pride and joy, bequeathed to her by her own maternal grandmother) with a small bouquet of Sweet Williams in it. Her father grew them religiously in the garden, as both of his 'girls', as he referred to his wife and daughter, had a fondness for the scents given off by the carnation family.

'A dance might be nice,' she said. It was easier to keep her mother sweet than to argue with her that she was in no hurry to marry and start producing babies. And Brian – who was a local hero due to his prowess with a rugby ball – was a nice enough lad. And a good dancer!

'Mind you don't go out to these student places at night, then, my girl,' her father said, putting his foot down, making his daughter regard him fondly. As if his word was still law, Trudy thought with a slight pang. She wasn't his little girl any longer. If either DI Jennings or Dr Ryder thought she needed to go out at night, then she would have to!

But Trudy Loveday hadn't reached the ripe old age of nineteen without learning how to handle her parents.

'Yes, Dad,' she said meekly.

She wondered just what she should wear tomorrow. Mentally, she began running through her rather meagre wardrobe. She wasn't sure she had anything really suitable. After all, Oxford women students were all bluestockings from wealthy backgrounds, and their clothes were, of course, of the best quality. She was pretty sure her Woolworths glad rags wouldn't fit the bill!

How she wished she had the nerve to ask Dr Ryder if she could buy some more 'upmarket' clothes, in order to fit in more easily and be accepted as one of the gang. But she just couldn't see herself asking him for money for a fancy hat! And the look on DI Jennings's face if she were to put in an expenses claim for a new outfit was just too comical – and horrific – to even contemplate!

Chapter 6

Reginald Porter (Reggie to his family and very few friends) leaned nonchalantly against the wall surrounding the Ashmolean Museum, and glanced casually up and down Beaumont Street. On another hot summer's day, the place was crowded with shoppers and tourists. Down the way a little, a couple of students were sitting on the steps leading up to the world-famous museum, smoking French cigarettes and talking animatedly about something to do with Oriental art. With a sneer of contempt, Reggie ignored them. What did it matter what the overeducated, overprotected little sods thought?

Two business types in a pair of matching neat, pin-striped, dark-blue suits and bowler hats swept past, discussing the tennis.

'I tell you, mark my words, the men's finals will turn out to be an all-Australian affair this year,' one of them said to his companion, with a shade of bitterness in his Home Counties accent. 'Wimbledon nowadays seems to belong to them.'

'Really? Which one do you think will lift the silver then? Rod Laver or Neale Fraser? Not that I really care – I'm more of a cricket man myself. Have you been following the second test against South Africa? Disgraceful, I call it…'

They passed on, their equally banal chatter about meaningless sport wafting past and over him. Instead, Reggie kept his eyes fixed on the progress of his quarry. He'd followed him all the way down the Broad after he'd stepped out of his college gates. Mind you, Reggie mused viciously, it was easy enough to keep track of him, with that head of hair so ostentatiously fair it was almost white, and his swagger telling the world he thought he owned it.

Right now, he was crossing the road alongside the Martyr's Memorial, and was heading, of course, for lunch at the Randolph hotel. Where else, Reggie Porter thought contemptuously, would someone like Lord Jeremy Littlejohn go for a snack?

He'd been keeping tabs on the peer now, off and on (as his working hours permitted), for over a month. Because of this, he was working up a general picture of the man and his habits. Which was why Reggie knew all about His Lordship's select little list of eateries.

He sighed as the fair head disappeared into the hotel. He'd been wearing his usual trademark white – today, in the form of a crisp white shirt and white linen summer jacket over pale-grey flannels.

It hadn't taken Reggie long to notice that his quarry had an affectation with regard to the colour, and again his heart twisted bitterly in his narrow chest. What a poseur! What a nancy boy! And how inappropriate! That Lord Jeremy Littlejohn of all people should favour white – the supposed colour of innocence! He just couldn't understand what Rebecca, his little sister, had seen in him.

As he thought of Becky, Reggie felt his heart give a sickening lurch. Just where *was* she? What had happened to her? Had she really run away to London as everyone insisted? And if she hadn't, where was she? He had to find out. It was killing him, not knowing.

He remembered her being brought home to the house by his parents when he was barely seven years old. A tiny scrap of a thing, he'd resented her at first for turning his life upside down, and threatening to steal all his parents' love, which had once been his alone.

But he'd been fascinated by her not long after – as a squalling infant, and then a chubby toddler, taking her first steps. As a child, she'd been simply adorable, with a riotous mop of fair curly hair, just tinged with the faintest hint of copper, and a pixie-like, gamin face. Precocious, funny and a little wild, naturally, she'd soon been able to twist him around her little finger, just as she had everyone else.

As soon as she'd hit her teens, she started to sing and dance, wear too much make-up and express an interest in being a 'star'. Somehow, the naivete of her extravagant dreams had only led to her family indulging her all the more. Of course, underneath all her pseudo-sophistication, she was still a total innocent.

His face twisted as he thought of her now, alone and helpless somewhere in the big, wide, nasty world, without her family to protect her. It was then that he noticed a woman passing by with a shopping basket in one hand giving him a startled look, and hastily stepping out past him.

Quickly, he wiped all expression off his face. He knew that, with his shock of very red hair and heavily freckled face, he wasn't exactly inconspicuous, so it wouldn't do to draw any further attention to himself. After all, the last thing he wanted, especially now, was for people to start noticing him.

Surreptitiously, he took out his notebook and made a note of the time and jotted down Littlejohn's movements that morning. It gave him pleasure to know he was building up a blueprint of the man's life. Learning his routines and foibles. All his dirty little secrets.

It made it so much easier to torment him.

And the tormenting wouldn't stop until he'd found out what had happened to Becky – because he was sure the aristocratic swine knew something about it.

He sighed and stretched, realising that, soon, he'd have to

leave off his surveillance and go back to work. He was currently the under-manager of a shop selling bicycles on the High, but he confidently expected to be made manager soon. Old Huddlestone was due to retire next winter, and the job was sure to be his. Even so, he couldn't afford to neglect his duties, and having to fit his campaign of attrition against Lord Jeremy Littlejohn in around his day job was enough to drive him to distraction.

So far as he could tell, the steady spate of poisonous and ever-more threatening anonymous letters he'd sent to the peer didn't seem to be having any outward effect on the appalling little dilettante. He still carried on with his wild parties and disgustingly lazy lifestyle as if the world were his oyster. As it no doubt was, damn him.

But Reggie had plans for escalating the pressure ever further. Then they'd see how long His Lordship could maintain his display of indifference and bravado.

He smiled wolfishly as he remembered the events of last week.

The death of his sycophantic and dirty-minded little friend must have shaken him up all right, of that he was sure. Oh, yes – what had happened to Derek Chadworth must be causing the peer of the realm some sleepless nights!

Wearing a hat to hide his distinctive red hair, Reggie had managed to get a place in the coroner's court when the inquest was being held. He could tell Lord Jeremy had been as nervous as a cat in the witness box, even though he'd given his evidence in his usual annoying and laconic drawl.

But underneath, he'd been like a cat on hot bricks. Wondering how things would play out…

And very satisfying it had been too, Reggie Porter thought now with a predatory grin. Now, all he had to do was find one little crack in His Lordship's armour of wealth and privilege and keep working away at it.

He was going to find his little sister, or find out just what had happened to her, and nothing and no one was going to stop him. And he would do, quite literally, whatever it took.

His large, freckled hands shook slightly as he put his notebook away and, with a last, withering glance of contempt at the hotel's attractive façade, walked briskly away towards the High.

Chapter 7

Maria DeMarco twisted her hands together nervously in her lap as she regarded the alarming old man seated opposite her.

She'd gone into the Bluebell Tea Room to meet her friend Lucy for a farewell lunch, but, as usual, her somewhat flighty companion was late. She'd been about to curtly dismiss the man who'd taken a chair at her table, murmuring a bland 'Hope you don't mind if I join you for a few minutes', with a blistering reply that she *did* indeed mind – very much – when she recognised him.

'Miss DeMarco, isn't it?' Dr Clement Ryder said now, with a jovial smile on his face as he made a show of settling comfortably into his Windsor chair. 'Thought I recognised you. I hope you don't mind if I rest my weary bones for a short while?'

It was, of course, no coincidence that he'd run into her here. He'd gone to her college expressly to interview her, but, on the way, had spotted her walking on the pavement across the road, and had followed her to the little café.

Now he sighed elaborately. 'This heat isn't to my liking. But I daresay you're used to far warmer climes in Italy?'

Maria, brought up to be respectful of her elders, smiled nervously, wishing her friend would arrive, giving her an excuse to politely get rid of him. 'Yes, I suppose that is true,' she murmured casually.

'I just wondered if you'd had any more thoughts about the death of that poor young man,' he dismayed her by asking firmly, for she'd been trying to cast around for a subject that would steer the conversation away from any mention of the dead boy.

'I? No… Well, yes, naturally it has been on my mind,' she hastily corrected herself, feeling totally wrong-footed. 'It was such a tragic thing to have happened.' She tried to sound politely non-committal.

'Yes. His parents thought so,' Clement said dryly, very neatly scuppering her attempts to distance herself from the events of the previous week.

Maria felt herself go cold at this rather brutal rebuttal and nodded miserably. 'Yes – his poor parents! Oh, how I wish I had never gone to that wretched picnic,' the young girl said with sudden savagery.

And that, Clement thought cynically, was probably the first totally truthful thing she'd ever said to him.

'Yes. Life isn't always roses and chocolates, I'm afraid,' he agreed gently.

Maria flushed. 'Now you make fun of me, I think.'

Clement waved a vague hand in the air. 'My apologies. Miss DeMarco. Let me be frank. I'm not satisfied with the events in my courtroom regarding Derek Chadworth's death. Not satisfied at all.'

Maria drew in a swift breath, her dark eyes darting all around the tea room, looking for a possible means of escape. But the waitresses, dressed in their black-and-white uniforms, were busy delivering lunches, and nobody was paying them any attention. Over by the far window, two young men were smoking and chatting, with one of them eyeing her favourably, but she could tell he wasn't interested enough to disrupt her tête-à-tête with the older man.

She silently cursed Lucy for always running late, and tried to avoid the coroner's knowing eyes. 'Oh?' she mumbled unhappily.

'Yes. You see, I think people were lying to me. And that tends to make me cross,' Clement said mildly.

Maria blinked furiously. This was intolerable! That she should be put in this position at all...

'I hope you don't think *I* lied to you, Dottore?' Maria, forced on the defensive, met his eyes boldly.

'No,' he surprised her slightly by saying. 'I don't think any good Catholic girl could place her hand on the Holy Bible and lie, at the peril of her immortal soul.' He gave her another kind smile.

His words pricked her conscience, and she felt her eyes actually smart with unshed tears. Quickly, she swallowed them back. It wouldn't do to lose control of herself – and the situation – now.

'You are quite right,' she said, truthfully enough. 'I did not lie under oath.'

Dr Ryder sighed gently. 'But perhaps you didn't exactly tell the truth either?' he persisted.

Maria flushed. 'I said I didn't see that poor boy on the day of the picnic, and I didn't,' she said firmly.

'Hmm. So you and all the others said. But would it surprise you to know that some of your fellow students that day are now saying they might have seen him after all?' he asked curiously. And he wasn't exaggerating. Since speaking to Lionel Gulliver, he'd spoken to three other students, not called as witnesses at the inquest, but who had been at the party on the fateful day, and all three of them were singing from the same hymn sheet. Derek might have been there. But they, personally, couldn't swear to it.

He could see at once that this news *did* surprise Maria. She shot him a quick, puzzled frown, then shrugged.

Clement realised that whoever had sent out the word that, from now on, nobody was to be so sure Derek *hadn't* been present that day, had failed to get the message across to Maria.

Slowly he leaned forward across the table, planting his elbows on the tabletop, folding his hands just in front of him and resting his chin thoughtfully on top of his knuckles. He gazed at her openly across the expanse of cutlery and the little vase of daisies in the centre of the blue-and-white-checked tablecloth.

'Who is it that's pulling the strings, Maria?' he demanded softly. 'Lord Littlejohn?'

He saw her give a little start.

'Well, he is the obvious ringleader, isn't he?' he swept on, almost kindly. 'The head honcho of your little gang. The big chief of the Marquis Club?' He said the last sentence carefully, but caught nothing other than a brief moue of distaste on her face.

'Oh, that! A silly little club for silly little aristocratic boys who have no respect for women, and fancy themselves as rebels! Hah! What do I care about all that?' she asked, with the Latin flair for magnificent arrogance. 'I was only there because a boy I liked asked me.'

'And do you still like him?' Clement asked, amused by this eye-flashing display of temper in spite of the seriousness of the situation.

'No,' the spirited young girl shot back. 'Like I said before, I wish I'd never gone out with them on that day.'

Clement nodded. 'So… is there anything you want to tell me, Maria? Now that we're away from the courtroom, and away from prying eyes and ears?'

Visibly, the girl hesitated.

'Since you're going back home soon anyway? Back to Italy and away from all this and everyone here?' he wheedled. 'What you say to me will be in the strictest confidence, I assure you.'

Maria made a little face. 'It is true. I will be glad to get away from here,' she said, looking out at the city through the window. Past the gingham curtains, it looked particularly lovely today, with its soot-darkened Cotswold stone glowing golden underneath the grime, its ivy-clad walls looking mellow in the summer haze, and all the clock towers, which chimed so haphazardly on and around the hour. 'Oh, it seemed nice enough at first, this place, but underneath…' Maria sighed.

Then she straightened in her chair a little and shot the older man a solemn look. 'I think, Dottore, that you should be careful here. Oxford is a very… elite place. And you have not, I think, the kind of power you might need… if you started to… how do you English say?… ruffle the wrong kind of feathers?'

Clement Ryder felt a ripple of surprise wash over him. For a split second he thought the young madam was actually having the gall to threaten him. But then, as he met her slightly concerned gaze, he realised she was actually trying to warn him.

He bit back the urge to laugh, and instead nodded solemnly. 'I'm not without power and influence myself, Miss DeMarco,' he said quietly – and with some understatement.

For a moment, Maria considered this. She knew she must look as unsure as she felt. The trouble was, she was still, even after three years, a relative stranger here. And although she knew some things, she didn't know others. She knew, of course, all the myriad things her fellow students knew. So she knew she had to keep her mouth firmly shut about that awful afternoon on the river.

She didn't understand enough about the power base in this city to know who really had influence and who didn't. Of course, she knew all about the Marquis Club, and that the elite and rich members of that little clique all had families with influence and power. Sons of dukes would always be protected and cosseted. It was the way the world worked – whether you were in England or in Italy. Maria knew this.

However, she didn't know enough about the politics of the city to know if this man, this coroner, was right to feel so sure of himself. Oh, she'd heard he had powerful friends in high places. But were they powerful enough?

As she met his steady, compelling gaze, she felt herself weaken. After all, like he'd said, next week she'd be back home in Italy, and she could put this part of her life behind her. Her own family were powerful enough in their own country to protect her from any consequences.

'Miss DeMarco, a boy has died,' Clement said sharply, interrupting her line of thought. 'If you can help me, in any way, don't you think you should do so?'

Maria flushed. Yes, that was all very well. But a girl had to look out for herself. Also, it was not nice to be the tattletale.

She sighed. But perhaps just a hint or two couldn't hurt? After all, he'd promised nothing she said to him would be repeated.

'I know nothing about how that boy came to drown,' she said flatly, looking him straight in the eye. 'Do you believe that?'

'Yes. I rather think I do.'

'Very well then,' she said, with a hint of satisfaction. 'I can say nothing more about what happened that afternoon… but I can say this. That boy who drowned? I don't think he was a very *nice* boy.'

Clement blinked. Whatever he'd been expecting her to cough up, it hadn't been that. He slowly unfolded his hands and arms and leaned back in the chair to give her more space.

'Why do you say that?' he asked curiously, careful to keep his voice light. He certainly didn't want to spook her, just when she'd started to trust him. But he needed more information. 'I thought you said you didn't know him?'

'And I did not,' Maria confirmed sharply. 'But I heard things. Not much…' She quickly held up a hand to forestall him. 'Nothing specific. Just rumours, you understand. Somebody would say something, and I would overhear. Nobody spoke badly about him openly, or anything like that. But I could tell. It was in their voices. In the knowing looks that passed between them, whenever his name came up. There was something about that boy that was not nice. And that's all I can tell you,' she added firmly.

Then her face lit up with relief, and the coroner turned his head a little to see a tall brunette weaving her way through the tables towards them.

'Oh, Maria, sorry to be so late…' She paused, obviously expecting an introduction to her friend's companion.

But the Italian girl was already rising, and saying firmly, 'It's all right, Lucy. This gentleman was just leaving.'

Dr Ryder gave her a brief, somewhat sardonic smile, murmured something to the ladies, and walked away.

His face, though, as he walked out into the bright, sunny afternoon, was very thoughtful indeed.

Chapter 8

Trudy ordered the Welsh rarebit and a cup of tea at the counter, and hoped she didn't look anywhere near as nervous as she felt. Not that, to any casual observer, there was any obvious cause for her to be alarmed.

She was in a basement cafeteria underneath a bookshop just opposite the train station, a cheap and cheerful place, full of penniless students (according to them) and one or two shop workers, attracted to the place because of its cheap lunchtime menu.

The small, airless room was full of smoke, since nearly everyone had a cigarette lit, and she was finding it just a little hard to breathe.

She'd never liked the smell of cigarettes, and the few times she'd tried to smoke one, had coughed so hard it made her feel sick. Consequently, although all her friends smoked, she was one of the very few women in the café not puffing happily away.

She'd managed to strike up a conversation with three other girls in the queue, after she'd overheard them talking about an essay they were all writing and realised they were indeed students. Now she followed them hopefully with her tray as they set off for one of the few free tables. Just as she'd hoped, one of the girls caught her eye and offered her a place with them.

'Oh, thanks,' Trudy said gratefully, taking a seat. 'I hate eating alone, don't you?'

One of the girls, a tall brunette with her hair swept back in a neat French pleat, rolled her big blue eyes and sighed. 'Oh, yes! You feel so conspicuous, don't you? I'm Mavis Whitchurch, by the way, and this is Mary-Beth.' She waved at a very overweight girl with short hair so dark it was almost black. 'And that's Christine,' she finished, nodding at the final member of their group, a tall, blonde Amazon of a girl who looked fit enough to destroy anyone and anything found on a hockey field.

'Nice to meet you all. I'm Trudy,' she said, then could have bitten her tongue out. Wasn't she supposed to be undercover? Shouldn't she have given a false name? Or was that unnecessary? She felt a little flustered, and wished she'd had the sense to ask either Dr Ryder or Inspector Jennings exactly what she was expected to do – and not do – while picking up the gossip.

Then she told herself crossly not to be such a rabbit. She was simply going to talk to people, after all!

'I wish I'd had the rarebit now, instead of the shepherd's pie,' Mary-Beth said, prodding her plate of rather mushy-looking minced meat and mash potatoes disconsolately.

'Oh, you always wish you'd ordered something else,' her friend, the Amazonian Christine, put in flatly. 'What I want to know is, have any of you actually finished the essay for old Pinkers or not? And if you have, can I crib?'

'Not from me you can't,' Mavis said flatly. 'You are a lazy cat, Chris. Do your own work.'

'Well, that's nice,' the other girl shot back. 'You know how Pinkers takes on so if we're late.'

'My tutors are the same.' Trudy felt it was time to set out her own (false) bona fides, and rush in where angels feared to tread, otherwise she was never going to be able to lead the conversation where she needed it to go. 'I think they have a mania about timetables or something. As if we're all automatons who can produce work like machines. I have to say,' she swept on, rather enjoying herself suddenly, 'that I, for one, can't produce any really good work unless I'm in the mood.'

'Me neither,' Christine said triumphantly, glaring at her friend.

'Well, it's got to be done, hasn't it?' Mavis muttered rebelliously.

'Too true.' Trudy tried to sound rueful. 'Mind you, I think it can be a bit much when they don't take into account extenuating circumstances. For instance, like those poor students who were at that awful picnic, where that poor boy drowned! I don't suppose any of them were able to just carry on swotting!'

She took a bite out of her cheese on toast, hoping she hadn't gone in too fast, or been too obvious, and shot a quick, darting glance around the table to see how her sally had been received.

When she'd first set foot in the café, she'd been feeling distinctly nervous. Not only was she not convinced that she could successfully pass herself off as a bluestocking, but she also wasn't sure how good she'd be at lying either. Now, rather to her shame (with a little elation mixed in), she thought she might get quite good at it!

'Oh, cripes, no! I don't suppose they could have either,' Mary-Beth said morosely and transported a huge forkful of food to her mouth. 'It gives me the creeps, thinking about it,' she added, after swallowing noisily.

'And nobody seems to know exactly what happened either,' Trudy exclaimed, leaning forward and dropping her voice just a little. She knew from her own schoolgirl days just how well inspiring a feeling of conspiracy got people talking. 'From what I read in the papers, nobody seems to have seen it happen!' she all but whispered.

'Oh, well, that's not so surprising,' Mavis said briskly. 'Being one of the White Knight's little parties, I daresay most of them were four sheets to the wind.'

Trudy blinked. 'The White Knight?'

'Yes. You know – Lord Littlejohn,' Mary-Beth said, shooting her a quick, puzzled look.

'Oh, right,' Trudy said quickly, and hoped she wasn't flushing. In truth, her heart was suddenly beating like a hammer as she realised how easy it was to trip up. If she really had been one of them, she'd have known the nickname. To try and recover, she shrugged, and grinned a shade helplessly.

'I have to admit, I don't travel in those sorts of circles. And I've had to have my nose to the grindstone ever since coming up. I don't think my brains are all that top hole, to be honest.'

She held her breath, hoping her apparent honesty would win them over, and, sure enough, Christine came to her rescue.

'Me neither,' she said glumly. Then grinned. 'Not that I'd ever be invited to one of the White Knight's little soirees anyway. I don't fit in with their view of the fairer sex.'

'No,' Mavis put in with a grin. 'The men in the Marquis Club like their women dainty and brainless. That lets out Christine. Well, on one count, anyway.'

Christine picked up one portion of her chicken sandwich and eyed her friend over it. 'Are you saying I'm not dainty?' she asked archly, and all three girls suddenly burst out laughing.

Trudy, just a second behind, did the same.

'None of 'em would look twice at me, unless it was to say something beastly,' Mary-Beth put in, rather matter-of-factly.

'And I'm too wise to them,' Mavis said, rather darkly. 'So that lets me out.'

'Seems none of us measure up to His Lordship's expectations then,' Trudy put in cheerfully. 'Just as well, if you ask me. I'd still be having nightmares now if I'd been there that day. Just thinking about… well, that poor boy drowning… Ugh!' She gave a theatrical shudder, then hoped she wasn't overdoing it. 'I suppose he must have hit his head or something and just floated off and nobody noticed.'

'I daresay they were all too busy scrambling for the riverbanks themselves,' Mavis said laconically. 'I can't see any of that lot being concerned with anything other than saving their own skins.'

'Even so…' Trudy sighed. 'If they were all such great friends, you'd have thought somebody would have noticed he was missing from the party, and wondered about it,' she added casually.

She noticed the three girls shoot each other quick, thoughtful looks and held her breath.

'I suppose so,' Mavis said, but she didn't sound convinced.

'You know, I never could understand what that Chadworth boy was doing running about in the White Knight's set in the first place,' Mary-Beth suddenly piped up. 'Old Bodger told me he was only the son of some Lancashire solicitor or something. Not a title in his line – even going back donkey's years.'

'Yes, I heard something similar,' Christine remarked, finishing off one sandwich and starting on the other. At nearly six feet tall, and with a body that looked packed with athletic muscle, Trudy supposed she needed to keep herself well fed.

'Perhaps he wasn't actually invited to the picnic then.' Trudy played devil's advocate craftily. 'Perhaps he just gatecrashed. Maybe he didn't even know Lord… the White Knight.'

'Oh, no, he *did*,' Mavis corrected her at once. 'I've seen them around town now and then. Nightclub crawling and what have you. They seemed pretty bosom pals to me.'

'Yes, I've seen them together too,' Mary-Beth said complacently. 'In the pub at the head of the river, and that new place near the Pitt Rivers. In fact, I think both of them were being chucked out one night, when I was cycling past.'

'Humph! You ask me, that Marquis Club of theirs was formed just so they could go out on the razzle and pick up all the local girls and make a nuisance of themselves,' Christine said flatly.

'I wonder if he was asked to join the picnic so he could take photographs,' Mary-Beth put in, making Trudy really sit up and take notice. 'You know – as their sort of semi-official photographer and all that.'

'Oh, was he a keen photographer then?' Trudy asked. 'I hadn't heard that.'

'Oh, yeah, I've seen him about town lots of times with a camera, snapping away,' Christine said. 'Buildings and butterflies and people and all that arty stuff,' she added airily, with a sigh. Pushing her empty plate away, she started eyeing the piece of Welsh rarebit still lying untouched on Trudy's plate.

Trudy took the hint and, with a little yawn, pushed her plate to the middle. 'I'm full. Anybody want the spare piece?'

But before the Amazon could reach for it, Mary-Beth pounced and snaffled it away from under her nose, and the other two girls began such a good-natured ribbing of her that Trudy didn't feel comfortable interrupting. She might be new at this, but even she could tell that trying to turn the conversation back to the events of the river picnic now would be pushing her luck.

So, she was quite content to sit back and join in the fun. Besides, she'd learned quite a lot, and was well satisfied with her first foray into undercover work.

Twenty minutes later, she left the café and walked the short distance to the coroner's office. There, his secretary told her the doctor hadn't returned yet from his lunch hour, so she took the time to sit in the outer office and write up her notes. And to sit and think.

When, ten minutes later, Clement Ryder returned from his own interesting interview at the Bluebell Tea Room, she had a few questions for him.

Once settled in his office, they swapped information, and then Trudy leaned forward in her seat, and said, 'You know, Dr Ryder, I've been thinking.'

'Always a good way to pass the time, WPC Loveday,' he agreed, eyes twinkling.

Trudy grinned back at him. She was dressed in a dark-blue skirt and white blouse, with neat black shoes. It was the best 'undercover' outfit she could come up with out of her meagre wardrobe, but it still felt strange to be sitting in the coroner's office without her hot and heavy uniform on.

71

'It's about the third punt,' she said seriously. 'It seems to me, if there was anything really iffy about Derek's "accident", then it had to originate with the collision. Right?'

'Elaborate,' Clement encouraged her succinctly.

'Well, there are only three things that might have happened that day. One, Derek was accidentally drowned. Two, he was deliberately drowned. Or three, he committed suicide.'

The coroner nodded, his face serious. 'Go on.'

'So far, there's nothing to suggest suicide. His parents and tutors and friends all testified that he was acting normally. And he left no note back in his college room. So, for the sake of argument, we'll put that to one side.'

'All right,' the older man concurred agreeably.

'And I think we still agree, don't we, that an accident still seems the most likely of the three options,' Trudy swept on. 'And the students not wanting to admit he'd been a part of their group could just mean they wanted to distance themselves from it. Just in case anyone blamed them for not coming to his rescue, say. Or… well… for whatever reason.'

'Hmm…' he said, a shade less certainly.

'Anyway, let's leave that to one side for a moment too,' Trudy hastily swept on, before he could start picking holes in her reasoning (she knew from past experience just how well he could do this!) 'Let's just touch on number three. Murder.' She felt a little flush of excitement wash over her as she said the thrilling word.

'All right, let's touch on it,' Clement agreed, watching her with twitching lips.

'OK. Well, if someone *had* wanted to kill Derek, it seems to me they must have either arranged for the collision to happen, thus giving them an opportunity to hold Derek underwater and drown him, or else simply taken the opportunity offered by the accidental collision to kill him.'

'Sounds reasonable.'

'So surely we should be concentrating on the third punt – and those students on it?' she pointed out eagerly.

Clement hated to rain on her parade, since she looked so bright and happy with herself, but he had no other choice. 'Yes, that was the first thing I thought of too,' he said mildly, pretending not to notice the way her face fell. 'So, before I went to your DI asking for help, I'd already talked to all the students on the third punt and satisfied myself that none of them had anything to do with it. First of all, none of them knew either Derek or Lord Littlejohn, and none of them was a member of the Marquis Club. Furthermore, they were all engineering students who knew one another well. And the chap doing the punting explained to me just how the accident happened, and I was convinced he was telling the truth. He rounded the bend and found the two other punts blocking the river. He didn't have time to avoid them.'

'Oh,' Trudy said, a little deflated. 'And I take it that neither he, nor any of the other engineers, noticed Derek in difficulties?'

'No – none of them noticed anyone who was having trouble in the water. And those who weren't the best of swimmers all seemed to have pals helping them out.'

'Well, that means then, surely, that the collision itself was an accident,' Trudy persisted. 'So if it *was* murder, somebody at the picnic party took advantage of the accident to get rid of Derek in a way that would make it look like accidental drowning.'

'Perhaps,' the coroner said mildly, and his lips twitched again as he saw he had aggravated her with his temporising. 'But that's what we're trying to find out, isn't it?' he added, appeasing her with a smile.

Chapter 9

That afternoon, Jimmy Roper conscientiously mowed his back lawn and then retreated with the local paper and a deckchair under the flowering cherry tree in one corner. Tyke, with a sigh, curled up in the shade under the sagging bottom of the chair and began to softly snore.

With a sigh of contentment, the retired milkman turned to the sports pages first, thinking he might just get himself a cold bottle of Bass from the fridge, once his wife had gone into town on the bus for her regular shopping trip.

Still thinking on this pleasant and tasty possibility, he began leafing absently through the black-and-white newsprint, and was suddenly struck by the name of the student who had drowned a week ago.

Like the rest of the village, his wife had been full of it these past days, and when she'd realised her husband had been walking along the river not long before it must all have happened, she'd been hailed as a reliable source of information. But although she'd been extremely gratified by this turn of events, Jimmy didn't like to think on it too much.

He'd seen enough death in the war – all those young men… he didn't like to think of another waste of such a young life, right here on his back doorstep.

He almost hurried past the article, except for the little byline, which caught his eye. It was an appeal from the city coroner, one Dr Clement Ryder. He was asking for anyone who had been in the area that day, but who had not been called to court to give testimony, to get in touch with him at his office.

Jimmy frowned thoughtfully and somewhat reluctantly read on. The coroner was asking for any and all witnesses to come forward, no matter how little they believed they could help. He was interested in building up a picture of life on the river that day, and any and all information would be treated in confidence.

Jimmy sighed gently. Surely he had nothing to say that could be of any use? Like most people, his initial instinct was to have nothing to do with anything out of the ordinary and unknown. If the war had taught him one thing, it was to volunteer for nothing! Getting mixed up in any sort of unpleasantness when you didn't have to wasn't something your average British citizen longed for.

But also, like most decent, hardworking people, Jimmy had a respect for law and order, and it had been drummed into him from early childhood that you should do what was right and expected of you. Civic duty was something everyone had to consider carefully.

He sighed and reached down absently to scratch Tyke behind his black-and-white ears. 'Well, old boy. Any advice? Do I get in touch with this here coroner, or don't I?'

His old dog stretched and yawned, then went back to sleep.

But Jimmy Roper wasn't the only one who had read the coroner's appeal in the newspaper. Two others had also seen it, with somewhat similar reactions.

One was a Mrs Enid Clowes, a sixty-eight-year-old woman living in a little bungalow at the other end of Wolvercote, and her reaction was one of mixed alarm and excitement. Nothing much ever happened in Enid's world, which was run along lines of strict routine. This felt safe and secure, of course, but was also inclined to render her life rather stultifying and boring.

So anything out of the norm was a cause for both celebration and extreme caution.

She'd been out and about that day and, like the rest of the village, had been shocked and dismayed by the awful tragedy – as well as just a little bit excited (although she'd never have admitted this to herself, let alone anyone else).

But she couldn't think how what she had seen or heard could be of any possible interest to a man as important as the coroner.

A widow since the war, she was one of those dithering, easily flustered old ladies who usually made most people impatient within five minutes of meeting her. She was also of the same mind as Jimmy Roper, in that she didn't want to get mixed up in anything 'not nice'. What would her neighbours say, for instance?

Of course, it would make her the centre of attention if she were just to mention… But no. Better not. As her old mother had always said, 'Better safe than sorry.'

On the other hand… the notice in the paper did say they were interested in any little bit of information, no matter how apparently insignificant.

Not having a black-and-white mongrel to consult for advice, she spent the rest of the afternoon turning the matter over and over in her mind, while pottering about and doing her usual chores in her quiet, neat and lonely little home.

It was quite typical of her that, by the time it got to be dark, she still hadn't come to any conclusion or made any definite decision as to what she ought to do.

The third person to read the short article was a thirty-year-old man called Clive Horton. He had a respectable, if not highly paid, job as a clerk at an insurance company in Somertown, a nearby suburb of the city.

He lived with his widowed mother in a tiny flat not far from a very prestigious avenue, whose line of cherry trees they could see (if they strained their necks a little) from the bathroom window.

Clive, a short, thin, and – alas – rather chinless man, was enjoying the warm summer weather by sitting next to his bedroom window without a tie on, the top two buttons of his starched shirt daringly undone. He read the newspaper article in his usual meticulous and thorough way, then, rather more quickly, read it again.

Used to poring over documents with great precision, he was inclined to think long and hard before taking any course of action.

In the end, he decided it wouldn't be a good idea to approach the coroner in person. Someone from his company might see him enter the mortuary premises and start making enquiries. (Clive lived in mortal terror of any out-of-the-way behaviour on his part getting reported to the senior management of his company.) As the sole breadwinner for himself and his mother, holding down his job was his top priority in life.

But it was his duty to answer this direct call for information, since he too had been out and about near Port Meadow at the time in question, taking his usual constitutional. A man had a duty to remain fit and healthy, after all.

Not to volunteer such information as he had might somehow rebound on him and put him in a bad light should it ever come out that he had failed to inform the authorities of what little he knew.

Clive, it had to be said, was the sort of person who always paid due attention to the authorities. Be they his mother, God, or anyone in the civil service!

Yes, clearly, the diligent clerk thought pedantically, what was called for was a letter to the coroner's office, detailing all he had seen that day that might be of any interest whatsoever. Naturally, he would need to take his time over such an important letter. It might have to be used at some point in an official capacity and would certainly go on file somewhere. And anything that bore his signature would have to be accurate and worded so carefully that absolutely nothing could be made of it that might, in any possible way, rebound on him to his disadvantage.

So he wouldn't hurry. He would have to get it perfect.

He got out a pad and pen and began to make preliminary notes. After that he'd do a first draft, and then consider it carefully before starting a second.

And when he was finally content with it, he would post it.

With a second-class stamp, obviously, since he wasn't made of money.

Chapter 10

Celia Morrison pushed open the churchyard gate and ignored the usual creak it gave when it got past a certain point. She knew the sexton was supposed to keep it oiled, but really, who cared?

In her hand she held a large and fragrant bunch of colourful Sweet Williams, plucked from her front garden not a few minutes ago.

Around her, the pretty little village of Islip dozed in the soporific afternoon sun. Bumblebees droned in the wildflowers bordering the lane that ran alongside the churchyard wall and, over in the meadow, the river glinted silver and gold as it meandered through the pastures.

Her feet began to drag as they took her to the newest row of graves, for she was in no hurry to reach her destination. Instead she paused a little to look around. In the older parts of the churchyard, the graves tended to lean, and none of them had any colourful votive gifts of flowers or mixed leaves. Of course, with most of these inhabitants having been dead for more than a century, even their children had long since died themselves, leaving no one to remember them, or mark their passing.

As the rows became newer, however, you came across the odd gravestone bedecked with flowers, until, gradually, nearly all of those in the last (and thus most recent) two had colourful offerings of remembrance arranged around a loved one's name.

And then there were the newest ones of all...

Swallowing back a hard, bitter lump that had risen to her throat, Celia Morrison forced herself towards one of these. Bending down by the headstone of her daughter, she removed the fading flowers she'd left there last week, and poured out the green and stagnant water from the vase onto the grass.

'Here you are, Jenny, the first of this year's Sweet Williams. Your favourite,' she murmured quietly.

She set about pouring fresh water from an old pop bottle – lemonade, another of Jenny's favourites – into the vase, and then arranged the flowers. Setting them against the well-scrubbed and pristine stone, she finally leaned back on her heels and read the inscription she and her husband, Keith, had chosen for their only child.

'In loving memory of our dear daughter, Jennifer Elizabeth Morrison, who left us on the 12th of January, 1959. Aged 17 years. Safe in our Lord's hands.'

Safe. Yes, she'd insisted on that. For that was the only way she could bear to think of her lovely Jenny. Safe at last, and at peace.

Of course, there were those in the village – miserable, loveless, heartless old biddies mostly – who had been scandalised her daughter had been laid to rest here at all.

But the rector had been so kind and had fought her case with his bishop. In the end, they'd been allowed to bury her here, joining some of her aunts and uncles, one set of grandparents and four cousins. For the Morrison family had lived in Islip for generations. Well, on Keith's side, anyway.

Celia, a slight, dark-haired woman with big, brown eyes, sighed heavily, then felt something warm drop onto the back of her hand. When she looked down in surprise, she realised it was a small droplet of water.

It took her a moment to realise it was her own teardrop.

With a weary gesture, she reached up and, using the sleeve of her summer frock, wiped her face dry. What was the point of crying?

She stood up listlessly and walked slowly away, telling herself she had things to do and people to see.

She had to start getting Keith's tea on, for a start.

As the mother of Jennifer Morrison walked back to her home to start cooking the evening meal, Lord Jeremy Littlejohn, in his rooms at St Winnifred's College, Oxford, was getting slowly but comprehensively drunk.

It was something he was used to doing, and could do well. The art of drinking properly, as he'd told his amused friends, was to pace yourself and enjoy the process, otherwise what was the point? It was also a man's duty, he'd tell them loftily, to learn how to hold his liquor and behave at all times as if he were perfectly sober. And to achieve this accomplishment, you needed to practise.

This speech was usually met with cheers and encouragement, and an all-round agreement that he was right, and that they needed to practise too. But today he was drinking all alone. And he definitely wasn't in the mood to be amusing.

The young lord was stretched out in a large, rather battered, leather chair. Like most of the rooms in his ancient college, it had been furnished and decorated with the donations of past alumni. So the furniture could be anything from the 1600s to modern Danish. Likewise, you had to take pot luck with the art (which could be genuinely ghastly or utterly divine) as all manner of bizarre bequests had been left to the old alma mater in various wills.

He even knew someone who'd had to live with an elephant's-foot umbrella stand, left by some blighter who'd been a viceroy of India or some such awful thing. Apparently it stank in wet weather.

Lord Jeremy Littlejohn snorted as he thought about this, then lifted the bottle of Beaujolais to his lips. He'd already drunk one bottle and was making serious inroads into a second. It was good wine, but not of the very best. You didn't drink to get drunk on the best, naturally. He wasn't a philistine, after all.

But today there was no pleasure in his indulgence, and his eyes kept going, sourly, to the piece of paper resting on top of his desk, along with all the other detritus of student living – mostly piles of books he couldn't be bothered to study.

It was a small, white, cheap piece of paper.

And it contained small, cheap threats.

He'd begun to get them nearly two months ago. Death threats. Torture threats. Exposure threats. All written in a depressingly lurid and unimaginative style.

At first, he'd shown them to one or two friends, since it had given him the opportunity to be droll. Jeremy rather liked being droll. One of his heroes was Noel Coward. Although – somewhat to the surprise of one or two of his set – he didn't share that great man's sexual proclivities, Jeremy *did* admire enormously his dry wit.

He used the letters to show off, both with his magnificent dismissal of them and by mocking the sender's banal phrases. Not for the world would he have shown one drop of concern or real apprehension, like any normal mortal might.

Indeed, it was only when they'd become more specific as to his alleged crimes that he stopped sharing them.

And became worried.

Very worried.

And now this latest missive had him very worried indeed.

If only he could find out which envious little bastard had written them. At first, naturally, he'd been inclined to think it was one of his own set – most of them were poisonous, envious little sycophants, who'd take their first opportunity to stick the knife in. (Just the kind he liked!)

But then he'd begun to realise that the writer of the letters didn't know him all that well, since his list of alleged sins was more general than specific.

So he'd begun to wonder if it was someone outside the Marquis Club – a student who felt slighted at not being invited into the inner circle, perhaps? But he'd had to dismiss that idea too, when he checked and saw that all of the letters had come through the post. Not one had been hand-delivered. And to neglect such an obvious psychological ploy of slipping one of the nasty things under his door in person could only mean one thing.

The sender probably wasn't a student at all. He simply didn't have access to the college. Which meant it was a city boy. Town, not gown. It was this revelation that scared him most of all.

Because the young lord knew he had power here, in the hallowed halls of academia, where wealth, name and privilege ruled supreme; but out there, in the real world, his grip and reach were far less certain.

The idea of some faceless, nameless, ordinary little oik watching and judging him was beginning to get seriously on his nerves.

Not for the first time, he cursed the name of Derek Chadworth. The stupid bastard! Just what had he got them mixed up in, exactly? How far had he really gone? A fellow liked having his fun and games and all that, Jeremy mused morosely, but it was an unwritten rule that you never went *too* far. That was just understood. Well, it was if you were a gentleman.

The thing was, Littlejohn mused dispiritedly, Derek had never really been one of them, had he?

One thing was for certain. He would have to search Derek's old rooms at St Bede's before the bursar reassigned them. Because if the stupid little sod had hidden anything incriminating, it might have been in there.

Steadily drinking – and remaining, in fact, rather impressively sober – His Lordship began contemplating common and petty larceny. A bit of a comedown for one of his rank, naturally.

But still… it might prove to be rather droll.

Chapter 11

Later that evening, Clement Ryder returned to the well-maintained Victorian place in South Parks Road that had been his home for many years now. His children, Julia and Vincent, had both long since left the nest. A widower for ten years, it sometimes seemed to him a very quiet place. But he wasn't a man who feared silence and, after a hard or hectic day, was often grateful for the sanctuary his home provided.

Walking through the front door, he realised at once that his daily woman was still in residence, for he could hear her scuttling about in the kitchen, and the welcome smell of cooking was wafting through the hall as he pushed open the door.

'That you, Doctor?' she called, as she did most days their paths crossed. Who else she expected to come through the door, he never could ascertain.

'Yes, Mrs Lorne,' he called back, walking down the short corridor to the kitchen. There, with her arms lightly dusted in flour up to her elbow, a comfortably rounded, middle-aged woman glanced up from a mixing bowl and smiled. Her salt-and-pepper hair was kept up in a loose bun, and she wore her habitual all-over flowered pinafore over a plain, navy-blue dress. 'Just making you a raspberry and apple tart. I got some fresh lard from the butcher's this morning, so the pastry will be nice and short, just how you like it.'

He leaned over to regard the pastry crumbs forming in the bowl and smiled. 'It looks as if it's going to be very tasty indeed,' he complimented her. As he did so, he happened to glance up and caught a brief look of distaste quickly passing over the woman's face. It was instantly hidden, and she looked slightly embarrassed as she caught his eye.

Wondering what on earth that was all about, he moved smoothly away, thanked her and set about making a cup of coffee. Then he got out of her way. They'd been together long enough to know better than to get under each other's feet.

In the study, Clement sipped his coffee and read the papers, but his mind wasn't really on the local news. Instead, his thoughts drifted to the Chadworth case. If case it was. Was he really so bored or jaded that he was making a mountain out of a molehill? After all, apart from a few odd and irritatingly vague lies from a bunch of students, what did it really amount to?

On the other hand, there was definitely something about it all that reeked just a little bit.

His thoughts moved on to probationary WPC Trudy Loveday, and he allowed a small smile to cross his face. No two ways about it, he rather liked having her around. Not only because she was young and pretty and thus a refreshing and charming change from his usual, dull, daily fare, but because of her spirit and quick mind.

When he'd first approached that nincompoop Jennings earlier in the year to ask for a police liaison to help him out with a cold case, he hadn't held out much hope the Inspector would spare him one of his best and brightest. Of course, by that dull police officer's own estimation, nor had he! No, Jennings had been happy to foist the lone, young, female officer onto him, just to get her out of his station house.

But it hadn't taken Clement long to appreciate he'd been

handed a diamond in the rough. Oh, yes, she was as green as grass, and sometimes still startlingly and heartbreakingly young. But she was a determined little madam, and had guts too, as well as ambition and brains.

She'd acquitted herself well in the Marcus Deering case earlier in the year, which had turned out to be a case of murder, right enough. That had been the first time he'd worked with her, and he was perfectly willing to admit that, without her valuable help, it would have been much harder going to catch the killer.

He wasn't so sure about this latest affair, though. He was quite prepared to accept that the boy had accidentally drowned. Nevertheless… With a shrug, the coroner turned to the crossword page and reached for a pen. As he did so, his hand began to tremble wildly.

With a curse, he tried to ignore it. When he concentrated and began to fill in the first of the clues, he was gratified and mightily relieved to see that the letters were clear and free from shaking lines.

Trudy had gone home for her tea, but had left home again in the evening, telling her parents she was going to meet friends at the local youth club. In truth, she wandered instead into (and out of) a few pubs in search of more gossiping students. (This alone would have worried her mother sick!)

As it was, Trudy had to admit, if only to herself, that it was rather nerve-wracking. It was very odd to think that, had she been in uniform, she'd now be admonishing the landlords for turning a blind eye to the regulations governing licensing laws! Instead, she gave them a grateful smile for ignoring her obvious youth as she sidled past the bar in search of likely-looking groups of drinkers.

She finally struck it lucky in the third place she tried – a little backwater of a place off Walton Street. The Dog and Duck was tiny, dark and full of a rather 'serious' crowd, mostly comprising students reading politics, philosophy and economics. As she nervously took her glass of orange juice to a particularly noisy corner, she could only hope she wouldn't have to try and join in with any serious discussions. Because her woeful ignorance of any of those three subjects would quickly single her out as a fraud!

Although she'd often toyed with the idea of how nice it would have been to go to university herself, she'd always known that couldn't possibly happen. For a start, working-class girls like herself simply couldn't afford not to start work right after school. And there was no way her parents could have supported her – especially not at Oxford! And, if she were being strictly honest with herself, she knew that, although she had done all right at school, academia wasn't really her strongest suit. Oh, she liked her lessons well enough (well, maybe not maths!), but she was the kind of person who liked to be out and about and doing things and making a practical and helpful difference to people's lives.

Studying books all day long in dusty libraries would probably have driven her mad!

Luckily, though, the mixed group of three girls and four lads occupying the table around a filthy window looking out onto the street were arguing over the future, or not, of television.

Taking a stool and sort of shuffling it close to the group, she was able to listen in and await her opportunity. One of the lads noticed her at once, and gave her a speculative glance, making her blush a little.

'I'm telling you, all those people watching the coronation was a blip,' a rather horsey-faced girl said. 'My pops says it's a passing fad and won't have a set in the house, anyway. And what he says goes.'

'Poor you,' another girl, rather less horsey-faced, said in commiseration. 'My old nanny insisted on having one, and Mother always indulges her. Now both of them adore that woman who's just started working for the BBC to try and win us over from that Barbara Mandell.'

'Oh, you mean the one in *Town and Around*, Nan Winton?' one of the lads said with a shrug. 'Can't see the appeal myself in listening to yapping women – let alone actually watching one yap on television!'

As expected, this set up a riot of ripostes, both for and against. Trudy sipped her orange juice and waited patiently.

She'd dressed in her prettiest summer frock of white and orange, and left her long, dark, curly hair loose. Of course, she hadn't dared put on any make-up, for her mother would have spotted that at once, but she noticed, with something approaching relief, that none of the other girls was wearing any either.

Eventually, as she'd expected, the boy who had been eyeing her for a little while plucked up the courage to say something to her, allowing her to be drawn into the group. And in much the same way as she had before when talking to the trio of girls in the café, she brought the subject around to Derek Chadworth. Not that it needed much effort – clearly his untimely death was still a hot topic of discussion among his peers. Speculation about him ran rife. Since most of it covered the same ground as her talk with Mary-Beth and the others, she was content to sit and listen, until something new was said.

Which didn't take long.

'I wonder what that girlfriend of his is doing right now?' one of the three girls said pityingly. She was a rather overweight girl with very long blonde hair. 'I suppose she must be cut up about it.'

'I didn't know he had a girlfriend,' Trudy put in mildly.

'Oh, I think I know who you mean,' a lad said, snapping his fingers over his pint of Waddingtons. 'That rather pixie-like creature. But I think they'd split up, you know. She was from the city, wasn't she?'

Meaning, Trudy translated with ease, not 'one of them' and a student.

'Yes, I know who you mean too,' his friend, another lad with overlong hair, piped up. 'And I think you're right. I saw them out and about all over the place for a while, but for the last month or so there's been no sign of her.'

'Didn't someone say she'd gone off to London to seek fame and fortune?' a second girl drawled – rather cattily, Trudy thought. 'Thought that gamin little face of hers would be her meal ticket, I expect. Wanted to break into the pictures or become a clothes model for one of the catalogues or something. Huh! Good luck with that.' She snorted rather inelegantly.

'What was her name?' Trudy asked, anxious for some solid leads.

There was a mutual exchange of baffled looks, but it was the third lad, a quiet youngster with well-cut hair and impeccable manners, who provided the answer.

'Becky somebody, I think,' he muttered quietly, and went back to slowly but thoroughly consuming his pint of Guinness.

'That's right. And isn't there some weird chap with a flaming head of red hair who's going about asking after her?' one of his companions said.

'Oh, yeah, I remember him,' the catty girl said with another snort. 'Bit of a weirdo, if you ask me. Yeah, he was asking about her all right. And about Derek too, now I come to think of it.'

For a moment, it all went quiet, and Trudy felt her heart thumping fast. Was she on to something at last?

'What was so weird about him?' she asked artlessly.

Again there was that mutual exchange of looks and shrugging of shoulders. 'Dunno, really,' one of the longer-haired lads said, taking the lead. 'Kept banging on about where this Becky was, and what did we know about Derek. He was just a bit intense, you know?'

Trudy didn't. But before she could stop them, someone said something about a mutual friend who'd just gone down expecting to get only a third, or even a mere pass, and the talk turned to other things.

She stayed on for another ten minutes or so and then excused herself. Once outside the pub, she quickly retrieved her notebook from her handbag and jotted down all she'd learned before she forgot it.

Although she didn't quite see how much further forward it got them. So, the drowned boy had been going around for a while with a girl from the town called Becky, who had gone off to London to try and hit the big time in some unspecified way.

But what if Derek Chadworth had really loved her and drowned himself in a fit of black depression that she'd left him?

Trudy somehow doubted it. And this man with the red hair – where did he fit into the picture, if at all?

With a sigh, she set off back home, knowing that if she wasn't back before it was fully dark, her parents would have something to say about it!

Chapter 12

The next morning – but not exactly bright and early – Lord Jeremy Littlejohn made his way to St Bede's, Derek Chadworth's college of choice. The peer rarely rose before noon, and never liked to expend much energy on physical exercise, but that day he made an exception and set out at a fair clip, anxious to get his task over and done with. It was perhaps because he was so distracted that he failed to notice the tall, red-headed man who followed him openly and closely.

For Reggie Porter had decided that, instead of taking great pains to keep his surveillance secret, it was now high time to up the ante a bit and make the cocky son of a duke actually aware of his presence. And if the other man actually had the guts to confront him – well… that would be interesting too.

Reggie was sure he could take the languid-looking youth in a straight fight. But he might also have a lot of fun making the man's life a misery in other ways. After all, if Littlejohn accused him of dogging his footsteps, he could simply claim he was mistaken or off his head. A man had a right to walk the streets of Oxford, didn't he? Yes, he could play the innocent, and make the fair-haired man doubt himself. Or he could just admit to following him, and up the pressure of the anonymous letters with some verbal threats.

The thought of actually getting physical with the peer at last made Reggie's hands itch with longing. He could quite happily have taken Lord Jeremy by the throat and shaken him like a terrier with a rat, demanding he tell him what he'd done to Becky.

But he'd have to be careful. He'd have to make sure he wasn't seen, for a start. And that he attacked Littlejohn in some isolated spot where none of his cronies or innocent passers-by might come to his rescue. Yes – when he made his move, he wanted some privacy and the certainty that he wouldn't be interrupted until he'd got the information he wanted from the pansy-faced toff.

But as he strode out, almost on the heels of his prey, Lord Jeremy, rather ironically, was oblivious to the man's presence. Instead, his mind was on the task ahead. Getting into the college grounds should present no problem, as he was known to practically every porter in every college, since he had friends everywhere. But gaining entry to Derek's old room itself might be a bit harder. But there were always ways and means. A bribe to a scout, perhaps. He wasn't sure who it was who cleaned Derek's rooms, but he knew servants were always happy to oblige for extra cash.

But he also knew another chap who was up at St Bede's – and everyone knew that, sometimes, older doors to the student lodgings had locks that fitted the same key. Bursars were notoriously mean-fisted, and why fit every door with a separate lock and key when you could have one lock and key to fit all? Yes, that was worth a go, and he'd try that first. He could always tell Blinkers Blenkinsop to keep quiet about lending him his key.

As Jeremy reached the entrance to the college and ducked inside, Reggie Porter felt a sudden and unexpected wave of real rage wash over him. After having made up his mind towards action, he was now almost immediately forced to concede defeat.

But there was no way he could just waltz past the porter. His own physical traits made him instantly recognisable and the guardian of the gate would know he was not a member and had no business there.

Swearing under his breath, he retreated to the other side of the street and decided to wait in the more comfortable shade. Perhaps it was just as well he'd been given the opportunity to reconsider his strategy, he thought morosely. For now he had time to think things through, he was forced to concede that, should he tackle his quarry head-on, the chances were that Lord Littlejohn would use his influence to have him thrown into the jug. Perhaps even get him a hefty prison sentence for assault. And he couldn't find Becky if he was behind bars.

But as Reggie watched and waited and fumed, he promised that soon, somehow, he'd get the truth out of the leader of the Marquis Club. And the consequences be damned.

Chapter 13

Trudy (who, unlike a certain peer of the realm, had no trouble rising early) was at the coroner's office at nine o'clock to the minute, and wasn't particularly surprised to find the doctor already at work at his desk.

As they brought each other up to date on their various projects, Clement shared a pot of tea with her and some of his favourite Huntley and Palmer biscuits.

'So I think I should try and find out more about this girl Mr Chadworth was seen going out and about with, don't you?' Trudy concluded. 'I don't suppose any mention was made of a girlfriend at the inquest?'

'No,' Clement agreed thoughtfully. 'And his parents never mentioned her. But then it's possible they didn't know. Youngsters don't always like their parents to be up to speed with all their doings.'

Trudy, remembering her white lies of the previous evening, had to agree and only hoped she wasn't blushing. 'So what do we do next?' she asked instead.

The coroner snaffled the last of the biscuits from the plate and sighed. 'I think it's high time we bearded the lion – or, in this case, the White Knight – in his den, don't you?'

Trudy nodded. She was back in her uniform, since Jennings insisted she only be allowed to change into civvies when actively in pursuit of gossip from students, and she was careful not to drop any crumbs on her skirt.

Outside, it was another hot day and she was glad of her police cap keeping the scorching sun off her bare head, even if she did feel uncomfortably hot in the rest of her dark clothing.

As it happened, they arrived at Lord Littlejohn's college barely a few minutes after the man himself returned from his own morning's activities.

When he heard the knock on his door, Lord Jeremy was morosely contemplating an open bottle of Scotch and growling about the need to exercise – for once – some restraint. Normally he'd drink whatever and whenever he damned well pleased.

But since he'd found nothing at all in Derek's room worth tuppence ha'penny, he was very much aware he needed to keep a sober and clear head if he was to make any headway with saving his own skin.

So when he realised he had visitors, he was not best pleased. Expecting to find on the other side of the door a friend or group of revellers calling to invite him to some amusement or other, he was taken by surprise at the sight of a distinguished older man and a woman in police uniform.

For a second, he wondered if a group of his pals were playing an elaborate hoax on him. That policewoman's uniform was a hoot! It couldn't possibly be real, though!

Mind you, the woman inhabiting this particular uniform was very pleasing to the eye indeed. No doubt Derek would have… He shut off the line of thought and told himself that now was no time to start indulging his fantasies. It was time to keep a clear and cool head. For a while, anyway, he needed to keep a low profile and be a good boy. At least until the furore over Derek's death died down and was forgotten.

Nevertheless, he couldn't resist letting both eyes run over her fine features, which included quite lovely, dark-brown eyes, a very neat waist and curves that not even ugly black serge could disguise.

And yes – the little minx was actually blushing! It gave him quite a kick to see that the colour had more to do with anger and resentment than anything else.

For once, he felt like applauding his hangers-on for presenting him with something a little different, and he almost reached out to pull her into his room and find out just how much her ferocious stare was an act, and how far she intended to carry it.

But then, just in time, he realised he'd seen the man's face before, and instinct prevented him from saying anything too outrageous. But if this was some sort of a wheeze, and these two had been put up to something by one of the Marquis Club in order to pull a gag on him, he'd have something to say about it.

It was one thing to pull a stunt on someone else and make a fool of them, but he'd be damned if he was going to put up with it himself.

'Lord Littlejohn?' the old duffer was saying, and the voice struck an even deeper memory within him. In a rush, he realised who it was.

And felt just a little sick. To think he'd come within a cat's whisker of making such a colossal mistake.

'Dr Ryder, I believe,' he drawled, recovering instantly. He was quite proud that his voice came out so smoothly. He'd never had a particularly good memory, but he wasn't lacking in the brains department. If his studies were languishing and his tutors were always admonishing him, it was simply because he couldn't be bothered to study. After all, what was the point?

'Yes, my Lord.' The coroner somehow managed to make the polite use of his title sound ironic and just a bit grating. 'This is WPC Loveday. May we come in?'

'WPC Loveday. Really? What a name to conjure with,' Lord Jeremy couldn't resist teasing. 'A lovely name for a lovely lady. But… good grief, I didn't think they actually let women into the police force. I thought that was a myth, perpetuated and spread by the more undesirable members of Fleet Street.'

Trudy bit back a rude reply and forced herself to step inside the room and carefully and quietly shut the door behind her.

Her first sight of Lord Jeremy Littlejohn had instantly set her hackles rising. He was too good-looking to be true, and therefore he seemed somehow unreal. He was wearing white summer trousers so spotless they almost dazzled her eyes. His sunbeam-fair hair was artlessly ruffled, and with such a pointed chin and sharp cheekbones he reminded her somehow of a cat. Cruel, selfish and heartless – but able to purr and charm at will.

But it was the way he'd looked at her, as if she meant nothing, and then the hateful way he'd drawled at her with that sneering, cut-glass accent…

She forced herself to take a deep breath, and only then realised that her hands were instinctively clenched into fists. She was glad Dr Ryder was doing all the talking, for right then and there she felt the really strong desire to kick this insolent and indolent young man in his shins. Or somewhere even more painful.

'We have a few more questions concerning the death of Derek Chadworth, my Lord,' Clement said mildly.

'Derek? I thought that business was all done and dusted,' Lord Littlejohn said sharply. And for the first time something other than amused insolence flashed in his eyes.

'The inquest is, yes, but with an open verdict given the investigation goes on,' Clement corrected him, allowing a wolfish smile to cross his face. At around five-foot-ten, the peer was shorter than him by a few inches, and he rather enjoyed looking down on him. Just as much, he could tell, as Littlejohn resented having to look *up* at him.

'Really?' the younger man said casually, throwing himself somewhat theatrically into a large armchair. 'Well, have a seat, why don't you?' he demanded gracelessly and reached across to a gold cigarette casket standing on a table and lazily extracted a cheroot. 'Want one?' he offered indifferently.

'No, thank you,' Clement said, deliberately keeping his voice mild and his wolfish smile in place. 'There's something that's been puzzling me, and I was hoping you could help.'

'Oh?'

'The dead boy.'

'What about him?'

'He was a member of your little club, wasn't he?'

'Which club would that be?'

'The Marquis Club.'

'Good grief, no! He was much too much of a nobody to be a member of that!'

'Ah. I did wonder. And yet, you and he were friends.'

'I'm friends with lots of people. A very amiable chap, that's me.' He smiled through the plumes of smoke he was emitting, his eyes narrowing as he regarded the still-standing man.

'I'm sure you are, my Lord,' the coroner conceded blandly. 'And that's why you invited him to the picnic party? Being so amiable.'

The younger man shrugged magnificently, but said nothing. Instead he let his eyes deliberately slide over to the pretty girl with the mass of dark hair hidden under her pert little cap.

His eyes began to gleam lasciviously.

Trudy's face froze.

Lord Littlejohn smiled lazily. 'Do you carry handcuffs, Police Constable Loveday?' he murmured insouciantly.

'Yes, sir,' Trudy shot back, hard and fast. She would very much have liked to use them on him right now, drag him back to the station, and have the extreme satisfaction of slamming the cell door shut in his smirking, knowing face!

Lord Jeremy, almost as if reading her mind, suddenly grinned widely. He only wished he was enjoying himself half as much as he was pretending to.

True, it was rather delicious (and a true novelty) to bait the police like this, but he was very wary of the older man. Dr Clement Ryder, he knew instinctively, could become a real problem. He was smart and had influence in this town. Yes, he'd want watching all right.

'Well, if that's all you wanted to know…' he said, beginning to rise to his feet.

'I can assure you, Lord Littlejohn, that we've only just begun,' Trudy said, her voice flat and hard in an effort to control her anger and take command of the interview.

'Well, that's too bad,' Lord Jeremy said, turning to blow a smoke ring in the direction of the window. 'Because I have an appointment in—' he ostentatiously consulted his watch, a Patek Philippe and an eighteenth-birthday present from his old man '—good grief, five minutes ago! Have to rush. You can see yourselves out, I trust? Having lunch with the local MP, don't you know,' he lied outrageously.

And just like that, they were dismissed.

Or so Lord Littlejohn would have liked. But he was soon to learn, as so many other people of rank and power had learned before him, that Dr Clement Ryder was not so easily got rid of!

For, in the doorway of his rooms, Clement suddenly turned and smiled at him. 'You forgot to answer my question, Your Lordship,' the coroner said placidly.

'Really?' the younger man drawled. 'Which particular one?' His eyes twinkled with either amusement or repressed anger – it was hard for Trudy to tell which.

'Did you, or did you not, invite Derek to your punting picnic party?' Clement said clearly.

Littlejohn sighed heavily and waved a hand vaguely in the air. 'Oh, dear me, do you have to be so pedantic, man? I really have no idea if I did or didn't,' he said with theatrical exasperation. Then, seeing Trudy open her mouth, intent on demanding a proper answer, he swept on, no doubt with a view to aggravating her further. 'I certainly didn't issue him with a printed card, with his name written on it and a demand for him to RSVP, if that's what you mean. But then it wasn't that sort of an event, as you can well imagine.'

'What sort of event was it, sir?' Trudy asked, determinedly refusing to use his proper title.

But if the privileged youth noticed the slip, he made no sign of it.

'Oh, you know how it is,' he responded airily. 'A group of us got together and planned it. Then everyone went away and invited someone else, and names kept getting added and taken away… It was all meant to be spontaneous and come or not as you please.' He shrugged elaborately. 'Nothing formal at all. I just laid on a load of champers and nibbles for a hundred or so, to be on safe side, and thought no more about it.'

Trudy couldn't help but gasp at the sheer carelessness of this largesse, and instantly his eyes darted to her, and a sardonic twist came to his lips. 'Anything left over and brought back from jaunts like this, the scouts always fall on like ravening wolves, anyway. So don't worry your penny-pinching little heart, WPC Loveday – nothing went to waste,' he mocked. 'You can keep your working-class morality to yourself, please.'

Trudy felt the insult hit her almost like a physical blow and turned away. Clement stepped quickly into the brief, tense silence that followed.

'How very charitable of you, my Lord,' he said dryly. 'To feed the starving college servants.'

This time it was the student who paled slightly, but he affected a light laugh, nevertheless. 'A bit over the top, I agree,' he said laconically. 'But now, I really must prepare for my appointment.' This was stated very pointedly, and Trudy, for one, was glad to move through the doorway and head off down the spiral stone staircase.

What an insufferable man!

A minute later, standing in the shade of the college cloister, Trudy could feel herself boiling with resentment.

By her side, and wisely deciding to let her fume in peace for a while, Clement Ryder was far more thoughtful. Unless he was mistaken – a circumstance so preposterous as to be almost impossible – the White Knight was a badly shaken man. Under all that playacting and indolence, Clement was sure the arrogant little puppy had got the wind up him well and truly.

But why?

Everyone they'd spoken to so far about that afternoon on the river had said that Lord Littlejohn had gone into the water along with everyone else, but had instantly set out for the nearest riverbank. He himself had said as much at the inquest, admitting that, although he was a reasonable swimmer, he wasn't that experienced. And, on his journey from the capsized punt to the shore, he'd been accompanied by quite a few of his fellow partygoers, who'd all crawled out onto the grass more or less in a mass.

Nobody had ever intimated that he might possibly have had the opportunity of finding Derek Chadworth in the scrum of flailing arms and legs, let alone somehow managed to drown the boy unseen and undetected.

So what had got the blond-haired Adonis in such a sweat?

'Of all the arrogant…' Beside him, Trudy began to vent her spleen, but Clement listened with only half an amused ear. Of course, he hadn't missed the way the peer had deliberately set out to goad her. But again he was sure that had been partly out of habit, and partly out of sheer devilment. Apparently, the Lord had an eye for a pretty girl.

'I'd like to show him my handcuffs all right…' Trudy fumed on.

Clement let his thoughts drift to other things. He could have sworn Littlejohn's fear had kicked in when he'd been told the investigation into Chadworth's death wasn't over.

So what was he so worried an ongoing investigation might reveal?

'So, are we?'

He suddenly became aware of Trudy's insistent voice, and her tone suggested she'd become aware of his distraction.

'Are we what?' he asked mildly, confirming her suspicions.

Trudy glowered at him. 'Are we going to arrest Lord Littlejohn!'

'On what charge?' he asked, even more mildly.

Trudy bit back the urge to say something that would really get her into trouble. 'He was… he was… hateful!'

'Yes, he was, wasn't he?' Clement agreed, and then, before she could really let fly, held up a hand. 'And he got under your skin. Which has prevented you from thinking clearly. Which, don't you rather think, might be just exactly what he hoped for?'

Trudy opened her mouth, then abruptly closed it again. Slowly, she began to get her anger under control, conceding her friend probably had a point. Clement, watching this process, which was written plainly on her face, nodded in approval. 'Good. Now you're using your noggin again, WPC Loveday, tell me… what struck you most about his attitude?' he asked curiously.

As they began to walk through the college gardens, Clement reached out to admire a particularly fine stand of roses – Peace, one of his favourites – and, to his horror, noticed his hand was trembling visibly.

Quickly, he snatched it back, but not before Trudy had noticed.

She felt instantly ashamed of herself. She'd been thinking the older man hadn't cared about the way Lord Littlejohn had acted. That he'd taken it for granted a man could treat a woman like that and she should just have to put up with it. But clearly, all along, he'd been as angry as she was – literally trembling with rage too.

But he, unlike her, had controlled himself.

Well, if he could, so could she. And the next time she met Lord Jeremy Littlejohn, she wouldn't give him the satisfaction of getting under her skin!

'Well?' Clement demanded, a little impatiently, and Trudy

quickly got her mind back on track. Working with Dr Ryder was a marvellous opportunity for her, but she was well aware she had to keep on her toes. The coroner wasn't one to suffer fools gladly.

Quickly, she went over the interview, filtering out her anger, and then nodded.

'He was acting the ass,' she said flatly. 'But only because he was… scared. Of us!' she added, with great satisfaction.

'Which means?'

'He's hiding something.'

'Yes. I rather think he was. Want to find out what it is?' he asked her, eyes twinkling, and his trembling, telltale hands stuck firmly in his flannel trouser pockets.

'Oh, yes,' WPC Trudy Loveday said, her fine eyes flashing. 'There's nothing I'd like better.'

And if, while walking back to the coroner's office, she let her imagination run wild with delicious thoughts of arresting a certain peer of the realm for… something or anything… well, who was to blame her?

Trudy and Dr Ryder weren't the only ones making their way to the latter's office that hot sunny day.

Jimmy Roper – had he but known it – was just hopping off the bus that had been driven into town by Trudy Loveday's father. He'd been driving buses for nearly thirty years, and as he watched his passengers alight, it never crossed his mind that one of them was on his way to talk to his daughter.

Jimmy had decided to leave Tyke behind on this occasion. His dog could be a bit of a nuisance in the city, as he tended to get overexcited and dive under people's feet. He had to stop to ask several people the way to Floyds Row, where the mortuary was, and felt a shiver of discomfort at having to go there. But the coroner's office was in the same compound, so he had no choice. He was wearing his best summer togs – his wife had insisted he look the part – and felt vaguely uncomfortable in his smart shoes.

He only hoped this wasn't going to take long.

He found the right place by following the well-posted signs, and a pleasant woman in the outer office assured him the coroner had just come in. After asking his business, she went into another room and came back less than a minute later.

Jimmy – not sure whether to be relieved or worried that he wasn't going to be kept waiting – found himself being ushered into a pleasant, book-lined room, where dried flowers were artfully arranged in the unlit fireplace, and a tortoiseshell butterfly was hovering around an open window.

A distinguished-looking older man half-rose from behind his desk, and a young, pretty girl in a police uniform, who was seated in one of the chairs to the side of the desk, gave him a brief smile.

'Oh, hello,' he said to the girl first. He hadn't expected the coroner to have company.

'This is WPC Loveday,' Clement Ryder said. 'She's liaising with me on the Derek Chadworth case. My secretary tells me you have some information?'

'Yes. Well, I'm not sure it's anything important…' He hesitated uneasily.

'Please, take a seat,' Trudy said with a smile.

Jimmy went to the other empty chair in front of the desk and sat down nervously. Clement, summing him up in one glance, smiled beneficently. 'I take it you saw my appeal for information in the local paper?'

'Yes, that's right.'

'You were on the river that day?'

'Yes. But before the accident took place,' Jimmy explained quickly. 'I was taking Tyke for the usual morning walk, and I passed the group of students just as they were setting up their picnic. I walked past them, you see. Later, around the bend in the river, I saw another punt full of people.' He paused to take a breath and shrugged. 'I assume they were on one of the punts that was involved in the accident.'

'You didn't see it happen?'

'Oh, no! I walked on towards some trees and sat in the shade for a while. It was a jolly hot day. Then I went back home again. But I took a small detour around the picnic party. I didn't want to intrude on the young people – well, you don't, do you? When other folks are having fun, you feel a bit of an interloper, pushing in. So you see,' Jimmy concluded hastily, 'I didn't really see anything of any interest. But I thought I should just come along and… er…'

'And I'm so glad you did,' Clement said heartily. 'I wish everyone was as public-spirited as yourself.' He added this rather dryly. So far, his appeal for help from the public hadn't netted him much in the way of new information. So now he had someone new to question, he wasn't going to let him go until he was squeezed dry.

'So, you set off for this walk at your usual time?' he asked smoothly.

Jimmy Roper agreed he had and offered up a rough estimate of the hour at which he'd passed the students, which matched with their own statements.

'And before you reached this party of youngsters, you didn't see anybody else in the vicinity?' Clement pressed, as Trudy faithfully jotted down the witness's statement in her fast, Pitman's shorthand. 'Perhaps another dog walker, for instance?'

'No,' Jimmy said positively. 'No other dog walkers. Tyke tends to bark at other dogs and make such a racket… oh, but there were the two fishermen.'

Both the coroner and the policewoman looked gratifyingly interested in these, and Jimmy gave them as good a description of them as he could manage. 'But I noticed,' he added with scrupulous fairness, 'that when I walked past that part of the river on my way back, they'd both gone. I daresay that makes sense – the noise those youngsters were making must have frightened every fish for miles.'

Clement smiled. 'I daresay. So you walked on – and noticed the students. Can you describe them?'

'Well – not sure I can really,' Jimmy said apologetically. 'They were just youngsters, like. Dressed like they are nowadays,' he added with a grunt. 'Oh, but I noticed there was more girls than boys. The girls were setting out the food, like, and the lads were just lolling about on the grass... Oh, yes, there was that one odd-looking boy, standing off a bit to one side. I'm not sure if he was part of their group or not. He was about six feet or so away from the nearest group to him, and was standing staring down into the river. The others were all sort of lolling about in groups and talking to one another, but none of them seemed to be paying much attention to him. I got the feeling he might have been someone on his own –you know? He just happened to be there, taking a walk maybe and just passing through, but wasn't part of the main party. He wasn't eating or drinking either, now that I think of it.'

'Oh?' Clement said sharply. 'Can you describe him?'

'Oh, yes – I remember *him* all right,' Jimmy said. 'He was a bit of a beanpole of a chap – tall and thin, you know – but the most memorable thing about him was his red hair. A really shockingly bright carrot-top he was. Freckles... can't remember what else, though.' He frowned thoughtfully.

Carefully, Clement took him over the rest of that morning, but apart from the two fishermen and the slightly mysterious red-headed lad, Jimmy had nothing else to offer.

Nevertheless, the coroner thanked him fulsomely for coming in and, by the time he'd left the office, feeling rather pleased with himself, Jimmy Roper had forgotten he'd ever been nervous about coming in.

Once he was gone, Clement stretched and yawned. 'Well, it might be something, or nothing. You might like to check with local anglers' clubs – see if you can find those two fishermen. They might have seen something useful.'

Trudy gave him a long-suffering glance. She knew a long shot when she heard it. But still, it was her job to do the boring, routine things, as well as the more exciting stuff.

'What about this red-headed man?' she asked eagerly. 'Could he be the same one who's been asking questions about Derek Chadworth's girlfriend, do you think? Have you come across him before?'

'No, this is the first time he's cropped up,' Clement said thoughtfully. 'When you next go trawling the student hotspots for gossip, see if you can find out who he is.'

Trudy nodded happily enough. At least a tall, thin lad with red hair would stick in most people's memories, so he shouldn't be hard to track down.

If he was a student, that was.

Chapter 14

Keith Morrison stepped through his back door and walked across the lawn. His large garden, located on the outer edge of the village of Islip, enjoyed a fine view across the water meadow, where the river skirted the boundary of their property to the south.

But although it was yet another hot and sunny day, Keith was oblivious to the singing birds and flitting butterflies as he made his way to the new pond he'd recently created, and stood staring down absently into it.

Most of the silt and dirt had settled now the first month had gone by, and the oxygenating plants he'd put in had begun to clear the water nicely. He noted that evidence of the small trench he'd dug to the river's edge less than twenty yards away, and which he'd used to fill the newly excavated hole with river water, had almost completely disappeared, and that the grass was growing up over it again nicely. Once the asters and dahlias he'd planted around that side had taken root, nobody would ever know it had been there.

A yellow and grey wagtail darted towards the pond, spotted him and, with a chinking flick of its long tail, darted away again, giving a small alarm call.

He thought how pretty it had looked, and – with a great lance of pain – how much his daughter, Jenny, would have loved to have seen it. She'd been a bit of an artist, his little girl, sketching flowers and the neighbour's cat, and birds and all manner of other things in her notebooks.

But Jenny, of course, would never see any of those things again.

Morosely, he stared down into the dark pond. At forty-eight, he stood at just over six feet, and was rather on the broad and beefy side. With a lot of iron-grey hair and deep-set eyes, he was still what most people would have considered a fine-looking man, but right now his face had a drawn, tight look. He owned a small manufacturing workshop in Cowley, producing the Morrison moped, a reliable little scooter that had made him and his family a modest fortune. But much good that would do them now, he mused bitterly. What was the point of working hard and buying a nice house in a nice village, and leaving a nice little business, if you had nobody to give it to?

When he and Celia had married nearly twenty-two years ago, they'd both thought they'd have a large family. But, in the end, only the one child had been given them – a girl.

They'd called her Jennifer.

And a brighter, prettier, more loving child was hard to imagine. From the moment she'd been born, they had both adored her.

Always small, she'd first wanted to be a jockey – the first woman to win the Derby and Grand National and all major horse races in between! And at the age of seven she'd looked adorable in her riding kit, with her small, triangular face, mass of dark-brown hair, and big, blue eyes. And then, when she'd been about fourteen or so, she'd changed her allegiance to dressage – to the relief of her parents, since it was a far more achievable goal. But then, somewhere, somehow, around her sixteenth birthday, she'd changed from the bright and easygoing girl they knew and become almost ruthlessly ambitious, pushing herself to succeed. The small local girls' school she'd attended hadn't been enough for her, and her parents had willingly spent money on private riding lessons.

Her dream was to become an Olympian, and she had the next Olympic Games firmly in her sights.

Her old friends fell by the wayside, and she became uncommunicative and withdrawn. They put it down to her fierce desire to make the grade in the horse world, and for a while hadn't seen the danger in the change that had swept over her. Teenagers were notoriously moody, after all. Girls, especially, could be difficult. Even Celia, her own mother, thought she was just struggling a bit with that difficult period when girls became women.

But she had become more and more quiet and withdrawn. A little absent. Even secretive, which wasn't like her. You'd be talking to her and suddenly realise she hadn't heard a word you'd said. Sometimes, too, Keith had caught her looking at him with a mixture of puzzlement, pity and something almost like contempt in her eyes.

It had been a shock to see that. From Daddy's little girl she'd become someone he hardly knew. Celia had counselled patience.

But then, a few weeks after Christmas last year, they'd lost her.

Later, they'd pieced it together – her family, and that nice police inspector who'd been given Jenny's case. How she'd gone round to a friend's house for tea, and then later, using the excuse of needing to use the upstairs bathroom, had ransacked the master bedroom, where she knew the mother of her friend kept a dose of sleeping pills in her bedside cabinet.

And then there was the bottle of whisky she'd purloined to take with the pills, this item having been kept in the Morrisons' own house, and which had been opened only that Christmas.

It had been Celia who'd found her. Asleep, or so she'd thought, in her bedroom. No note. No explanation. It was even more puzzling given that her riding and dressage tutors were pleased with her improvements in the sports arena.

Keith continued to stare down into the dark water, watching the reflections of the clouds and noting the odd, manic, swirling motion of a whirligig beetle – as if he could find an answer there, somewhere in the randomness of nature. But there were no answers for him here, in this place – a solution of sorts maybe, but no real relief from the questions that plagued him.

'Why, Jen-Jen?' he muttered at last, his voice sounding gruff and out of place in the pretty garden setting. 'Why did you do it? There was no need, sweetheart. I would have continued paying off the bastard!'

A few miles away in Oxford, Reggie stared scornfully at the uncomfortable girl wriggling about on her seat, and bit back a sigh of impatience.

He'd spotted Minnie 'Mouse' Hartley, Becky's best friend since primary school, slipping into the café on his way back to work, and couldn't resist the opportunity to follow her inside.

There, he'd been pleased to see she was on her own and, ruthlessly ignoring the way her face had fallen when she spotted him, he'd joined her at the table. Even offering to buy her tea and cakes failed to bring a smile to her face. A chubby girl, with more curly, mousy-brown hair than she knew what to do with, she would normally have been delighted with the display of cakes the waitress had just set down.

Now, however, she stared across the table at her friend's big brother with wide, worried eyes.

'Honestly, Mr Porter, like I told your dad, I dunno where Becky is,' she whined. It was the same old story she'd told ever since the Porter family had found Becky's letter, left behind in her bedroom, saying she was leaving home and not to worry about her.

Reggie bit back the urge to take the silly little chit by her shoulders and rattle her until her teeth popped out, and instead forced a brief smile onto his face.

'Come on, Mouse. You and Becky were always thick as thieves. And I know what you girls are like. You couldn't keep a secret from each other if your life depended on it.'

Minnie miserably helped herself to a slice of Battenberg but left it untouched on her plate. Right now, she couldn't eat a thing. Of course, Becky had always said her big brother was a real killjoy, always watching her like a hawk – worse than her mum and dad put together. And, in truth, Minnie had seen for herself just how protective he could be. Always hanging around at the youth club to walk her home, and always asking her questions about her boyfriends. Downright creepy, she thought.

It was no wonder Becky hated him! Now she wished he'd go away and leave her alone. But she could tell he wasn't going to.

'Honest, she never said,' Minnie lied stubbornly. At nearly twenty, Minnie had worked at the greengrocer's at the end of her street ever since she'd left school at fourteen. She was a grown woman, used to earning her keep. It felt silly to let the likes of Reggie Porter intimidate her.

She knew Becky had certainly never let him get the better of her, for all he'd tried to lay down the law with her. No wonder she'd left home and run off to London where she could have some fun. The kind of fun Becky had come to like. But she could say none of this to the grim-faced man sitting opposite her.

'Look, Mr Porter,' she wheedled. 'Becky always said she wanted to do stuff with her life. That she didn't want to stay in Oxford for ever. She was always going on about London, the bright lights and all, and about wanting to become a model or break into the films, like.' This was true enough. But she didn't dare say anything about what Becky had done to finance her dream. It still made her sick to think of it, but then… well, Becky wasn't like her. Never had been.

Reggie felt like screaming in frustration. 'Of all the stupid… How many girls do you think head for London every day with the same silly dreams in their heads?' he demanded. 'Thinking they can just waltz into a modelling agency and be taken on just like that?' He snapped his fingers angrily. 'Get their faces in the magazines and get "discovered" by a director and whisked off to

Pinewood? Hundreds! Probably thousands,' he thundered contemptuously. 'And just how many do you think actually ever make it, you dunderhead? For every Vivian Leigh or Margaret Lockwood, how many others do you think never even get to... oh, this is pointless! If you know where she went, tell me now, or so help me...'

Minnie, alarmed by the growing wildness she could see in his face, swallowed hard. 'Honest, Mr Porter, I dunno,' she wailed. Which was sort of true.

Before she left town, Becky had been full of herself and her plans for the future. And if they did, indeed, include doing the rounds of the modelling agencies, she hadn't been as silly or airheaded as her big brother seemed to think, Becky mused resentfully.

For a start, she had a plan as to where she could live. Both of them knew of someone else from their secondary school who had gone to live in the capital, and Becky had managed to find out her address. So she would have a place to stay.

What's more, Becky knew that, to get taken on by an agency, you had to have a decent photographic portfolio – done by a professional photographer, and including glamour shots and everything. And she'd got one of those done – well, sort of – before she'd left.

Anyway, Minnie thought with a mental toss of her head, she for one wouldn't put it past Becky to do just what she said she was going to do, so there! She had grit, had Becky, and determination. For all she looked like an innocent little pixie, she was hard as nails underneath.

But she had more sense than to say anything like this to her big brother, who still thought her a veritable little angel. How Becky had laughed about him behind his back. 'Honestly, Mouse,' she'd say, 'Reggie still thinks I'm a sweet little kid of six!'

'She must have told you something,' Reggie roared now, making her jump, and making the customers at the next table look across at them and frown.

'No, she didn't,' Minnie lied bravely. 'She only said she was going to hitchhike to save money on train fares.' Which, again, was true enough. In fact, Becky had been confident she could get a ride with a lorry driver. According to Becky, they were always ready to have a pretty girl sitting up front in the cab with them.

At the news of this latest folly, Reggie Porter went white with fury and worry.

If this was true, she might not even have made it to London. You heard such bad things nowadays about young girls who went missing…

'And what about that bloke she was hanging around with?' Reggie refused to contemplate the unimaginable. Instead, his eyes narrowed as the chubby girl in front of him began to wriggle even more uncomfortably on her chair. 'That student chap, and his cronies,' Reggie persisted ominously.

Minnie swallowed nervously and prepared to lie some more.

Back at the station, Trudy stood in front of DI Jennings's desk and delivered her latest report on the coroner's investigation. She described what they'd learned so far, none of which seemed to impress or interest her superior officer much.

'So he's not bothered talking to any of the parents of the students then?' was all Jennings wanted to know. He looked relieved when Trudy shook her head.

'No, sir. Although Dr Ryder wants us to drive up north tomorrow to talk to Mr Chadworth's parents. He wants to learn more about their son, now some of the shock has worn off and they're back on their home territory.'

'Yes, yes, fine,' DI Jennings said airily. As far as he was concerned, the annoying coroner could badger the dead boy's parents as much as he wanted. Just so long as he refrained from asking the powerful and wealthy parents of the other students involved any questions – especially the Duke, Lord Jeremy Littlejohn's father.

His Chief Constable had already told him that the Duke expected the whole unfortunate incident to be decently and quietly swept under the carpet forthwith. And what the Duke expected, the Chief Constable had promised. And woe betide any mere Detective Inspectors who failed to get the message!

'And you've only talked to Lord Littlejohn the once?' he asked again sharply.

'Yes, sir,' Trudy said patiently. This was the third time her DI had asked her this. 'I didn't like him, sir,' she said somewhat rashly. 'He was very rude and condescending and…'

'When I want your opinion, WPC Loveday, I'll ask for it,' Jennings said, brutally cutting her short. Trudy paled and nodded.

'Yes, sir,' she said smartly.

'All right. Trail up to… wherever the hell it is Ryder wants to take you tomorrow. Let him ask as much as he wants to about the dead boy. But keep me posted.'

'Yes, sir,' Trudy said, glad to get away.

Back in the outer office, she began to ring around the angling clubs, trying to find a line on the missing fishermen witnesses, but most of the people she spoke to weren't of much help. Certainly, none of the local clubs had organised a fishing competition that day. 'Sounds to me like your fishermen were just passing the time, like. I only hope they had the right licences or the river bailiff would like as not have given them a fine!'

With a sigh, Trudy rang off and pushed the task of finding the fishermen to the bottom of her to-do list. Even if she managed to track them down, they probably wouldn't have anything interesting to say.

'That's a woebegone sigh if ever I heard one,' PC Rodney Broadstairs said, oiling over to her and perching one buttock cheekily on the edge of her desk. 'Doing anything exciting then?' he laughed, knowing what her answer must be. 'Me and the sarge are on those warehouse robberies out Botley way,' he boasted.

'Nice for you,' Trudy said, through gritted teeth.

'So who were you on the blower to then?' Rodney demanded. A tall, fair-haired man, he was both literally (and figuratively) the blue-eyed boy of the station. Jennings regularly gave him the best jobs, and even their sergeant, Mike O'Grady, seemed to rate him.

'Local angling clubs,' Trudy reluctantly said. 'I'm trying to track down two potential witnesses to a death,' she added pointedly.

For a moment, Rodney, who'd been leering at her chest, looked put out. Then his handsome brow cleared. 'Oh, you mean that drowned student thing. Oh, yeah, we heard you was back working with our loopy coroner!'

'He's not loopy!' Trudy said hotly. 'He's got more brains in his little finger than you've got in your head.'

'WPC Loveday!' The voice wasn't that of DI Jennings, she was relieved to hear, but that of their sergeant. Even so, the admonitory bark made her wince.

Mike O'Grady, she knew, liked her well enough, but he, like nearly everyone else at the station, didn't really believe women had a place in the police force. Now he walked over, and Trudy watched, with a slightly obstinate look on her face, as Rodney surreptitiously removed himself from her desk and stood up a bit straighter.

'I'll remind you that you are still a *probationary* woman police constable, Loveday. As such, you will show the proper respect to those of your fellow officers who have successfully completed their own probationary period. Is that clear?'

Trudy bit her lip. 'Yes, Sarge.'

'And as for you, Broadstairs, stop lounging about and get on with some work. Or haven't I given you enough to be getting on with?'

Trudy bit back a smile as the blue-eyed boy slouched off.

The Sergeant gave a long-suffering sigh and swept on.

Trudy wisely put her head down and waited patiently for clocking-off time. The thought of being away from the station for a whole day tomorrow made her feel like cheering.

Chapter 15

'So this is the motorway,' Trudy said the next morning. 'I've never been on it before.' The MI had opened the previous year, in 1959, a masterpiece of engineering, or so her dad had always maintained. When she'd told him she and the coroner would be using it, he'd been almost jealous, and had confessed he'd like to take his old bus on the new road, just to enjoy the sensation of wide-open road and fast, free-flowing traffic.

Now, as she looked around the vast expanse of almost traffic-free space, she glanced at the speedometer of the coroner's car and saw with a thrill of excitement that it was nearly touching sixty!

'Like it?' Clement said, with an appreciative grin for her excitement. She was wearing her uniform, of course, but her cap was off, and with the windows open on yet another warm day, her long, curly, brown hair was flying back from her face. She'd also, at his insistence, left her black jacket draped across the backseat, and had rather daringly rolled the white sleeves of her blouse up to her elbows.

'It's smashing!'

'At this rate it won't take us long to get where we're going,' Clement agreed, looking at the long, empty road ahead of him. 'This is the future of motoring and no mistake!'

*

The Chadworths lived in a mock-Tudor house on one of the new little housing estates that had sprouted up on the edges of towns the length and breadth of Britain just after the war.

Both Anne and Paul Chadworth were waiting for their arrival, the boy's father having arranged to take time off from the small solicitor's office where he was a partner.

'Please, won't you come in?' Derek's mother was dressed in a plain, navy-blue summer dress with white trim, but her face looked exhausted underneath the layer of carefully applied make-up. The dead boy's father was dressed in lightweight summer trousers and a shirt and tie. He had a tight-lipped expression that never once wavered during the course of the interview.

The coroner, after doffing his hat in the hall, and Trudy, now appropriately dressed in her full uniform, followed the couple to a small front room that was obviously seldom used.

The couple sat on a small sofa, and Trudy and Clement took the two matching armchairs that were offered. The room smelt of furniture polish, and Trudy could imagine Mrs Chadworth or her daily woman whisking around in here to make sure everything looked spic and span.

'Thank you, we won't take up much of your time,' Clement began, addressing Paul Chadworth, who nodded briefly. 'As you know, an open verdict means the inquest was unable to come to any definitive conclusions regarding your son's case. As a result, it is still being investigated. I've come with my police liaison officer—' here he nodded at Trudy, who had brought out her notebook '—because we'd like to learn a little more about your son.'

Anne Chadworth, who was clutching a handkerchief in one white-knuckled hand, sighed softly, but said nothing.

'We don't want to cause you any undue distress,' Clement swept on, 'and I hope you won't find any of our questions too intrusive.'

'Ask anything you want,' Paul Chadworth suddenly said, his voice as grim as his face.

Clement looked at him thoughtfully. Did the boy's father also believe there was something 'not quite right' about his son's death?

'We've been making enquiries,' the coroner began carefully, 'and it seems your son was seen in the company of a local girl, quite often, in the months before his... before he died. Do you know who she was? Did he mention her name to you at all?'

Trudy saw husband and wife exchange quick, puzzled looks. But it was the boy's mother who spoke. 'No. He never mentioned anyone specifically. Oh, we knew he had girlfriends.' She gave a small smile. 'Derek was a handsome boy, and he had a way about him. My mother, his granny, always said he could charm the birds out of the trees. But he told us, when he went up to Oxford, that he was going to devote all his time to studying. Girls and courting and all that could wait. That's what he said.'

Her voice trailed off as if she had just run out of breath.

Her husband abruptly took over. 'I know what you're thinking,' Paul Chadworth said, his chin beginning to jut out. 'That that was all so much pie-in-the-sky, said for our benefit. I know what youngsters are like when they leave home for the first time. They can be a bit wild. So I don't suppose our son was any angel, and he might well have been running around with this girl. But let me tell you something, Dr Ryder...' He leaned forward on his chair a little, the more to emphasise what he was about to say. 'My son had great ambitions. We did all right for him – provided him with a good, handsome home, and paid his fees at a good school. But right from when he first left primary school, he made it clear he wanted more from life than this.'

Here the dead boy's father waved a hand around the room, taking in the respectable cul-de-sac of houses to be seen outside the window. 'He wanted to stay down south, for a start, and find work either in Oxford or London or Surrey, somewhere like that. He said anywhere north of the Thames was too provincial.'

His wife gave a little sniff of distress, but the boy's father sounded rather more proud than censorious of this rather sweeping statement. 'He wanted to go places and make something of himself. He said our generation didn't understand modern times – that the war was long in the past and a new order was coming. A world where a man could rise as high as he wanted, if he was prepared to work for it. Derek intended to do just that.'

'And you endorsed this ambition?' Clement made it more of a statement than a question.

'I wasn't going to hold him back,' Paul Chadworth said grimly. 'Why would I? Good luck to him, I said, and when he told me he'd become friends with the son of a duke, I couldn't have been more pleased. As I always said, in this world, it's not what you know, but who you know, that counts.'

Trudy kept quiet and took notes.

'Ah, yes… Lord Littlejohn.' The coroner picked up the cue smoothly. 'What did your son say about him, exactly?'

Again the boy's parents exchanged a glance, and it was the mother who spoke.

'He didn't really talk to us much about college and Oxford when he came home for the holidays, Dr Ryder. He knew we didn't really know anything about that world. Instead he showed us his photographs, and talked about his plans for the future.'

'Oh, yes. I heard he was a keen amateur photographer,' Trudy said, speaking for the first time and giving the other woman an encouraging smile. 'Do you have any of his work here?'

'Oh, yes, I kept an album,' the proud mother said. Needing no encouragement, she got up and walked to a big, dark-wood utility cupboard standing massively in one corner, and, reaching down to one of the lower doors, opened it and pulled out a large, red, velvet-covered tome.

'When he was younger, he used to enter his photographs in

local competitions. He used to win things too – camera equipment mostly. Once he had a photograph published in a local magazine.'

'Oh, so he was really good then,' Trudy encouraged, as the woman returned to the sofa and laid the album on the small wooden coffee table between them.

'Oh, yes. But he said there was no real future in it. That you couldn't make any real money…' Again her voice trailed off, as if she were too exhausted to carry on speaking.

Trudy leaned forward and turned some pages over, noticing the coroner was eyeing them too.

Most were black-and-white 'atmospheric' shots of Oxford and the northern countryside. Some were wildlife shots. Some were headshots of unknown people – family members, most likely.

'They're good,' Trudy said, and meant it. Not that she was an expert in any way, but she could tell the photographs had a certain sense of style.

Having relaxed the atmosphere a bit, Trudy glanced up at Clement, her eyes telling him to take over again.

He shot her an appreciative glance and said smoothly, but not altogether truthfully, 'He sounds like a good lad. But had you noticed any change in him in recent weeks? When was the last time you saw him?'

'Easter,' Anne Chadworth said at once. 'He came up for two weeks.'

'And he was much as normal?'

'Oh, yes. He was cheerful and bright and happy. He took us out to the Hotel Carrisforth for lunch on the Saturday before Easter Sunday. The Carrisforth is a five-star hotel. The menu was French.' Clearly Mrs Chadworth held this establishment in high esteem.

Paul Chadworth sniffed. 'They have a fancy French chef there. All our friends were whooping it up and Derek said we should go. He would pay.'

Again the coroner found himself regarding the boy's father thoughtfully. His first thought on hearing this was to wonder how a student could afford the prices at this sort of hotel. Had his father wondered the same thing? Was he trying to tell them something?

'I see. He didn't seem worried about anything then?' Clement asked mildly.

'No. He was much as usual,' Anne said sadly.

'Did he mention this picnic-and-punt party?'

'No. But he was always going out and about,' Paul Chadworth said shortly. 'Derek said cultivating the right social life was almost as important as getting a good degree.'

Trudy sighed slightly, and continued jotting down notes.

'Is there anything you can tell us, anything at all, that strikes you now as odd? Something he might have let slip?' Clement asked, looking at the father closely.

But if Paul Chadworth had been trying to tell them something, he wasn't going to come right out and say it. Perhaps he couldn't.

After another ten minutes or so of fruitless questioning, the Chadworths walked them politely to the door and stood on the threshold, watching them until they got in the car and drove away.

'So, did we learn anything new?' Trudy asked, once they'd left the cul-de-sac behind.

'I'm not sure. But I think we might have,' Clement said cautiously.

Trudy watched him as he drove, wondering with a sigh if she'd ever be able to learn to drive herself. She knew Rodney Broadstairs had put his name down at the station to take driving courses, and she was sure he'd be accepted. But she already knew it would be pointless to sign up for them herself, as she could almost hear DI Jennings's scornful voice telling her she should be happy with her bicycle!

'What was the big sigh for?' Clement asked, sounding amused, and Trudy gave a small smile.

'I was just thinking how nice it would be if I could drive a car myself.'

Clement's brown eyes crinkled in puzzlement. 'So what's stopping you?'

Trudy laughed. 'The police force won't pay for women to learn to drive! I can't afford private lessons, and I don't think Dad would be any good teaching me – he's used to driving buses! Besides, we don't have a car I can practise in. Dad gets a lift into work and back with a friend.'

She heaved another sigh. 'Most men think women drivers are a menace anyway.'

Clement quickly glanced across at her, his lips twitching. 'Do *you* think they are?'

Trudy smiled. 'No, I don't, actually. I saw a lot of bad driving when I did a stint in traffic, and nearly all the accidents were caused by men – especially after rolling out of a pub at night. I think women drivers are more sensible and cautious.'

'So?'

Trudy shrugged. 'It's no good,' she said philosophically. 'DI Jennings won't believe I could learn to drive, so he'll never put my name down for it.'

'Do *you* think you're incapable of learning to drive?' Clement demanded briskly.

Trudy shot him a slightly angry look. 'I don't see why I should be!' she said, with some asperity. 'My Aunt Margaret drove an ambulance in the war – and during the Blitz too. And if she can do it, I don't see why I shouldn't!'

'Well said!' Clement grinned. 'Tell you what. Get a licence and I'll teach you how to drive if you like.'

Trudy gaped at him for a few seconds, not sure what to say. She felt elated, and then terrified. What if she really couldn't do it? She'd feel such a fool. Or worse, what if she pranged his car? He'd never let her work with him again.

'What's the matter – getting cold feet?' Clement asked, casting her another quick look, and feeling proud when he saw her shoulders straighten and her chin come up.

'Of course not,' Trudy said staunchly. 'But you'll have to give me a few months to save up the money for the driving licence fee.'

Clement blinked, then forced himself to nod casually. Sometimes it took him by surprise, this difference in their circumstances. Of course, he could afford to buy her the licence just like that and not even notice. But instinct warned him not to make the offer. He didn't want her to think he saw her as a charity case.

'Done – it's a deal then. Let me know when you want to start. Now, back to the case. You know what I was thinking, when Mr Chadworth was telling us all about his son? I wondered where the boy got his money.' He went to change gear but fumbled it as his fingers gave a quick spasm. He swore, and the car jerked slightly before he used the clutch and found the right gear.

Trudy, seeing his hand trembling on the steering wheel, felt a sudden cold feeling wash over her.

Was the coroner the worse for drink?

The traitorous, nasty little worm of a thought slipped into her mind before she could stop it. And then she remembered how he'd almost stumbled on the staircase when they'd gone to talk to Lionel Gulliver.

At the time she'd thought nothing of it… but in her training, she'd been taught that most anti-social behaviour was a result of too much alcohol and the signs of inebriation had been drummed into her. Slurred speech. Unsteady gait. Clumsiness.

She shot him a quick look, but he seemed alert and bright enough. But then, everyone knew some people could hold their drink. Sergeant O'Grady said that sometimes you'd never be able to guess someone was drunk, if they were used to drinking heavily regularly.

'What do you think?' Clement asked, making Trudy blink. And

when he shot a quick look at her, he saw that she was blushing a little.

'Think?'

'About where Derek's money came from?' the coroner prompted, a shade impatiently. Had she not been paying attention? 'He was a student, yet he could afford to pay for three people to dine like emperors at a fancy five-star hotel? Didn't that strike you as odd.'

'Oh… oh, yes, it did,' Trudy agreed. 'It's not as if *his* father is a duke, is it? I suppose his parents did give him some kind of an allowance, but even so…'

Clement nodded. 'I think, you know, that when we ask around about him, we're going to discover that our ambitious and upwardly mobile dead friend never seemed to be short of a bob or two.'

Trudy frowned. 'You think Lord Littlejohn gave him money?'

'Possibly,' Clement said, although, in truth, he didn't think so. For one thing, he rather doubted that Lord Littlejohn was in the habit of giving out money – unless he was lending it to someone from his own set. And for another, he suspected Derek Chadworth would have gnawed off his own foot before asking his upper-class pal for a loan.

Someone in Derek's precarious position (namely that of a middle-class lad swanning about in aristocratic circles) must surely always have been at pains to pay his own way and act at all times as if he was used to flying high.

No. Unless he was very much mistaken, the dead boy had somehow found a lucrative source of income to fund his lifestyle.

And who knew – if they found out what that was, they might be a lot further forward than they were now!

By his side, Trudy was trying to push her unhappy suspicions about her friend's sobriety to one side. Even so, when she got back to the station that night, she might just ask someone what they knew about the habits of secret drinkers…

Chapter 16

Bernie's Boxing Gym was a small, nondescript building just off New Inn Hall Street, sandwiched between two much more imposing buildings. Nobody quite knew how the eponymous Bernie had managed to set up shop there, but the establishment had become something of a 'pet' with the rowing blues who also liked to box. As a consequence, it was one of *the* places to hang out if you were a student with time to spare, especially since the owner (not named Bernie, funnily enough) looked the other way when his 'boys' smuggled in liquor.

Naturally, because of all of the above, the little gym attracted a lot of hangers-on who would never have thought of getting into a boxing ring, and was, consequently, one of the abodes where a number of members of the Marquis Club liked to hang out. It was so seedy and down at heel as to be catnip to their jaded palates. Also, the fact that Lord Jeremy Littlejohn had set up a gambling ring there, wherein full-length boxing matches were held, with some very long odds put on rather good amateur pugilists, had only increased the club's revenue and popularity.

So it was that the second son of the Duke paid the gym a visit, not long after rising that morning. Ever since his unsatisfactory search of Derek Chadworth's now-vacant college rooms, he'd been wracking his brains trying to think where his dead friend might have stashed anything incriminating, and had suddenly remembered he'd been a member of the gym. And, like all members of the gym, he'd been given a small locker.

As Littlejohn pushed his way through the front door, he wasn't surprised to find the main room and boxing ring empty. The students and city boys who used the gym did so mostly in the evenings; nevertheless, the owner kept it open all day, with what he liked to call a skeleton staff. This consisted of one cauliflower-eared giant called, naturally, Tiny, who spent most of his time dozing in a corner with a copy of the racing pages over his face and a crate of beer at his feet.

Tiny was there in one corner now, snoring like a stegosaurus through his ruined, flattened nose. Littlejohn ignored him and went through the small door at the back, where the changing room and lockers were.

Barely two minutes later, curious and cautious, Reginald Porter popped his head around the door, his eyes widening at the sight of the empty boxing ring. In the next instant, he heard the snoring man in the corner and almost bolted. But the fact that the room was totally deserted, not to mention his own compulsive curiosity, stopped him just in time.

Instead, and holding his nerve, he looked around the less-than-salubrious room and, wrinkling his nose a bit at the sour aroma of stale sweat and – incongruously – cleaning fluid, he moved slowly to the only other door he could see, halfway along the back wall.

Here he paused, listened, very cautiously opened the door, and listened again. In front of him was a small maze of lockers, benches and wire-mesh cupboards of the kind so beloved of sports changing rooms everywhere.

He almost bolted again. The last thing he wanted was to get caught snooping in a boxing gym of all places. After all, who knew how many bruisers were here who might be happy to oblige

Littlejohn – for a fee – by giving a nosy man a good thrashing? But then he realised that this room, like the other, was very quiet. That is, he could near no buzz of conversation at all. But coming from one corner of the room, there was a faint sound.

Emboldened by the tall and concealing rows of grey-tin lockers that almost touched the ceiling, he manoeuvred himself stealthily towards the sound. He felt his heart begin to thump a little sickeningly in his breast, and began to sweat with tension.

Taking a long, slow breath, he peered very cautiously around one particularly dented locker and saw the now-familiar back of Lord Jeremy Littlejohn.

As usual he was wearing white – today, a white cricketing jumper over a pale-blue pair of slacks. His fair head gleamed dully in the sunshine pouring through a high-set and incredibly grubby window. He was clearing and frantically searching a locker.

Just how Reggie knew it wasn't his own locker, he couldn't have said. He just knew it wasn't. Something about the speed of the search and the anger of the other man's movements, perhaps.

He felt a trickle of sweat run down his forehead and forced himself to ignore it, despite the almost uncontrollable urge to wipe the annoying little trickle away with his shirt sleeve.

He was very conscious that they were totally alone here, and even the smallest sound, like the rustle of his clothes, might alert his quarry to his presence. Although he had no real fear about taking on the other man in a straight, one-on-one fight, he was very aware of the sleeping presence of the giant in the other room.

One call for help from His Lordship, and Reggie could find himself being beaten to a pulp.

He forced another slow, quiet breath, and concentrated on what the blond-haired man was doing. Why was he here? Whose locker was that? What was he looking for? And could it be of any possible use to find out…

Then he almost jumped out of his skin as, suddenly, the blond-haired man swore savagely and gave the locker a vicious, frustrated kick – sending a tinny, clanking noise echoing around the room.

Like a rabbit suddenly spying a snake in the grass, Reggie froze, sensing imminent danger. Clearly His Lordship hadn't found what he was looking for and was now going to do something else.

And here Reggie was, right in the line of fire if the other man should spot him.

The sweat that had broken out on his forehead now popped out all over his skin, making him feel shaky.

Luckily, though, when Littlejohn slammed the door shut and span away, he set off down the narrow passageway on the other side of the row of lockers from where Reggie was hiding; otherwise the redhead would have had no other option but to make an undignified run for it.

As it was he held his breath as the hated Littlejohn passed by harmlessly – and in total ignorance – just a few feet away from him. When he was gone, Reggie heaved a sigh of relief and sagged weakly against a locker.

It took him a moment or two to regain his equilibrium, then he stiffened his backbone and made his way to the violated locker and searched it himself, seeking some much-needed answers. For the strange actions of the blond-haired Littlejohn had intrigued him.

There, books and some letters made it clear the locker had belonged to Derek Chadworth.

Paydirt!

Quickly, and as Lord Littlejohn had done just a few minutes earlier, he frantically searched through the bags of old sports clothes, some law books and other detritus. But there was nothing to help him find out where Becky might have gone. No diary with jottings that brought news of her, or train-ticket stubs that might give him a clue where the dead boy had spent time away from Oxford. No sign he might have rented a place for someone else, no letters from his sister – nothing.

Ironically, just as Lord Littlejohn had done before him, he swore and kicked the locker.

Then Reggie calmed down and became thoughtful. He shut the door and looked at it curiously. In the centre, it had one of those open-ended square tin slots, where a piece of white card could be inserted, with the owner's name written upon it. This one was empty – but then, not everyone bothered to mark their ownership.

But as Reggie quickly began to prowl up and down the rows of lockers, he soon found one that bore the name of Lord Jeremy Littlejohn.

Perfect. It wasn't even locked! After all, the people who used this place probably thought it was safe enough. It wasn't only anonymous; tough ex-boxers also patrolled it! But when Reggie searched it, he found it contained nothing much except a few shorts and vests, a couple of towels and two bottles of unopened Scotch.

With a grim smile, Reggie closed the locker carefully and gave it a few seconds' thought. Then he nodded.

Now he knew about this place, and how easy it was to sneak in during the day, the next time His Lordship opened his locker, he'd see to it that the first thing that met his eyes was a very nasty surprise indeed.

A dog turd, maybe? And with the excrement he could leave a nice little note. Saying something along the lines that he was a living turd himself.

Yes, Reggie thought with a satisfied smile. That would wipe the lazy, supercilious smile right off His Lordship's face. And help soften him up nicely.

Or was that a bit too juvenile? Perhaps it needed to be something more threatening? He frowned. He would have to give it some thought. He was sure he could come up with something better, given a little time.

Carefully, Reggie Porter tiptoed past the sleeping boxer in his corner chair and stepped outside into another bright Oxford day.

Things were going to come to a head soon. He could feel it!

Blissfully unaware of the nasty shocks in store for him, Lord Littlejohn made his way back to his college, disgruntled and disappointed. He'd felt sure the locker at the gym was the obvious place for Derek to have stored his stuff, and the fact that it was another dead end annoyed him considerably.

Given the fact that the nosy coroner was snooping around, he'd have to find it soon, or things could get very awkward indeed. His dear papa would most assuredly not be amused at having to bail his second-born out of yet another jam. Jeremy was very much aware that his father's patience wasn't unlimited.

Trust Derek to die and leave him in an even bigger mess than he might have been if… His thoughts came to an abrupt halt as he approached the entrance to his college gates and saw a familiar female figure, in police uniform, sitting on a low wall near the lodge entrance, taking advantage of the shade cast by the tall building.

He tried to tell himself he was amused rather than dismayed, but he was aware of feeling uneasy as he approached her. He wasn't used to being made to feel uneasy, and he didn't like it.

'Well, well, well, if it isn't the officer of the law,' he said, taking the initiative and forcing his voice to sound charming and care-free. Before she could stand up, he sat down beside her and eyed her feet, which had been swinging gently to and fro as she waited. 'Good grief, those have to be the ugliest shoes I've ever seen,' he drawled, eyeing the black, flat, lace-ups with distaste. 'Pretty girls should be wearing pretty shoes on a day like this. Some of those little strappy sandal things, perhaps.'

'I doubt I could chase down a suspect in those,' Trudy shot back smartly, but she knew she must have gone an ugly shade of red and could have kicked herself. After all, what did his scorn matter to her?

'And do you do a lot of chasing, WPC… mow what was your rather remarkable name?'

'WPC Loveday, my Lord,' Trudy said stiffly. 'And I have a few more questions I'd like to ask you.' In truth, she knew she shouldn't really be here. For sure, DI Jennings wouldn't approve, and she hadn't even told Clement she intended to question His Lordship again. But it rankled to think she was being forced to treat him with kid gloves, and she just couldn't see why he should enjoy yet more special privileges. She was determined to treat him the same way she would anyone else.

'Ask away, dear heart,' he drawled, channelling his hero, Noel Coward, for all he was worth. And as she flushed most attractively in anger at the mocking endearment, he wondered suddenly what Derek would have made of her. How he would have drooled…

'We wanted to know why Mr Chadworth was a member of your club, sir,' she began smartly. 'As we understand it, to become a member of the Marquis, you had to have a title.'

'Oh, not all of us. One chap just has a father who owns half of Cumbria. No title at all – but oodles and oodles of land. A mere farmer, in fact, you might say. Besides, who says he was a member?' he challenged her.

'But Mr Chadworth's father is a solicitor,' Trudy pointed out firmly, ignoring his last sentence. Now she understood he was trying to make her angry on purpose, she had no intention of letting him get the better of her again.

'Oh, yes. How plebeian is that?' the Duke's son drawled.

Trudy had no idea what the word meant and guessed at once that this man would know she didn't. She promised herself that, the next chance she got, she'd look it up in a dictionary! Her fingers curled more tightly around her pencil as she scribbled down her shorthand. But, oh, how they itched to withdraw her small, neat truncheon and bring it down hard on this man's impeccably clad kneecaps!

'How did you even come to meet him?' she persisted with enforced calm.

'Oh, how does any chap meet another?' he asked laconically. 'Probably at a pub.'

'And you were so impressed with him that you became instant best friends.' She allowed the scorn to drip from her voice.

'Hardly!' Littlejohn said with a smile. Of course he couldn't tell this annoyingly attractive girl how the whiff of corruption rising from the ordinary-looking chap had set his antenna twitching. Always bored, and always on the lookout for something different, Derek Chadworth had caught his attention like rotting meat attracted flies.

He had been amusing, had Derek. So unashamedly coarse and vulgar, while all the time sounding and acting like a prim and proper little lad from 'oop north'. And some of the things he'd come up with had surprised even the most jaded palates of the oldest and most dissolute members of the Marquis Club – himself included. Oh, it had been so much fun at first. Corrupting all those respectable city girls, who were so ripe for exploitation. It had been such a delicious, and slightly dangerous, little game…

Until it became clear that Derek, the little toad, had been in it strictly for the money. Which was so grubby. There they all were, thinking themselves the rightful heirs to the Hellfire Club or what have you, and this avaricious son of a second-rate solicitor had only been intent on filling his pockets. What a disappointment. And yet, even then, he'd still held a certain fascination for them all. It was almost as if they kept him underfoot just to see what the bumptious, appalling little creature would do next.

But how could he explain any of this to this green, utterly respectable member of Her Majesty's Constabulary?

He turned and looked at her, and was struck once more by how pretty she was, how naïve and innocent, and how her severe uniform and that ridiculous WPC's cap only added to her sex appeal.

He smiled at her lazily. 'You know, WPC Loveday, I'm beginning to wonder why you're so interested in me,' he drawled, leaning a little closer so the tops of their arms touched.

'What?' Trudy said, alarmed and bewildered by the sudden shift in atmosphere.

'Oh, it's all right, you don't have to be shy with me,' Littlejohn said smoothly, delighted to see the way her angry colour came and went. She was so clueless it was really delicious. Corrupting someone like her… He reached out and slowly, with one forefinger, tapped her knee. 'I dare say, underneath here—' he ran his finger over the dark material of her thick skirt '—you're wearing some awful pair of regulation knickers?' he asked casually.

Trudy went hot, then cold. Never had anyone said something so extraordinarily insulting and offensive to her.

She saw the corners of his eyes crease into a smile and, with a sense of shame and shock, shot off the wall abruptly. She wasn't exactly sure what she would have done next, but she didn't have a chance to find out, for Littlejohn lithely stepped off the wall as well and then pulled her towards him, a suggestive leer marking his usually handsome face.

Before she could say anything, he suddenly reached out and drew her close and placed one hand insultingly over her left breast. Even through the thick material of her uniform jacket, she could feel the pressure of his fingers. Hot shame, revulsion, sudden fear and then a burst of overpowering anger shot through her in rapid succession.

Instantly, before she could even think about it, her knee came up and connected with his privates. It was her Aunt Margaret who'd taught her that particular move. Margaret, who'd served in the war and knew all about the quickest and easiest ways to put wayward soldiers in their place.

Littlejohn's face went a satisfyingly puce colour and he instantly doubled over, letting go of her, allowing her to take a few steps backwards.

'You little bitch!' the aristocrat wheezed viciously. 'You'll be bloody sorry you did that!' He gasped, leaning back against the wall and looking around furtively to see if anyone had seen the incident.

One or two men clearly had for, as they passed them by on the pavement, they were hiding smiles. His already puce face became almost purple.

'Keep your hands to yourself in future,' Trudy said shakily. She hesitated, uncertain what to do next. Something told her she should do *something* – but she had no idea what. After a moment or two, feeling very shaken but trying not to show it, she turned uncertainly and walked away.

Lord Jeremy Littlejohn swore savagely, and when he was sure he could straighten up without too much pain, did so. Very carefully he walked stiffly through the lodge gates, hoping she wouldn't have the guts to come back and follow him in here.

Trudy didn't follow him. Instead she walked numbly away, before slowly beginning to smile softly to herself. First, she had been the one to get under *his* skin! She wasn't sure exactly how, but she'd ruffled his aggravating, superior calm and made him angry. That was the only reason for his clumsy pass at her.

Then, when he'd assaulted her, she'd defended herself. And very satisfying that had been too!

With a feeling of triumph, she walked almost cheerfully back to the station. Nevertheless, in the back of her mind she felt a certain amount of panic. There had been real venom in his voice when he'd threatened retribution. She knew she could be vulnerable, patrolling the streets on her beat as she did, on her own.

Should she tell someone? DI Jennings, perhaps? But no, her thoughts instantly shied away from that. It would be too hideously embarrassing, and besides, it would only reinforce his prejudice against women in the police force.

Dr Ryder then? But what could he really do? He couldn't walk her beat with her!

No. Criminals made threats all the time, her teachers had warned her. The thing to remember was that they seldom followed through.

At that moment in time, Dr Ryder wasn't far away from her, as the crow flies, since he was sitting in Dr Vincent Pettigrew's rooms at St Bede's College, sipping a very nice fine malt whisky. He didn't often drink during the day – in fact, he rarely drank at all – but when a man was offering a fine vintage such as this, you didn't turn it down.

Dr Pettigrew was a lecturer in jurisprudence, specialising in tort, and had been one of Derek Chadworth's tutors. A small, lean man, with rather more jowls than one would have expected, he reminded the coroner somewhat of a French bulldog. He had a neat cap of almost black hair and nearly black eyes that watched the world with a rather sorrowful expression.

He'd seated Clement in a very comfortable chair opposite his crowded, green-leather-topped desk, poured out the drinks, and gave every indication of being the sort of man who had nothing much to do, and all the time in the world in which to do it.

Now he sighed, took a sip from his own glass, studied the colour of it for a moment or two and then gave a brief nod. 'Chadworth. Yes. A tragedy, that. I expected that boy to go far in life. That sort usually does,' he added pointedly.

The Doctor of Law had shown no particular surprise when the coroner had made an appointment to talk to him about his late student, and didn't seem to feel any reluctance about discussing him – for that, Clement was glad. Sometimes the colleges could be very protective of their reputations, to the point that they could become obstructive.

But from the tutor's relaxed attitude, Clement surmised that the principal of the college had given him permission to talk freely. Perhaps he, like so many others, was assuming the worst of the Chadworth case was now over. Or it could simply be that the law tutor considered he was a law unto himself, and felt no need to toe the party line.

'A boy of "that sort"?' Clement echoed the other man's words back at him, and raised a questioning eyebrow.

Pettigrew smiled briefly. 'Overwhelming ambitions and, between you and me, not too worried about sailing close to the wind.'

'Ah,' Clement smiled. 'One of those.' He looked at the smaller man speculatively over the rim of his glass. 'Would I be right in thinking that you didn't like him much, Doctor?'

Pettigrew smiled wanly. 'Ah, but we mustn't speak ill of the dead, must we? Or so we're told.'

'Mustn't we?' Clement mused, using that particular, droll, one-man-of-the-world-to-the-other tone of voice that was so instantly recognisable. 'It's my opinion that the dead are precisely the people we *can* speak ill of, since it hardly matters a tuppence ha'penny to them! Don't you think the world would be a better place if we refrained from speaking ill of the living?'

The law tutor gave a small start and then a wide grin. 'You are a maverick, sir! Congratulations. I have to say, as a youngster, I might have made a good maverick also. Alas, the comforting regularity of my annual stipend and a wife and family put paid to all that.'

Clement gave him a sympathetic shrug. 'So, young Chadworth…' He drew the conversation firmly back to the matter in hand. 'You expected him to do well in his exams?'

'Oh, yes. He was bright enough. And, unlike some, he put in the hours and the study. Had to, of course, if he wanted a first.'

'Hmm. Ambitious, you said. What area of law did he want to pursue, do you know?'

'Oh, criminal law,' Pettigrew said quickly and with a grunt. 'I think he'd have done rather well, defending the wealthy and the perennially guilty, Dr Ryder. It's a very lucrative field, you see. Keeping gangsters and corporate sharks out of jail.'

'Ah. He was a man who lusted after filthy lucre then?'

Pettigrew grinned. 'Nothing filthy about it, as well you know! And yes, Chadworth gave me the impression that he would always be in pursuit of it. His trouble, if you ask me,' the smaller man said, settling more comfortably into his chair, 'was that he grew up with not quite enough money in the family to satisfy him. Had he been poorer, he'd have better off. As it was, his middle-class upbringing couldn't quite compare with the lifestyle of his more affluent friends here. This is where he really came off the rails, of course,' the Oxford don said complacently, waving a hand at the window, where the city, behind the college walls, went about its daily business. 'Oxford gave him the chance to see how the rich can really live.'

'Ah, yes. The Marquis Club,' Ryder said ironically. 'Did you know he ran in Littlejohn's crowd?'

The law tutor sighed heavily. 'Yes. But that was typical of Chadworth, of course. Attracted to the money.'

'As opposed to the lure of the aristocracy? He was no snob then?' Clement put in sharply, watching the other man closely.

'No, I don't think so,' the boy's tutor said slowly, with a slight frown. 'I never got the feeling that he yearned for that *particular* pot of gold. If so, he could probably have married some ladyship or other. He was certainly attractive enough and had a way with the ladies. But I don't think having an aristocrat for a father-in-law would have suited him somehow. Having to say "yes, sir" and "no, sir" and minding his Ps and Qs all the time. He thought far too much of himself to have to put up with that! No, I always got the feeling young Chadworth needed to be his own man. The king of his own particular heap.' He waved a hand vaguely in the air.

'And you think he wouldn't have much cared what he had to do to acquire the heap?'

'Hmm?'

The coroner took another sip of his drink. 'Earlier, you said you didn't think he'd have minded sailing close to the wind.'

'Oh. Oh, yes. Mind you,' Pettigrew said, with his first intimation of caution, 'that was only my impression.'

Clement nodded quickly. 'Oh, yes. I'm only after your impressions of the lad. Nothing about our chat is official.'

Pettigrew nodded, satisfied. 'In that case then… yes. If he'd lived, I could have seen him setting up a very successful law practice – and making a lot of money for himself in the process. And not having any scruples about how he came by it.'

Clement finished the last of his drink and leaned forward to put his glass down on the desk. 'In other words, Doctor, you thought he was a wrong 'un,' he clarified with a twist of his lips.

'Quite so,' Pettigrew said with a mild smile of his own and, leaning forward, held up the decanter of whisky. 'A refill?'

Clement shook his head. 'Not for me. But please don't let an ex-surgeon's abstemiousness put you off having a second glass,' he said with a smile. 'But it's so hot, I wouldn't mind a top-up of soda.'

'Of course,' Pettigrew said, moving to comply.

And then a curious thing happened.

As the law tutor leaned forward to fill his glass, it brought their faces close together over the desktop, and when Clement held up his hand and said, 'that's fine, thank you', he noticed a quick flash of distaste cross the other man's face. He quickly leaned back in his chair, feeling puzzled. The other man's movements and attitude had given the coroner a vivid sense of déjà vu. Once again he was back in the kitchen of his home, where his daily woman had done the same thing. Pulling away from him as if somehow offended.

For a moment, Clement wondered uneasily if the hot days had made him smell rather ripe! But of course, he washed assiduously every morning – and he wasn't so overweight that he sweated unduly. Was his aftershave particularly pungent and not to the law tutor's taste, perhaps? The thought made his lips twitch again.

But then, with a flash of understanding that made him suddenly go pale, he understood the problem.

One of the symptoms of Parkinson's disease could be halitosis!

A flash of angry shame swept over him, almost catapulting him to his feet. 'Well, I won't keep you any longer,' he heard himself say briefly. Realising he still had his glass in his hand, he tossed back his drink and deposited it back on the desk.

He then thanked the smaller man for his time, careful to keep his distance as he shook hands so as not to inflict his bad breath on him a second time. And then, feeling stiff-jointed and absurd, he left the man's office.

Only once outside did he feel able to pause and take stock. Not that it took him long. He felt humiliated and stupid. And angry. This damned disease just kept heaping one indignity after another upon him. Unsteady gait, bouts of trembling. How long before he heard himself slurring the odd word or two?

And now this! Bad breath!

Grimly he set off towards Cornmarket Street, where he could find a chemist. He would just have to buy packets of the strongest breath mints he could find.

From now on, he'd have to be careful to use them regularly – and especially whenever he expected to come into close contact with any of his friends and acquaintances!

Chapter 17

Reggie Porter didn't like his father much. That was no big secret in the Porter family, but it did, inevitably, lead to clashes. These had eased somewhat when Reggie was finally able to move out of the family home, but the two men still trod warily around each other, even then.

Since Becky had remained in the family home after he'd left, whenever Reggie visited, his father usually took himself off to the local pub. His mother, June, the perpetual peacemaker of the family, tried to remain neutral in their ongoing hostilities, but in reality she sided with her children every time.

When she'd married Stanley Porter, he'd been a handsome man in uniform, with good prospects as a motor mechanic. In many ways, he'd fulfilled his part of the marriage bargain they'd made. He'd provided a roof over their heads, via a council house in Cowley, and, due to the thriving Morris car industry, was in constant work and brought home a regular wage packet. They'd had two strong, healthy children, but, even so, their union wasn't altogether successful.

This was mostly due to Stanley's liking for beer and his way with his fists when he became dangerously drunk. At first, June had taken the brunt of it, but later, as Reggie had grown into puberty, for some reason Stanley had transferred his drunken rage onto his son.

This had only lasted a few years, coming to an abrupt end when Reggie – a big-for-his-age lad at fifteen, had turned around and thumped him back. Luckily, Stanley had always adored his daughter and never touched a hair on her head. Otherwise, Reggie might seriously have killed him.

Now, on a sunny May evening, Reggie sat facing his father over the kitchen table. His mother was outside in the garden, trawling the vegetable beds for something for their tea. With a quick and experienced eye, Reggie could tell his old man had only had about three bottles of the dark beer he preferred and would thus not become belligerent just yet.

'So you haven't heard from her then?' Reggie asked persistently.

Since Becky had left home, he didn't trust his father to keep him in the loop. It would be just like him to keep his son in the dark if she *had* been in touch. Just to torment him. Becky had been able to twist the old man around her little finger and had always been canny enough to keep him sweet. If she had written to anyone, Reggie had to acknowledge with an inner growl, it would be Stanley.

'No, she ain't then! I already told you!' his father snapped across the table at him.

'I can't get anything out of her friends,' Reggie said angrily. 'They keep insisting she went to London to become a model or an actress. It's absurd!'

His father grunted. 'She always wanted to be a star,' he said indulgently. 'And I reckon she could be, too. She's got the looks and the talent. She can dance like that French bird… what's-'er-name?'

As he spoke, he looked across to a Welsh dresser, an heirloom from June Porter's side of the family. On one shelf was a large photo-portrait of a striking-looking girl, with short curly blonde hair, and a very sharp chin and cheekbones. She had a certain gamin look that went beyond mere prettiness. 'She'd look right good on the silver screen, I reckon,' he said fondly and a shade wistfully.

Reggie stirred angrily on his chair. 'Don't tell me you've got silly visions of her coming home rich and famous! The darling of Pinewood! Dad, grow up! A girl like Becky, in the big city…' He shuddered. 'She'd be prey for every con artist and who knows what. She might think she's smart and street savvy, but compared with the sharks down there… We've got to find her!' He slammed his hand on the table in frustration.

It made Stanley jump and spill a bit from the bottle of beer in his hand. Instantly, he turned ugly brown eyes on his son. He was a big man, running to fat now, and almost completely bald. His neck was thick and the hand not holding his bottle of beer curled instinctively into a fist.

In his day, he'd played amateur football and had been known for his crushing tackles on the field. He was also 'known to the police' for several drunken and vicious brawls that had taken place outside pubs after closing time.

The neighbours were scared of him, and he knew it. It gave him a great deal of pleasure to be known as a hard man.

But as his son stared back at him, totally unimpressed, he was the first to look away. 'Ah, well, we all know why you want her back, don't we?' he sneered.

Reggie stiffened. 'And what's that supposed to mean?' he asked softly.

Stanley shrugged. 'You always did mollycoddle her,' he said, backing off a bit, and staring at the photograph of his daughter morosely. 'I reckon half the reason she left was because you was always breathing down her neck, like, demanding to know where she was going, and who with.'

'Somebody had to keep an eye on her,' Reggie shot back swiftly. 'You never cared a damn about her!'

'Oh, didn't I then?' Stanley raged, getting up and thrusting back his chair so violently it toppled over and hit the floor with a crash. In a flash, Reggie was also on his feet, ready to duck the swinging fists.

Outside in the garden, with both the doors and the windows wide open in this hot weather, June Porter heard the commotion and looked anxiously back towards the house. But she made no move to go back inside.

Inside the kitchen, father and son glowered at each other. 'Oh, didn't I care about her then, aye, laddie?' Stanley raged. 'Didn't I do my best for her! Didn't I give every penny I had to…'

For a second, Stanley faltered, aware he was saying too much.

But Reggie was in no mood to let him get away with anything. 'You! Spend money on something other than beer and fags and football season tickets! Not on your life, you selfish git!'

Enraged, Stanley strode over to the dresser, took a key from his pocket, squatted down and unlocked a bottom cupboard door. From the back he withdrew a large, brown envelope.

'Don't believe me, huh? Well, there you are then, there's the proof!' he bellowed, slamming the envelope back down on the table. 'But don't say I didn't warn you! When they came in the post, with a demand for money to keep them from being circulated, don't you think I paid up? Hmm? Of course I did! For our Becky's sake…'

Suddenly he slumped down on the chair, all the fight going out of him. He glanced up at his son's tight, white, uncertain face, and smiled mirthlessly.

'Yes. You can look like that too, laddie. You thought your little sister was so innocent. So perfect…' For a second Reggie had the astonished thought that his old man was going to cry.

Of course, he didn't. Instead, he swigged thirstily from his beer.

With a slightly trembling hand, and with the feeling that he was standing on a precipice it would be wise to step away from, Reggie Porter reached out and took the envelope.

And looked inside.

Chapter 18

The moment Trudy stepped into the station house she felt the atmosphere. Rodney Broadstairs didn't even grin at her, but shot her a quick, almost gentle look.

It was left to PC Walter Swinburne, one of the station's oldest constables, to tell her the bad news.

'DI Jennings wants you in his office right away, Constable Loveday,' he said formally. Then added in a hissed whisper, 'He's in a right tizz! What on earth have you been doing?'

Trudy gulped. Feeling slightly sick, she approached DI Jennings's office and tapped timidly on the door.

'Come in!' The voice roaring the instruction did indeed sound very sharp and unhappy. Straightening her shoulders, she opened the door and walked in.

Jennings watched her approach, his face tight with fury. 'I've just had a phone call from Lord Jeremy Littlejohn, Probationary Constable Loveday.'

At these dread words, Trudy's heart leapt into her throat, making her feel momentarily as if she was going to be sick. With an effort, she swallowed the nausea back down.

'He tells me you physically assaulted him,' Jennings continued grimly, his voice level, flat and hard. 'Naturally, I expressed my deep surprise that this could possibly be the case, but he insisted.'

'Sir, I…'

'Be quiet! And let me finish,' her superior officer interrupted with a raised bark. Trudy flinched, knowing his voice could be heard in the outer office.

Feeling the sweat break out on her forehead, Trudy forced herself to be still. And to think.

Suddenly, she remembered Dr Ryder telling her how she couldn't let her emotions cloud her thinking. How, if she allowed herself to be distracted by fear or excitement or anger or anything else, her antagonist had already won. And now, she realised, was a good example of the need to keep a clear head.

She blinked, forced back her feelings of indignation and fright, and watched the Inspector closely.

'I told His Lordship that no officer under my command would ever attack a member of the public. Let alone someone of his standing in the community,' Jennings proceeded, his voice tight with suppressed fury. 'You can imagine my surprise, then, when he insisted that you had done so. What's more, out in the street, where everyone and their grandfather could see you do it!' Again, his voice had risen to a shout, but although she flinched, she kept her mouth firmly closed.

In the back of her head, though, a tiny voice of panic was rising. She was on probation, and would be for the next thirteen months. An incident like this was something DI Jennings could leap on as an excuse to be rid of her.

She needed to stop him doing so somehow. Think! Think! What would Dr Ryder do?

'Well, Loveday! Don't just stand there like a stuffed dummy,' Jennings snarled. 'Did you…?' And here he finally lowered his voice to a near squeak. 'Did you knee the man in his groin?'

'Yes, sir,' Trudy said boldly. And before he could carry on, added quickly, 'It was the only way I could think of to bring the situation under control without causing more embarrassment to

His Lordship or bringing the station house's reputation into disrepute, sir.'

Jennings, his mouth open to rip into her, paused for a fraction of a second. Into Trudy's mind flashed the realisation that he looked a bit like a bullfrog, caught mid-croak. She had to bite her lip to stifle a sudden, hysterical desire to giggle.

'Explain yourself,' Jennings contented himself with saying.

'Sir, I was talking to Lord Littlejohn just outside his college when he… er… made a rather clumsy but very public assault on me. I'm afraid he was a little the worse for drink.' She lied without compunction. 'He… er… grabbed me… er…' She knew her face was flaming now, but that she had to persevere. She could feel the sweat trickling down her spine and felt shaky at the knees, but ignored both sensations. 'He grabbed me in a certain place on my, er, upper torso, and made as if to do more. We were on the pavement, sir, and I needed to get the situation under control before an undignified scuffle broke out. And, of course,' she added with a flash of inspiration, 'that last thing I wanted to do was be forced to arrest him for common assault on a police officer.'

She knew from the look on her superior officer's face that she'd scored a direct hit there. 'Naturally, sir, I knew you wouldn't want to have to explain to the Duke how his son had been arrested after publicly assaulting me. If the press got hold of it…' She allowed her voice to trail off. 'So, I did the only thing I could, sir, and disabled him as quietly and neatly as I could, then left him to collect himself. Luckily, I think, only one or two passers-by noticed, but they didn't interfere. I came straight back to the station in order to apprise you of the situation—' she added the lie almost without a pang of conscience '—in the hopes that you could help make sure it could all be nipped in the bud. I have to say I'm surprised Lord Littlejohn wanted to pursue this further. Er… I take it that he asked for me to be reprimanded?' she asked, using her best guileless voice.

Jennings slowly leaned back in his chair. Some of the fury was gone, and now he looked a shade uncertain. It was, under the circumstances, the best she could hope for.

'Yes, he made it clear he wanted you to get a good dressing-down, at the very least,' Jennings confirmed absently. In fact, the aristocrat had demanded she be fired instantly.

But now warning bells were beginning to sound in Jennings's ear.

'You say his assault on you was witnessed by members of the public?' he asked quietly.

'Yes, sir. I daresay I could find them again easily if you wanted their statements, since that area is on my beat, and I'm sure I recognised two of them…' She again lied without the least hesitation.

'That won't be necessary, Constable,' he said sharply, and Trudy nodded, relieved to hear he'd now dropped the threatening word 'probationary' from her title.

'Of course not, sir.'

Jennings sighed heavily. 'I was able to persuade His Lordship not to press charges against you,' he said flatly. 'But for pity's sake, Constable, you should have learned by now how to fend off men's advances without going to such extreme measures!'

Trudy bit back an angry retort, swallowed hard, and said meekly, 'Yes, sir. Sorry, sir.'

'All right. Get out of my sight. No, wait!'

Trudy, who had half-turned with weary relief to head towards the door, once more stiffened her backbone and turned back.

'Yes, sir?'

'What were you doing questioning His Lordship in the first place? I thought I told you to keep Dr Ryder reined back when it came to talking to the witnesses who have influence in the city!'

'Yes, sir,' Trudy said. 'I… er… thought it best to speak to Lord Littlejohn myself, sir. I thought Dr Ryder might be rather more… er… inclined to be… er… somewhat brusque and…'

She felt an inner sense of shame at throwing her friend to the wolves like this, but she was sure he wouldn't mind. In fact, when she told him about it later, she rather expected he would congratulate her on her quick thinking. For the coroner had made no great secret of the fact that he didn't regard DI Jennings particularly highly.

'Yes, yes, I understand. Well, in view of the mess you made of the interview, I hereby order you to keep away from Lord Littlejohn in future. Is that clear?'

Trudy blinked hard, but nevertheless managed to force out another meek-sounding 'Yes, sir' before saluting smartly, turning and walking away.

But as she walked to the door, she was already telling herself she'd be damned if she was going let that last order prevent her from finding out what had happened to Derek Chadworth.

She opened the door and carefully closed it behind her. Aware that she was the focus of all eyes, she lifted her chin, walked to her desk amidst the eerie silence, and began to empty her satchel of her accoutrements. In dignified silence, she threaded a piece of paper, a carbon and a backing sheet into her Remington typewriter and began to type out her report.

Around her, the office broke out into murmured conversations again, and she began to breathe easier.

Chapter 19

On the way out of the station house that evening, Trudy sidled over to the craggy-faced Walter Swinburne's desk. At forty-eight, he was the station's oldest PC, and most experienced.

'Can I ask your advice about something?' she asked quietly.

'Sure, but I have to be off in a minute?' He glanced at his watch tellingly and Trudy sighed. The trouble with Walter was that he had no ambition – or curiosity. A nice enough bloke who did his job efficiently and without complaint, but all he really wanted to do was shoot off home to his wife and his beloved allotment. Sergeant O'Grady maintained stoutly that he earned his keep if only because of his long list of snouts. No one could argue that he didn't know every villain on his patch – from the minors to the big players. But Trudy hadn't been at the station for more than a month before she realised that nobody really rated Walter.

Still, since he was neither for nor against her, he made for a handy – and neutral – point of reference. 'What can you tell me about secret drinkers?' she asked bluntly.

'Eh?'

'You know. People who drink too much and try and hide it.'

'Oh, them. Functioning alcoholics, the medical men call 'em,' he surprised her by saying. Sometimes, PC Swinburne showed unexpected flashes of learned intelligence which tended to discon-cert everyone, and the Sergeant most of all! 'What do you want to know?'

'Oh – you know. How you can spot them,' Trudy said casually.

'Not always easy that,' Walter said, leaning back in his chair and smiling slightly. 'I knew a man once, a pickpocket out Abingdon way, who could drink enough to put a carthorse under the table and still go out and lift someone's wallet without them ever being the wiser.'

'But surely you could tell he'd been drinking?' Trudy protested.

Walter shrugged.

'But most people, you know, slur their words and aren't really steady on their feet, that kind of thing?' she persisted.

'Oh, sure – most of 'em show signs of it, if they've been drinking more than usual. But if they're hardened drinkers and their bodies have acclimatised to so much booze in their systems, you'd be surprised how "normal" they can appear, even when completely sozzled. Mind you, they're often very careful of how they speak – a bit slowly, like, being careful not to get muddled.'

'So – slow and careful speaking.' Trudy made a mental note. 'Anything else?'

'Well, it's not always easy,' Walter said cautiously. 'Some of them can be really sly and creative. Especially the secretive drinkers – they're usually the higher-ups, who have the most to lose. Not like your average working-class Joe, who does their drinking on the up and up in the local boozer.'

'So, a professional man then…' Trudy prodded delicately.

'Oh, yes, they're the sort who stash little bottles of this and that in hiding places and have a crafty nip when none of the family is looking.'

'And there's nothing else to give them away?'

'Well – there's their breath, of course,' Walter said, wiping the side of his nose with his forefinger thoughtfully. 'Can't always hide the smell of booze on the breath, see, even if they're drinking vodka or gin.'

'So they'd have the smell of alcohol about them,' Trudy said, a little impatiently. She'd already figured *that* out for herself!

'Not so fast, WPC Loveday,' Walter mocked her gently. 'I never said nothing about that.'

'You said their breath gave them away,' Trudy protested, puzzled.

'Yeah. But on account of the breath mints, see.'

'Breath mints?' Trudy echoed. Then her frown cleared as she caught on. 'Oh, right! To disguise the smell of spirits or beer!'

'Exactly. You need a strong scent to obliterate booze, and a good, strong mint does the trick.'

'Right,' Trudy nodded. 'Well, thanks for that, Walter.'

The older PC dismissed her with a wave, and then quickly set about clocking off. He liked to be home dead on time for his tea, and it was rissoles and chips tonight. One of his favourites!

Trudy went on her own way a little while later, but as she walked home for her tea she was rather thoughtful.

She'd never smelt alcohol on the coroner's breath – or mints either, for that matter. And he'd always talked normally. Perhaps she was jumping the gun a little, and thinking the worst?

At home, her mother was just putting the mashed potatoes on top of the shepherd's pie to brown in the oven, for her father was due home any minute from his shift on the buses.

She kissed her mother absently on the cheek in greeting, then went upstairs to change out of her uniform and have a quick bath.

Tomorrow she was back in plain clothes, since she had more student hangouts to haunt in the hopes of picking up information on the dead student, the mysterious, red-headed stranger, and that unspeakable Lord Littlejohn. Even now, she squirmed at just how easy it was for him to put in a phone call and almost get her sacked from her job. He'd probably done it without a qualm, too, never even stopping to think that he might have ruined her whole life.

It simply wasn't fair!

She sighed and went down to tea, listening to her parents good-naturedly arguing about whether or not to fork out and start renting a telly, and eating her meal without really tasting it.

Her thoughts kept shifting resentfully to Littlejohn. He was such a nasty piece of work; she didn't have any doubts at all that he would have been capable of killing his friend. But had he?

Telling herself that, from now on, she'd have to be careful not to let her dislike of their prime suspect cloud her judgement, she skipped the jam roly-poly for pudding, and went to bed early. One thing was for sure – whatever happened, she mustn't give the Duke's son any more ammunition to use against her.

But it wasn't going to be easy. She was beginning to positively hate him – and all that he stood for.

The next morning, still in civvies, Trudy went first to the coroner's office to bring him up to date on her findings and confess about the incident with Littlejohn. She was extremely gratified when Clement laughed heartily at her description of the elegant, white-clad lord doubling up in pain and going puce.

Even so, he gave her the same warning DI Jennings had – namely, to leave Littlejohn strictly alone from now on.

'I don't think it's a good idea for you to question him without me along in future,' Clement said firmly.

And with that stricture still buzzing – somewhat resentfully (for surely she'd proved she could look after herself?) – in her head, she made her way to a bookshop that was also half-coffee shop, in a little side alley not far from The Ship Inn.

There she bought herself a cup of something she'd never heard of (some kind of weird coffee) and walked with it to a table where a group of female students were lounging around, discussing some bloke called Spinoza.

'I still think his philosophy…' one large-boned, but rather striking, redhead was saying as Trudy approached.

'I say, I hope you don't mind if I bag this spare chair,' she said casually. 'Only the place is rather full.'

'Sure, we don't mind,' a small brunette said, smiling at her in a friendly way. 'You reading PPE?'

'Uh, no. English lit,' Trudy said, thinking it was a subject she might just be able to bluff her way through, if necessary.

'Then don't mind us. We're having an argument as to which philosopher was the maddest.'

'Sounds fun.' Trudy laughed. 'Makes a change from talking about that poor student who drowned,' she added carefully.

'Oh, Derek!' The large redhead rolled her eyes meaningfully. 'Yes, he was the last person you'd have expected to get himself drowned, wasn't he?'

Trudy tried not to look too keen. 'Oh, you knew him personally?'

'Not *that* personally, praise be!' the smaller brunette said, making the third member of their group, a string bean of a girl, grin widely. 'It wasn't always a good idea to get *that* close to him!'

Trudy took a sip of the coffee, almost choked on its bitterness (she liked a load of a sugar and cream whenever she had it) and put the cup hastily down. That would teach her to stick to good old tea! 'Oh? A bit of a ladies' man, was he?'

'Wasn't he just,' the string bean of a girl said. 'How they stood him, I don't know. He gave me the creeps.'

'Oh, he was all right,' the small brunette objected. 'He was good fun, and a brilliant photographer. That moody black-and-white he did of the swifts over the Radcliffe Camera won him a prize in some magazine or other.'

'He might have been a great photographer, but I'll bet he was a lousy boyfriend,' the big redhead snorted. 'Just ask that poor little thing he used to go around with, Jenny Morrison. He dropped her soon enough when someone better came along.'

Trudy would have loved to ask who Jenny Morrison was, but didn't feel confident enough in her 'spying' technique to risk it. Both Dr Ryder and DI Jennings had dinned into her that the art of getting information was to listen more, and ask questions only when really necessary. And now she had the talk centred around the dead man, she didn't want to risk sounding too nosy.

'Well, he never was the faithful type,' the small brunette said. 'I saw him one day with this pixie-like girl, really striking she was, arms all around one another and her giggling away, and then the very next day – and I do mean, literally, the day after, he was with some other girl.'

'So there were probably a few broken hearts around after that punting accident then,' Trudy said with a somewhat exaggerated sigh.

The girls agreed, rather hard-heartedly, that there probably had been – and then the argument about mad philosophers continued.

Trudy, happy to leave her still-full cup of coffee on the table, eventually excused herself and left.

But she didn't go on to her next student hangout, as she'd originally planned. Instead, she went straight back to the station house, wondering why the name Jennifer Morrison rang a distant bell.

In the main building, she slipped into the records office, not really expecting anything, but meeting with success almost at once. Perhaps today was going to be one of those wonderful days when everything just seemed to go right?

It seemed that one Miss Jennifer Morrison had committed suicide last year. The coroner, she was interested to note, had not been Dr Ryder, but one of the city's other officers of the court.

She made notes on the case, and then went to her desk to write up two reports – one for Dr Ryder and another for DI Jennings.

Chapter 20

Enid Clowes got off the bus opposite her favourite department store, Elliston & Cavell, and wondered if she should visit the tea room and have a little treat. She still felt a little bit fluttery about her errand, and a nice cup of tea and a bun – or maybe even a scone – would help settle her nerves. But then she saw a small group of Teddy Boys pass in front of the shop, and quickly turned away.

Really, it was extraordinary what the youth of today got up to. Going around on those noisy Vespa mopeds, and looking so outlandish with their pointy shoes and slicked-back hair. She was only glad she'd never lived in Brighton, with all the trouble they'd had down there with Rockers and whatnot!

Instead, she turned and set off determinedly in the direction of Thursby College, where, she somewhat vaguely believed, the coroner's office was situated. She was sure, anyway, that the people in the post office in St Aldate's would be able to direct her to the right place, which they very kindly did.

Enid didn't like to think the mortuary was so close by, but when she knocked on the door of Dr Clement Ryder's office she was mightily relieved to be ushered into a very nice room by a kind-eyed and rather motherly woman.

She was a little flustered again when she had to admit she hadn't made an appointment. 'Oh, how silly of me. Of course, I should have realised... an important man like the coroner would need... oh, dear...' But when she told the great man's secretary she had come in response to the newspaper appeal for witnesses who were abroad in the Wolvercote area on the morning that unfortunate young student had drowned, she was quickly reassured.

Her name was ascertained, and she was shown a seat, while the secretary tapped discreetly on an inner door and disappeared inside. After a moment or two, she reappeared, and Enid was shown into the inner sanctum, where a very handsome gentleman indeed rose from behind an impressive desk.

Clement Ryder summed up Enid Clowes in a second and smiled gently at his secretary. 'I think a nice cup of tea is in order, don't you, Mrs Clowes?'

'Oh, yes. Thank you,' she accepted nervously. She clutched her 'best' handbag tightly in her hands. She was dressed in one of her Sunday outfits, and her neatest pair of lace-up shoes. She'd had her hair done yesterday, and now had to fight back the urge to pat it and make sure her newly permed curls were all in place.

'I really don't know if I'm doing the right thing or not, er... Sir... er... Dr Ryder,' she began, flushing a little as Clement came around the desk and pulled a chair out for her.

'Oh, I'm sure you are, Mrs Clowes,' he said gently. 'My secretary tells me it's about the fatality in Wolvercote a little while ago?'

'Yes, it is.'

The secretary returned with a cup of tea in a very nice cup and saucer so thin that Enid was convinced it had to be bone china. And with such pretty roses on it too. She took a sip, appreciative at finding it hot and sweet, just how she liked it.

Clement retired back behind his desk and ignored his own cup.

'You live in Wolvercote?' he asked mildly.

'Oh, yes. For many years now – so pleasant a place. Port Meadow is such an attractive feature to have on your doorstep, so to speak,' Enid gushed.

Clement nodded. 'Indeed,' he agreed. 'I take it you saw something on the morning the students were holding their picnic party?'

'Oh, no,' Enid said. Then, 'Well, perhaps. I'm not sure. Oh, dear, I knew this was going to happen,' she said miserably. 'When I read in the papers that you wanted people to come forward, I wasn't sure exactly what it was…' For a little while she bleated and dithered, and Clement, with hard-won patience, slowly, bit by bit, began to extract what it was that she had come to tell him.

It appeared that, on the day in question, she had been walking along the road, and had looked out across the meadow and seen the students beginning to gather.

'Did you see the accident itself? The punts colliding?' he asked.

'Oh, no. I think that must have happened after I passed by. Besides, you can't really see the river from the road, as it's down below the edge of the banks, you see.'

'Yes. But you saw the congregation of young people?'

'Oh, yes, indeed.'

'Good. Was there anyone else you saw? Someone walking their dog, for instance?' he asked, wondering if he could place the time she had been walking by, by linking her up to James Roper and his canine companion, Tyke.

'No, I don't think so. Oh, but I did see a fisherman walking away – probably after realising he had no hope of catching anything once the students began splashing about. They always do, you know – in the river, in summertime. I'm not at all sure it's healthy, though.'

Clement smiled. 'There were two fishermen, weren't there?'

'Oh, no. Well, there might have been, but I only saw one of them. He'd packed up his fishing equipment and was halfway across the meadow, heading towards the road. It was clear he'd given up trying to catch any fish that day.'

Clement nodded. He'd rather thought, from James Roper's evidence, that the two fishermen he'd seen had been friends and had come to the river together, since they were fishing so close to one another. But if they left separately, perhaps they had come to the river separately as well. Not that it necessarily mattered.

'And did you notice anyone else?'

'No, I don't think so.'

'And you don't remember anything about the students or the party that struck you as odd?'

'Oh, no. Well, apart from that young man with the really fierce red hair who stood a little way away, watching them,' Enid said, a shade breathlessly. She really was enjoying having the coroner's undivided attention. Such a nice man, and with impeccable manners too.

'Oh, yes, we know about him,' Clement mused. James Roper had also mentioned a red-haired student in the mix. 'You think he was watching them?'

'Well, he seemed to be.'

Clement nodded. 'You're sure he wasn't part of the group?'

'Well, he wasn't acting as if he was,' the older woman said. 'You know, he sort of kept his distance, and didn't talk to anyone. Like someone who was just out enjoying a walk along the river and didn't want to be a part of the revelry.'

Clement nodded. He would have to find out who this mysterious redhead was. If this second witness was also saying the as-yet-unidentified stranger had been taking a keen interest in the proceedings, while trying to hold himself apart, he might have seen something of interest.

He thanked Enid Clowes effusively, positively making her day by taking her arm solicitously and walking her to the door, telling her how he wished all members of the public were as civic-minded as she.

After she'd been gone for little more than ten minutes, he was surprised to see Trudy back again. After their early catch-up meeting, he hadn't expected to see her again until the end of the day.

But one look at her bright and shining brown eyes told him she was excited.

'I've discovered something that might be interesting,' she began. 'First of all, can you get the file of a girl called Jennifer Morrison? She committed suicide last year – not one of your cases, though.'

As she began to relate her conversation with the students in the coffee shop, Clement asked his secretary to find the file.

And after he'd finished reading it, he agreed a visit to the dead girl's parents was definitely in order.

Islip looked lovely in the sun. As Clement pulled in at the bottom of a steep and narrowly twisting lane, checking to see if he could see the number of the Morrisons' house on any of the pretty selection of cottages on offer, he couldn't help but admire the gardens.

Not a gardener himself, he nevertheless appreciated the show put on by those who had green fingers.

'There it is,' Trudy said, pointing across the road. 'The one with the old, dark-blue Riley in the carport.'

Clement nodded and parked the car.

The Morrisons' front garden was particularly crammed with flowering things and, as they walked up a neat, stone path to the front door, the drone of bees was almost deafening.

The door was answered quickly by a tired-faced woman who looked at the coroner's credentials with a tightening of her lips, but no other obvious sign of distress.

'I'm so sorry to disturb you, Mrs Morrison, but Constable Loveday and myself are investigating the death by drowning of a student out near Wolvercote way. You may have read about it?'

Celia Morrison frowned slightly and then shrugged. 'I don't really read the papers much, nowadays. Please, won't you come in?' She stepped aside and led them into a tiny hall that smelt of lavender furniture polish. 'Please, go on through to the lounge,' she said, indicating a door which opened out into a small room just off to one side. A couple of large armchairs and a new-looking sofa filled most of the space, but a set of French doors had been set in the far wall, letting the light flood in. Through them, the even more beautiful and much larger back garden stretched for a long way, revealing a neat section of fruit and vegetables, a large lawn area surrounded by herbaceous borders and several mature trees.

'What can I do for you?' Celia Morrison asked pleasantly. 'Would you care for a drink? Tea, coffee, orange squash? It's so hot, isn't it?'

'No, thank you,' Trudy said kindly. Since they'd agreed in the car on the way over that she should talk to the wife, and Clement to the husband, she smiled gently and said, 'Mrs Morrison, were you aware that your daughter, Jennifer, was a particular friend of Derek Chadworth? The boy who drowned recently?'

'My Jenny?' Celia said, looking and sounding genuinely surprised. 'Are you sure? She never mentioned anyone of that name.'

Trudy nodded gently. 'Yes, we're sure. Several of their... er... mutual friends mentioned it. They might only have been seeing each other for a little while, though. I don't think it was anything serious,' she added tactfully.

'Oh. Oh, well... I'm afraid my daughter isn't with us...' Celia's voice began to choke, and Clement smoothly interjected.

'It's all right, Mrs Morrison. We know what happened to your daughter. And we're very sorry,' he said softly.

They knew, from reading the girl's file, that she had visited the home of her friend Abigail White one night and, under the pretext of using the bathroom, had stolen all Mrs White's prescription sleeping pills – leaving her poor mother to find her dead in bed the next morning.

Now the older woman ducked her head a little and turned briefly away. Clearly, she felt incapable of carrying on a conversation. 'My husband is at home. He's in the garden. Perhaps you'd like to talk to him,' she said, jerking the words out staccato style, evidently desperate to be rid of them and the unbearable sadness their questions were bringing back to her.

Trudy felt herself tense guiltily. Although she understood that you had to ask questions in her job – in fact, that it was her duty to do so – she didn't have to always like it. And she certainly didn't like bringing pain back into people's lives.

'Yes, perhaps that would be for the best,' Trudy said swiftly.

'He's out in the back, playing with his newest toy.' Celia smiled bravely, trying to bring some sort of normality back into the proceedings. 'He's had a big pond installed,' she carried on, catching the coroner's quizzical eye. 'My husband loves his garden, Dr Ryder,' she explained, taking a shaky breath. 'He's always expanding it – putting in a rockery, trying out new hybrids, adding new varieties of fruit trees to the orchard, that sort of thing. But I told him, I don't know what he wants with a big pond, especially since the river forms part of our boundary at the far end!' Now she'd started talking it was as if she couldn't stop. 'But there you are – he said he wanted to start growing water lilies! You'll probably find him right down at the back far end of the garden seeing what's what,' she added, pushing the French doors open to their widest extent, since they were already standing a little ajar, letting the warmth and scent from outside seep into the room.

Trudy wondered if her erratic behaviour meant she was on some sort of medication herself.

'Just go along the patio, following the curve of the lawn to the right and carry on straight down. You'll see a stand of weeping willows that follows the line of the river. I'm sure he'll be down there somewhere,' the woman gushed, with a smile so wide it didn't look quite right.

Clement Ryder, too, wondered about the state of her nerves, but she wasn't his patient. Even so, he made a mental note to find out who her GP was and have a quiet word about her condition – professional to professional.

'Thank you, Mrs Morrison,' Trudy said gently.

They stepped out across the glorious garden in tense and thoughtful silence, both of them thinking hard.

Trudy wasn't that surprised the dead girl's mother hadn't known she was seeing Derek. More and more it was becoming clear that the drowned student was not what her parents would have called a 'nice' boy. And girls, Trudy had to acknowledge wryly, tended not to introduce 'bad' boys to their parents, but kept their existence very quiet.

She couldn't count the number of times her own friends had begged her to tell their parents they had been with her, when, in fact, they'd gone out to the pictures with somebody they knew their fathers wouldn't approve of!

Once they'd walked a few yards, they did indeed spot Mr Keith Morrison, and, sure enough, he was standing, peering down into a large, roughly round body of water that was only just beginning to show signs of settling in. The raw earth that had been gouged out to make room for the pond was banked around one half of it and had been planted with various small shrubs and some irises. As they approached, they saw him notice them and turn around to face them.

He was a big man, Trudy judged, maybe six foot and even a little over, with a beefy build and thinning, pale-grey hair. Perhaps because Celia Morrison had seemed so small and fragile, she was expecting her husband to be of a similar stamp. But as he watched them, his face showing no signs of either welcome or rejection, she recalled what she'd learned about him before setting off to visit the coroner.

A quick background check had quickly informed her that he was a successful businessman, the owner of a small works in

Cowley that produced the Morrison moped in impressive numbers. Their child, Jennifer, had been an only child, though, and she wondered who Mr Morrison would pass the business on to, now he could no longer expect to have grandsons.

'Hello? Can I help you?' he called gruffly, his eyes moving behind them, perhaps expecting to see his wife accompanying them outside. His gaze quickly returned to Clement, however, as the coroner produced his credentials, introduced Trudy, and told him they were enquiring into the death of Derek Chadworth.

'Chadworth? Derek Chadworth? Never heard of him,' he said bluntly. Then he added with a small frown, 'Wait a minute, though – he was the boy who drowned when those students got rowdy on the river a week or so back, wasn't he?'

His eyes moved constantly between the tall, obviously well-educated man and the unexpected figure of the young woman with long, curly, brown hair and big brown eyes, as if seeking some other explanation for their presence. He looked tired and a little ill at ease. Maybe even a shade impatient – as if they'd interrupted his quiet contemplation and he wanted to get things over with quickly so he could return to his own private world again.

'That's right. We believe your daughter Jennifer knew him,' Clement said mildly. 'And we were hoping she might have told you something about him that might prove helpful to our enquiries. We're trying to find…'

'Rubbish,' Keith Morrison interrupted him, somewhat rudely. 'I don't know where you get your information, but I doubt very much that my daughter knew this man, this student, you're talking about. She was a city girl, see – "town" not "gown". She had a grand little job on the cosmetics counter in Debenhams – went straight there from school. She was training for the Olympics, you know – dressage – so she didn't have much free time. But even if she'd been seeing a young man, it would have been someone from the village, perhaps, or someone of our own kind.

164

She wouldn't have had anything to do with students,' he maintained stoutly.

Clement shot Trudy a quick look, which she interpreted quickly and smoothly. Irate or testy fathers needed soothing, and she was far better at doing that sort of thing than the sometimes impatient and irascible coroner.

'I can understand why you might think that, Mr Morrison,' she said gently. 'But I've heard from several sources that Jennifer and Derek were stepping out together for a period of time last year. Did she never mention him at all?'

'No, and I still think you've got it wrong,' the other man insisted stubbornly. 'She knew the students were off limits – I told her often enough. It stands to reason – they're only in town for three years or so to get their degrees and then they're back off to wherever it is they come from. Most of them are toffs and nobs, out to sow their wild oats and have a good time – definitely not the sort who are looking for good and decent girls to marry. Her mother and I warned her all the time to keep away from them, and she did.'

Trudy sighed gently. It seemed Jennifer Morrison hadn't confided in either parent that she'd been seeing the dead boy. And with an attitude such as that of Keith Morrison, she wasn't surprised.

'I see,' she said, a shade helplessly, and glanced across at the coroner with a questioning look.

He gave a shrug so slight it was almost invisible, then turned and looked down at the pond. 'You've already got some newts, I see. Never takes nature long to colonise a new place, does it? Nice-looking pond you have there,' he said, in an effort to get the interview back on more friendly terms with a temporary change of subject.

With an effort, Keith dragged his eyes from the policewoman and scowled down at what his wife had called his new toy. 'Yes, it's coming along,' he said listlessly.

'I can see the marks of the trench you dug to the river are almost obliterated now. That creeping plant you have there covers the ground well, doesn't it?' Clement went on amiably. Then added simply, 'You must miss your daughter very much.'

Keith Morrison stiffened, clearly in no mood to be either mollified or sympathised with. 'If there's nothing else I can help you with,' he said coldly, 'I'd be obliged if you didn't bother us again. Especially my wife. She took our Jenny's... passing... very hard. Can you see yourself out?'

Thus summarily dismissed, Trudy and Clement nodded, murmured their thanks, and began to walk slowly back across the impressive garden.

Trudy felt vaguely down. They hadn't learned a single new thing about the dead boy. Except that Jennifer Morrison had had more sense than to tell her parents about him!

'Well, that was a washout,' Trudy said regretfully.

But Clement Ryder wasn't quite so sure.

Chapter 21

The coroner dropped her off at the station house and then went back to his own office, intending to tackle a mound of paperwork he'd been neglecting lately. Trudy, reluctant to go back to the office (since she was still smarting a bit from the dressing-down DI Jennings had given her over the debacle with Littlejohn), loitered on the busy pavement, casting about desperately for something useful to do that wouldn't include office duties.

She suddenly remembered that the dead boy had been something of a photography buff. She was pretty sure one of the students she'd been chatting to had mentioned that he'd even won prizes and got some stuff published in a local magazine. OK, it was a bit tenuous, but who knew, she might find out something new.

A quick trawl in the library soon put her on to *Oxford through the Lens*, a monthly magazine dedicated to local photographers and their work, and whose back issues did indeed contain several 'Chadworth' originals.

She found their headquarters in a little alleyway not far from the site of the old prison. In the tiny office she found only one person, a tall, thin, rather desiccated-looking old man, but he recognised Derek Chadworth's name instantly.

She introduced herself, showed her credentials, and told him why she'd come.

'Oh, yes. Poor Derek! He was such a loss to photography, my dear young lady. Er, sorry, officer. I always told him he could become a professional if only he would devote more time to perfecting his art. Alas, he was more interested in his studies and er… well, yes,' he broke off, looking at Trudy a shade uneasily.

Trudy grinned, guessing what he'd been about to say. No doubt Derek had made no secret of his appreciation of the fairer sex.

Sensing she wouldn't get very far now with this witness unless she went down the official route, she reminded him crisply that the constabulary was still investigating his death.

'So I was just wondering what you could tell me about him, sir,' she said, keeping her voice matter-of-fact, and bringing out her notebook in order to look even more official. 'Did you like him?'

'Like him?' The old man, who'd introduced himself as Richard Fosdyke, looked surprised by the question. 'Well… er… I'm not sure… I liked his *work*. He did some wonderful black-and-white shots of the city at dawn. We've published a fair few of those in the magazine over the past year. I encouraged him to enter one or two into a nationwide competition, and I believe he won quite a prestigious prize.'

'So he was very good then,' Trudy agreed briskly, not interested in his prowess with a camera. 'Did he seem different to you in the weeks before his death?'

'Different?'

'Yes. Perhaps he was moodier. Or afraid of something? A little edgy?'

'Oh, no. Nothing like that. He seemed his usual ebullient self,' Richard Fosdyke said with a wry twist of his lips. 'Never lacked self-confidence, did Derek. Mind you, I suppose he had every reason to be happy. He was confidently expecting to do well in his exams, and he was very popular with the women.

And obviously he was never short of money,' Fosdyke swept on, failing to notice he suddenly had the pretty young WPC's full attention now. 'I suppose he was another trust-fund lad, like most of them in this fair city of ours,' he mused – a shade enviously, Trudy thought.

But Trudy, who knew differently, smiled widely. 'Oh? What makes you think he was in funds? Always dressed smartly, did he? Free with his cash, perhaps?'

'Hmm? Oh, no. Well, not especially. I mean, I was thinking of his studio. All the best photographic equipment, the best cameras, and a darkroom that, quite frankly, was even better than mine here,' the old man said, his envy quite obvious now.

'Photographic studio?' Trudy echoed, her detective's blood beginning to race. Surely this was the first they'd heard about this? Clement certainly hadn't mentioned it. Nor had the boy's parents. 'Do you know where this was?'

'Oh, down Jericho way somewhere, I believe. Overlooking the canal. He rented a place – used to be a double garage, I think.'

'Yes, sir. Do you have the address?'

'No, don't think so. But he took me there once, to show me some stuff he had drying... Would you like me to draw you a map?' he asked helpfully.

Trudy could have kissed the old bird. Instead she gave him a dazzling smile that quite made his day.

'Yes, sir, that would be smashing,' she said.

More or less on the other side of town, Lord Jeremy Littlejohn pushed his way through the boxing-club doors and noted the usual bruiser, sleeping in his chair. With a curl of his lip he anticipated the moment when he could kick the chair leg, thus waking the man up and demanding a bout of sparring in the empty ring.

He was just in the mood for punching something solid and stupid for an hour or two.

He made his way to the back room and walked towards his locker, slipping the bag containing his athletic kit from one shoulder and dropping it onto the floor.

He shucked out of his jacket and opened the door, his hand automatically reaching inside to extract one of the wire coat hangers that habitually hung from a pole at the top of the locker space.

But before his hand could connect with the wire, something fell out and landed with a dull thud on the top of his immaculately polished Oxfords.

Lord Jeremy Littlejohn, on seeing what it was, gave a muffled yelp and jumped back, fastidiously shaking the pathetic, furry body from his shoe.

His heart leapt unappetisingly into his throat, and for a second or two he had to swallow back bile.

For a moment he stood, staring down at the dead rodent. Its two protruding yellow teeth curled obscenely from the jaw, and its two front legs were slightly curled up, ironically enough, as if in a pugilist's pose. Then, distastefully, he reached down and very delicately plucked it up by the very tip of its tail.

A faint scent of malodorous decay reached him, making him retch slightly.

His first outraged thought was to take the little corpse into the other room, drop it into the sleeping man's lap, and then demand to know what good he was if he couldn't prevent intruders from leaving such calling cards in the members' lockers.

But common sense quickly prevailed.

The last thing he wanted was for it to get out that he was being targeted in this way. Besides, the more tightly he kept control of the situation the better. Until he could find a way of figuring out exactly what was happening, the less other people knew about it, the better.

So, instead, he went to a rear door that led out to a tiny cobblestone back courtyard where they kept the bins, and disposed of the little body with the rest of the rubbish.

Then he went to the men's rooms and washed his hands feverishly, several times, in hot water, using the hard cake of carbolic soap that had been there, it seemed to him, since time immemorial.

No longer in the mood for sparring, he collected his jacket, made a mental note to be assigned another locker, and slipped back outside.

Although he tried to reassure himself that his sang-froid wasn't seriously disturbed, he was nevertheless aware that his heart was beating much faster than he'd have liked, and he felt in need of a stiff drink.

With her newly acquired piece of paper clutched in her hand as if it were gold, Trudy went to the first public phone box she could find and rang Clement's office. When she told him what she'd found, the coroner quickly agreed that his paperwork could wait.

Agreeing to meet up at the bottom end of Walton Street, and with Fosdyke's map to guide them, they set off into the maze of rather rundown and seedy streets that comprised the little area known as Jericho.

Here, tiny, mean, terraced houses crammed together, overlooking narrow streets that were interspersed here and there with such signs of commerce that proliferated in the poorer, working-class areas in any city in the country. Pawnbrokers, betting shops, HP shops hiring out aged and poorly repaired electrical goods. Several children playing in the street watched them with curious and rather hostile eyes as they tracked down Derek's studio.

Set in a small square of old garages and low-level commercial offices, with weeds growing through the tarmac and not a clean window in sight, even the air managed to smell dank on such a warm summer's day. Courtesy, no doubt, of the Oxford canal which must have run just out of sight, behind the buildings.

'Not exactly grand, is it?' Trudy said wryly, as they finally came to the small, square, concrete box that was indicated with an X on Fosdyke's map.

'Doesn't need to be, does it?' Clement said thoughtfully. 'It was just somewhere he could develop his photographs. Cheap to rent, and out of the way. I doubt he kept his cameras here, mind you. They'd have been nicked in a trice. I daresay he kept them in his room at college. But developing fluid, paper and whatnot – no market for a burglar or thief to make it worth their while breaking in for stuff like that.'

The building did indeed look as if it had started out life as a double garage. Two tiny and filthy windows set high up would have let in little light, but both Trudy and the coroner could see that thick, dark-coloured curtains had blacked them out anyway. So, they were in the right place. A small door had been rather inexpertly cut into one set of the big double doors, and had been kept shut with a simple padlock and hasp arrangement.

Clement rattled it, but the lock held true. 'The key was probably among Derek's effects,' the coroner said blandly, making Trudy groan.

So now they'd have to traipse all the way back to…

'Lucky for us, then, that I thought to bring the set of keys from evidence,' he carried on, smiling at her look of relief. 'I asked his parents if I could hold on to some of his things until the investigation was concluded. Now… ah, that looks like a padlock key to me.'

He held up a tiny, shiny, square-shaped key, and thrust the notched end home. It turned with ease and, ushering her in ahead of him, they stepped through the door. While Trudy felt along the side of the wall nearest to her, groping for a light switch, Clement closed the door behind them.

The smell of chemicals and paper was still faintly present on the air, and when Trudy finally flicked a switch, and a dim, somewhat reluctant, single light bulb flickered on overhead, it illuminated a surprisingly neatly arranged space.

In the centre was a large wooden table. On one wall was a bank of large, green, tin filing cabinets. A wooden partition at the back, going from floor to ceiling and set at right angles to the wall, was clearly his darkroom, for a small, red-coloured bulb was set at the top of it.

Inside, no doubt, there would be infrared lighting only. Trudy, who knew next to nothing about photography, knew enough to know that natural daylight could spoil film.

Along one blank wall, she noticed several six-foot-tall columns of paper, which she suspected had either painted or photographic backdrops on them, for pushed against the wall was a large, red-plush ottoman. She could imagine someone sitting on it, with a backdrop of the Leaning Tower of Pisa, or whatever, behind them.

She hadn't known Derek Chadworth did portraits as well as landscapes. Odd that no one had mentioned it.

A single bed, with a sheepskin rug thrown over it, was pushed away to one side, catching Trudy's eye and making her frown uncertainly. Surely Derek wouldn't sleep in this place? Not when he had a nice, warm room at St Bede's College?

Hanging from the ceiling in long loops were pieces of string, and attached to them were several pieces of paper, white on the back, but obviously exposed photographs on the front, which were attached by one corner with clothes pegs.

'Look – he'd been drying some photographs out just before he died,' Trudy said, walking across to them.

When she was just a little way away, however, her footsteps slowed. She drew in a long, sharp breath.

'Dr Ryder,' she said sharply. 'Look at these! They're… they're… disgusting!'

Reacting to her tone of voice, Clement, who had been about to go to the nearest set of filing cabinets and begin rummaging among the files, moved instead to join her. As his eyes, not so sharp as hers, started to take in the images on the now fully dried photographs, he felt his lips curl in distaste.

'So this was his little game,' he said flatly. Reluctantly, he reached for one and drew it off the peg and looked at it calmly, mentally distancing himself from the subject, as he might have done in his junior doctor days when having to examine a naked female patient.

Trudy tore her eyes away from the image of a very pretty girl, topless and smiling provocatively at the camera. She was sitting on the red ottoman, and behind her was a cityscape of New York. Trudy felt herself blushing. Which was silly. They'd learned all about pornography and that sort of thing in training college.

'Well, this changes everything, doesn't it,' Clement said dryly.

'Do you think he sold these to dirty magazines?' Trudy asked, trying to sound matter-of-fact.

'I'm sure he did.' Clement headed for one of the filing cabinets and began to rootle through it. 'And I wouldn't be surprised if he didn't make up packets of them to sell in the local pubs as well,' he said, after finding a ledger, of sorts, with columns of figures and the names of several well-known nightclubs in the seedier areas of town.

Trudy sighed. 'Why do girls do it?' she mused, turning away from the string of photographs and going to another filing cabinet. Here, though, were only folders of his landscapes and more respectable work, along with a few newspaper cuttings lauding his prize-winning efforts.

She left these in the drawers and turned to the next cabinet, pulling out the first folder.

Opening it up, her eyes widened and she knew she must have made a distressed sound, for suddenly the coroner was beside her. Hastily, she shut the folder and thrust it wordlessly out at him. But the image she'd seen before her brain had had a chance to warn her was still clear in her mind's eye.

No coy, coquettish, topless poses these. But a young man and a girl, both naked on a bed and in the act of…

Trudy paced the room restlessly. This was awful. Silly. She felt

sick and at the same time like giggling inanely. But she must not
– and *would* not – do either. She was a professional, and she
would damn well act like one!

'I need to inform DI Jennings of this, Dr Ryder,' she forced
herself to say crisply. 'Clearly these fall under the obscene mate-
rials act. The vice squad will have to be informed.' She was already
walking steadily to the door.

She needed air.

'Yes, of course,' Clement said flatly, walking beside her. 'You
report back, and I'll keep guard here.' His matter-of-fact tones
matched hers and he was careful not to meet her eye.

Trudy nodded and stepped outside into the fresh air and took
several deep gulps. Then she set off briskly for the station. But
she wasn't particularly looking forward to reporting her find to
her boss.

Normally, getting onto a racket like this would be a real feather
in her cap, and a proper career boost. But, given the possible
ramifications, she had the feeling DI Jennings wasn't going to be
very happy with her for raking up such a potentially nasty mess.

He wasn't. But he dutifully arrived back at the studio with her
half an hour later, bringing along an inspector from the vice
squad with them.

Clement was waiting demurely outside, but he hadn't wasted
his time alone. As soon as Trudy was gone, he'd gone through
some of the more lurid photographs with crisp efficiency and
deep distaste, and had found just what he'd expected to find.

It wasn't the girls' faces he'd been interested in so much, but
the identity of the men in the photographs. And he was pretty
sure he recognised at least four of them as being on his list of
witnesses called at the inquest into Chadworth's death. Which
meant they were probably all members of the Marquis Club – and
almost certainly members of the student body.

Like Trudy, he knew only too well that this had all the makings of a scandal that could rock the university to its foundations. No wonder Jennings looked at him with undisguised loathing.

'Dr Ryder, this is Inspector James Hewson, from the vice squad.'

Clement nodded at the older, chubby man, who looked at him with curiosity and a brief grin. 'Found something in my line, I understand?' he asked blandly.

Clement waved a hand at the building behind him and moved away. 'We'd better leave you to it,' he said mildly. 'I take it WPC Loveday has informed you of the circumstances that led us here?' he said to Jennings. 'Still inclined to think there was nothing untoward in Chadworth's "accidental drowning"?' he added quietly, making sure it didn't reach the ears of the man from vice.

Nevertheless, Jennings scowled at him. 'Must I remind you, Dr Ryder, that this is a police matter now? A separate, ongoing, active investigation in fact? I can trust you to be discreet about this?' he demanded aggressively.

'Of course,' Clement said smoothly. 'My lips are sealed.'

Jennings sighed heavily and, catching sight of Trudy, who was hovering nervously a few feet away, said crisply, 'That's all, Constable. You can go back to your duties. And back into uniform, please,' he snapped.

He supposed he should be grateful to her for finding this nasty little place first. If a journalist had stumbled upon it… he shuddered to think of the ramifications. Nevertheless, he couldn't help but feel she'd dropped him right in it and, right now, just the sight of her was making his blood pressure rise.

Already he could imagine his superiors breathing down his neck to cover it up. But at least that would be vice's headache, he thought complacently. Not his.

'Yes, sir,' Trudy said primly and turned away. She'd always known that, as a humble probationary WPC, she wouldn't be allowed to investigate the case further, but even so she felt a certain amount of chagrin. If it hadn't been for herself and Dr

Ryder, the city police wouldn't even know about this trafficking in obscene material.

'I take it that boss of yours has already warned you not to say a word about this?' Clement said to her quietly, as they began to retrace their steps back towards the centre of town.

'Yes. In fact, he told me I'd be out on my ear if word leaked to anyone in the office even,' Trudy said, sounding a little surprised.

'Surely you can guess why that is?' Clement said with a grunt. 'I think you'll find that, although the young ladies in the photographs might be of little interest to the powers that be, their erstwhile swains most definitely will be.'

Trudy blinked. 'Sorry?'

'Our Derek might have wooed, bribed or coerced the women into posing for his dirty pictures, but I think the men in them were all eager and willing volunteers. Didn't you recognise any of them?'

Trudy drew in a sharp breath. 'I can't say as I looked at them all that closely,' she admitted grimly.

'Well, I did. Several of them were definitely students – and, I'd be willing to bet, members of the Marquis Club.'

Trudy stopped dead in the street, staring at the coroner in amazement. Then, slowly, she began to smile. 'Oh, please tell me Lord Littlejohn was one of them!' she begged.

But Clement had to shake his head. 'There were some photographs of a lean man with flowing blond locks, yes, but he was careful to always be photographed from behind – and not even in side features. Rather canny of him that, when you think about it,' Clement said dryly. 'While his pals might have been too gung-ho or drunk to care about being captured on celluloid for posterity, our Duke's son was too careful to be caught out. In fact, I wouldn't be surprised if he hadn't insisted on seeing all the negatives and destroying any photographs that might prove his involvement.'

Trudy's shoulders slumped. 'I suppose he would! He'd always take care to look after his own skin, that one. And Derek Chadworth did seem to be very much his creature, didn't he?'

'Was he, though?' Clement murmured. 'You know, I'm beginning to wonder! And I wouldn't be at all surprised if our drowned student didn't have his mind set on bigger fish than the earnings to be accrued from a bit of private enterprise in pornography.'

'What do you mean?' Trudy asked, fascinated. She could feel her heart beginning to thump with excitement. Something told her they were nearing the end of this investigation now – and that soon the solution to everything would be out in the open.

'Think about it,' Clement said. 'The dirty pictures were a nice little earner for a poor student working his way through his university years. It certainly explains how he came by his money, paying for the photography equipment and so on, and keeping his end up when running with the likes of the Marquis Club. Standing a round when it involves bottles of champagne wouldn't have been cheap! But if we've learned anything about him in the last few days, it was that he was ambitious and a planner, with an eye to his long-term future. What's the betting that, in the years to come, when all the male "stars" of his pictures had made their names and careers and had safely married respectable women, our Mr Chadworth wouldn't come calling. With copies of his very interesting photographs in hand?'

'Blackmail!' Trudy yelped, reaching out to clutch Clement's sleeve in her excitement. 'He'd have them all over a barrel!'

'Exactly. And he might not just have demanded money, either. The men he'd have under his thumb would prove very valuable to an up-and-coming man of the law in all sorts of ways. Captains of industry, magistrates, politicians… He'd be able to call the shots and ensure all of them helped him climb the slippery slope to success and power.'

Trudy shuddered. Then her jaw almost dropped. 'Oh! No wonder they had to kill him!' she breathed.

Clement sighed gently. 'Don't go so fast,' he warned her cautiously. 'We need to sit and think this out. Let's go back to my office.'

But once back at Floyds Row, sitting around the coroner's desk and sipping fresh-made tea and nibbling on biscuits, Trudy could hardly sit still, she felt so excited.

'But it all makes sense now,' she insisted, pacing up and down on his carpet, while he watched her with carefully concealed amusement. 'Derek must have overplayed his hand! Maybe they found out he was selling the porn on the open market and didn't like it? They were doing it for fun or kicks or whatever other sick reasons of their own, but he was in it strictly for profit. Or perhaps one of the Marquis members suddenly sobered up and realised just what an insidious position they were in, having let themselves be photographed like that... and decided to do something about it! After all, it might have seemed like a bit of a laugh at the time, especially if they were all drunk and off their heads on dope or something. But once they'd had time to realise how stupid they'd been... wouldn't they have felt vulnerable?'

'Maybe,' Clement said. 'Then again, don't forget just how powerful they are. Littlejohn alone could have squashed him like an ant if he'd so chosen. He could easily have hired someone to torch the studio, and threatened to kneecap Chadworth if he tried anything on.'

But Trudy was unwilling to listen. 'It has to have been Littlejohn,' she insisted urgently. 'He set up the party.' She ticked off the items on her fingers one by one. 'He was the big cheese, and everyone took their orders from him.' Another finger tick. 'And he had the most to lose out of all of them, if any of those photographs had come to the attention of his father, the Duke. We have to confront him!'

'With what?' Clement asked reasonably. 'We don't have the photographs – they're in the hands of vice now and, through them, in the hands of the powers that be. And even if we did have copies of them, Lord Littlejohn isn't identifiable in any of them. After all, any number of young men can have rather long, fair hair.'

'Wasn't there a mole or birthmark or something that would identify him?' Trudy pressed hopefully.

'I'm afraid not. Besides, I don't think those photographs are ever going to make their way into a courtroom, do you? No matter how much that nice inspector from vice complains.'

'What do you mean?' Trudy demanded suspiciously, coming to a sudden stop in the middle of his carpet.

'Come now, you can't be that unaware how the world works,' Clement told her gravely. He didn't like to have to be the one to shatter some of her illusions, but sooner or later, any young constable in the police force would have to be made aware of some of the more unsavoury and harder facts of life. 'The boys in those photographs all come from some of the so-called "best" families in the land. Their relatives are people of power and influence, and you can bet your life they'll move heaven and earth and call in every favour they need to, to make sure they're destroyed. Do you really think the university will want a scandal like this either? Students and girls from the city, caught on film, in flagrante delicto? They'll want the problem to disappear as much as the students and their families will. Perhaps even more so!'

Trudy stared at him, the colour slowly fading from her face. 'They're going to cover it up, aren't they?' she said helplessly. 'That's why DI Jennings insisted I told nobody, not even our own people, about it.'

Clement spread his hands helplessly.

'But they can't! It's evidence!' she cried.

'Of what?'

'Murder!' Trudy all but yelled, exasperated. 'Surely this can't all be a big coincidence! You must be sure now that Derek Chadworth *was* murdered?'

'Oh, yes,' the coroner agreed quietly. 'I've thought so for a little while now. But we're a very long way from proving it,' he added hastily, putting up a hand to ward her off as she opened her mouth to contend with him. 'And we're certainly not going to be allowed to use those photographs we just found to back up our contentions.'

Trudy slumped down in one of the chairs by his desk and felt like crying. It was all so unfair! 'Are you going to let them get away with it?' she asked bitterly, glaring at him fiercely, her brown eyes sparking vim and vinegar.

Clement Ryder smiled grimly. 'As touching as I find your faith in me, WPC Loveday, I'm not Superman or the Green Lantern,' he said, a shade wearily. 'I can't fight the authorities and the university, the Lord Mayor and who knows who else single-handed!'

'So that's it?' Trudy said bitterly. 'You're just going to give up?'

Slowly the coroner reached out for another biscuit and took a bite. 'Now who,' he said mildly, regarding his Garibaldi with interest, 'said anything about giving up?'

Chapter 22

Reggie Porter closed up the shop early. He couldn't concentrate and wanted to snap at customers and staff alike. Ever since his father had shown him those disgusting photographs of Becky, he'd felt as if he wanted to rage and shout at the world.

Of course, they hadn't come as a complete shock or surprise to him, since he'd found some topless photographs of his little sister just before she'd run away from home. Sitting on a red ottoman, with a white silk drape coyly wrapped around her shoulders, but falling open revealingly in front before pooling around her waist and draping oh-so-artistically to the floor. Her pretty, gamin face smiling with heartbreaking innocence at the camera, her pert little breasts exposed to any damned man who had the price to pay for a set of them.

He'd confronted her instantly, shouting at her, and even taking her by the shoulders and shaking her, frightening her badly, as he'd demanded to know who had taken them. Of course, eventually she'd given him Derek Chadworth's name. For nearly a week he'd trawled the pubs and clubs in the seediest part of town before he'd spotted the man, who was selling yet more photographs.

He'd even bought a packet, to make sure he got a good look

at the man who'd corrupted his sister. Luckily, when he'd checked through them, there wasn't a photo of Becky in his batch, or else he might have reached out and strangled the bastard right there and then in the pub, and the consequences be damned.

So he'd thought he'd known the worst. And when Becky left home, he'd blamed Chadworth for that too.

But what he didn't know was that his father knew about the photographs too. And had been paying blackmail money.

He also hadn't known about the *other* photographs. The ones his father had taunted him angrily with. Not mere topless photos but images of Becky – his little sister, Becky – going with men… laughing, ugly, filthy men.

Of course, he knew who they must be. Students, and almost certainly members of that bloody Marquis Club. Lord Littlejohn's band of debauched, filthy, rotten bastards.

After following Derek Chadworth from the pub and back to his college, it hadn't taken Reggie long to learn all about him, and his allegiance to the fair-haired Littlejohn and his corrupt little gang.

Well, Chadworth's hash had already been settled, Reggie thought savagely, as he made his way through the streets to a wine shop where he bought a bottle of the best champagne he could afford. He then went into a chemist's and, claiming to be diabetic, bought a packet of hypodermic needles. Then he went to Coopers, a big haberdashery store that sold all sorts, and bought some weedkiller and rat poison.

Now Chadworth was out of the way, it was Littlejohn's turn, Reggie Porter vowed viciously.

From raging hot with shame and helplessness after seeing those vile photographs of his violated little sister, Reggie now felt ice-cold and calm.

Derek Chadworth was dead.

And now it was time for the head of the Marquis Club to join him.

Chapter 23

'I can't believe you kept some of the photographs!' Trudy said, staring at the three images the coroner had just produced from inside his jacket pocket. He'd had to fold them a little to fit, but even so, they were clear enough for their purposes. 'Won't that detective from vice miss them?' she asked nervously.

When the coroner had told her what he'd done, she wasn't sure whether to applaud or feel appalled. Even as she looked at them now, she couldn't help but think what trouble she'd be in if DI Jennings realised she had them.

'How will he know there are any missing?' Clement asked cavalierly. 'I chose these three because they each have a different girl and man in them. We need to identify them all. I'll take the men. I'm pretty sure they'll all turn out to be part of Littlejohn's inner circle and it'll be easier for me to visit them in their colleges and find out which are our Prince Charmings,' he added, tapping the men's faces on the photographs.

'And I kept this one—' he tapped the fourth and last '—because of him.'

For a moment both of them stared at the back of a fair head. He'd been caught, naked from the top up, looking down at a girl lying on a bed with a sheepskin rug thrown over it. A backdrop

184

of Rome at night had been set up behind her in an attempt to create an aura of spurious romance and glamour. She was a rather small girl, but had a gamin, pixie-like charm to her face that made her stand out.

'You need to try and identify the girls,' Clement went on. 'Mind you, I think we already know the name of one of them.'

'We do?' Trudy said, taken off-guard. Then, after a second's thought, her face fell. 'Oh. Yes. Of course – Jennifer Morrison! That poor girl! She must have been taken in by Derek and… oh, how awful. She thought he loved her, that he was her boyfriend, when all the time he was setting her up to become involved in this disgusting…' Her voice trailed off, and she was unable to go on. 'No wonder she ended up taking her own life.'

'Which means it's more important than ever that we find the living victims,' Clement reminded her, his voice gentle but firm. 'Women who might just be prepared to speak up.'

'Right,' Trudy said, her chin coming up. 'But if Inspector Jennings gets to hear what I'm doing…' She held out her hands, her face going pale.

'Don't tell him,' Clement said flatly – and, again, far too cavalierly for Trudy's liking! 'As far as he's concerned, you're still talking to students about Derek's death.'

'He won't let me carry on working with you for much longer,' Trudy predicted miserably. 'Not after this.' It was all right for the coroner to be so offhand about things, she thought, a shade bitterly, but he didn't have so many people looking over his shoulder! What's more, people who could so easily wreck his career!

'Then we'd better get cracking, hadn't we?' Clement said brusquely.

Trudy stiffened her spine and nodded. 'Yes. I'll take the photograph of Littlejohn and start with the woman on the sheepskin rug.'

Clement's lips twitched. 'Why am I not surprised? You really want to see His Lordship in the mire, don't you? I can't say as I blame you – but remember. Leave him well alone for now and concentrate on finding out the name of his elfin companion.'

Trudy promised she would, and the two of them parted company for the day.

The next morning, Lord Jeremy Littlejohn stared down at the bottle of champagne that had been left outside his door. He'd just come back from the boxing gym, where, thankfully, his locker had been free of dead rats, but the sight of the bottle of bubbly still gave him pause.

Yesterday, on finding the deceased and odoriferous offering of rodent, his careful questioning of the so-called doorman at the gym had informed him that an unknown chap, tall and with red hair, had been on the premises earlier, asking about joining and membership fees and whatnot.

And now this.

Turning away from his door without touching the bottle, he made his way back to the porter's lodge.

There, he learned that the guardian of the gates had indeed noticed a tall, thin gentleman with a head of rather fine, fiery red hair entering through the gates with a small gaggle of other undergraduates earlier that morning.

For a moment, the Duke's son wondered if he should make a song and dance about it, and then decided that, for the moment anyway, discretion was perhaps the better part of valour. He didn't want word getting back to his father that he was yet again mixed up in something unpleasant.

He returned slowly across the quad, annoyed to find himself looking around every few seconds to see if he could spot anyone with red hair watching him.

Really, this was getting intolerable, he fumed. First the anonymous threatening letters, which, at first, had been amusing more than anything else. Then the dead rat in his locker, and now the anonymous champagne.

What, wondered Lord Jeremy Littlejohn uneasily, was coming next?

At his door, he picked up the bottle of champagne – sneering at the less-than-premium name on the label – and went inside. He took it straight to the window and examined it minutely. It looked OK – but he wanted to be sure. Rootling around in his desk drawer he found an old-fashioned magnifying glass the previous occupant of the room had left behind and peered at the top of the bottle intently.

And sure enough, there, in the golden foil, he could just see a tiny round hole that no doubt carried on through the cork. Someone had injected something into the wine.

In spite of himself, he felt a lance of fear shoot through him.

Was it really poisoned? Or was he being paranoid?

Perhaps one of his fellow Marquis members had left the bottle, injected with nothing more serious than some sort of laxative, just something to give him an embarrassing and inconvenient dose of the squits. It would be just the sort of infantile joke they might play on him.

Or was it possible that the death threats he'd been receiving were actually real? That someone out there – a tall, thin man with red hair – actually intended to kill him?

Then he thought of Derek. Dead Derek. Dead as a doornail Derek.

And the aristocrat thought that yes, it was perfectly possible somebody was out to kill him.

With a muttered curse, he flung open a wardrobe door, then dragged down a suitcase from the top shelf. He'd intended to go down next week, but right now he wanted to be as far away from Oxford as he could get. (It had always amused him that the Oxford phrase 'to go down' meant to leave college and the city. Whereas, for most of the world, when people 'went down' it usually meant they were being given a prison sentence. And more than one witty wag had often compared the two!)

Now, though, he was too agitated to find amusement in the quaint or the ridiculous.

He'd go to London first, obviously, probably the family flat in Mayfair, and then set off abroad somewhere. There were plenty of residences scattered around the globe he could choose from, after all, where generations of Littlejohns before him had lived and played.

Normally he'd call in his scout to come and pack for him as he had several cases to take his vast array of clothes. But he didn't want to waste any time.

Feverishly, he began to fling things into his case.

Outside, on the street, standing in a comfortable patch of shade, Reggie Porter waited and watched.

He already knew the college had very little parking room inside the ancient quads, so that most of the dons and students alike were forced to park their cars in the little side streets surrounding the college.

While he was hoping that, right now, His Lordship was already quaffing back the champagne, and that in due course he could watch with satisfaction as, first, an ambulance and then a mortuary van was called, he wanted to be prepared.

Just in case.

Because if the champagne didn't do the trick, Reggie Porter thought with a wolfish grin, there was always plan B.

The Oxford postmen, unaware of any of the various dramas being played out in and around them, made their usual rounds of the city, busily bustling through their daily routine. Over at the coroner's office, one of them dropped off some mail at the reception desk, where a secretary sorted it out and delivered it to the offices and personnel thus addressed.

As his own secretary brought in his mail, and with a smile dropped it onto his desk, Clement Ryder had no idea that one of those letters was going to change the course of his whole day.

And the course of someone else's whole life.

Trudy very carefully refolded the photograph in half, concealing the naked back of the blond-haired man, and then refolded it again, so only the face of the naked girl was visible. She then clamped her thumb and fingers firmly together so that the thick photograph couldn't spring open, back to its original shape. She might not know the identity of the girl, or what had led to her agreeing to do what she had, but she was determined to preserve her modesty and dignity as much as she could.

She walked into the eighth café of the day, another favourite with the city's students, but this time, instead of joining in the bantering or learned conversations going on around her, she turned to the café counter and the staff.

She'd already discovered that morning – to her cost – that talking about Derek was one thing. But actually showing a photograph around and asking direct questions was something else altogether.

She'd been getting funny looks from the students all morning, every time she showed the girl's likeness to people, and you didn't have to be a genius to figure out why. Gossiping about the death of a student in cafés and bars, where everyone was already interested and intrigued, was one thing. Producing an actual photograph, and asking for an identification of an unknown girl, was definitely something else.

It tended to make people who might have talked casually shut up pretty quickly.

So Trudy was glad she'd probably picked up all the titbits of information there were to be had about Derek already, since she was sure her 'cover' had now been well and truly blown. For although she wasn't in uniform again, who else but the police went around asking for specific information, as she had been doing all morning?

So it was perhaps not so surprising that the students she'd asked about the girl in the photograph so far had all looked uneasy, and had claimed not to know her. But whether this was true, or whether they simply distrusted Trudy herself, she wasn't sure. Perhaps they thought she had her own axe to grind. Or was even a madwoman!

Either way, they were being distinctly cagey. It was as the sergeants back at the station house had always maintained – members of the public didn't like to get involved in 'anything nasty', and could imitate the three wise monkeys well enough whenever it suited them.

Or perhaps their reticence could be put down to the fact that they recognised the girl in the photograph as a fellow student and, out of consideration for one of their own, pretended ignorance? Just in case this last scenario was true, she determined to try something different, and thus talked to the waitresses instead.

Perhaps because they were bored and found the chance to grab at a bit of excitement too much to resist, or maybe because they liked the look of her, Trudy found both of them more inclined to be helpful than anyone else she'd spoken to that morning.

To her delight and relief, one of them in particular claimed to know the girl in the photo.

'She was one of the regulars who used to come here, love,' the waitress, a middle-aged woman with a large bosom and a mop of curly, brassy-blonde hair informed her tiredly. 'You remember her, Maeve?'

Her friend shrugged, then nodded slowly. 'Didn't she usually come in with a group of giggling girls, with some fellows always hanging around hopefully. You know the type?'

Trudy smiled. 'Don't suppose you remember her name, do you?' she prompted.

The waitress snorted. 'Now you ask me.'

'Please, it's important,' Trudy insisted earnestly. 'Take a good, long look. She's rather distinctive, isn't she? Reminds me a bit of a pixie or…'

The other, older waitress suddenly snapped her fingers. 'Of course, now I remember. That's old what's-his-name Porter's young girl. The one that ran off to London a little while back. Lives up Cowley way, I think… or is it Osney… now what was his name…?'

As Trudy waited patiently for a waitress to remember a name, Lord Littlejohn finished throwing his clothes haphazardly into a case, slammed the lid down and locked it. For a moment he looked around the room, searching for something he might need and mustn't leave behind, then patted his pocket to make sure he had his wallet.

He was wearing cream slacks, with a white shirt and white linen summer blazer, and with a sigh of satisfaction at feeling the hard, flat, reassuring bulk of his wallet against his breast, he began to look around for his car keys.

He drove a Morgan (in racing-car green, naturally) and kept it just off a little alley a few hundred yards away. And already, in his mind's eye, he was letting her have her head on the A-roads leading out of the city and towards High Wycombe, leaving this place far behind him.

With a bit of luck, he could shake off whoever had been dogging him lately, and lie low until this whole Derek Chadworth mess had died down.

Whistling tunelessly, he located and pocketed his car keys, then hefted his suitcase from the bed and humped it down the stairs. It was dreary work. Although he didn't keep a valet at the college, he was still used to other people doing annoying little jobs like carrying luggage for him. Still, at least he didn't have far to go.

In a few days, he could be off – perhaps he'd go to Biarritz.

Or maybe the Caribbean? Come to think of it, didn't old Mungo 'Pesky' Peake-Smythe have a yacht he was always sailing to and from Capri? And if old Pesky had asked him once to join him on a jaunt or two, he'd asked him a dozen times.

Yes. Island-hopping in the Med might be just the ticket.

With a smile, Littlejohn nodded at the porter, stepped through the lodge double doors and out into the busy and noisy city beyond.

Within a few minutes he was stepping away from the busy streets and winding his way down one of the many little medieval alleyways that criss-crossed the city. So narrow, some of them, that a car couldn't get through.

He turned down one now where, on either side of him, the high, blank, outside walls of colleges and other commercial buildings crowded in on him. Here it was quiet, very quiet, without even a fellow pedestrian or some clerk or other using a shortcut to get to his office to bother him. He could barely hear the traffic on the High or Broad Street, and no little shop windows marred the pale, Cotswold stone walls.

It was then that Littlejohn heard a step behind him, and started to turn around to look.

As he did so, in his peripheral vision he saw a flash of red hair, brightly reflecting the sunlight.

And the blur of movement as something moving fast seemed to rush out of the stillness at him.

Chapter 24

Stanley Porter looked surprised to see the pretty girl on his doorstep. All long, dark, curling hair and big brown eyes, she was the total opposite in looks from his daughter, Becky, and yet something about her made his heart ache for his lost daughter.

But when she showed him her warrant card, he looked worried. And nervous. June, his wife, was out shopping, and since it was his day off work, he was supposed to be helping her, but they'd both known he would think up some excuse to avoid having to go, and the hot weather had been it.

Now he wished he'd put up with the boredom shopping always instilled in him and gone with her.

He reluctantly showed the WPC into the kitchen, where both windows had been thrown open to let in a rather warm breeze, which was perversely doing little to diffuse the scent of the breakfast bacon that hung tenaciously around in the air. The unwashed dishes still lay in the sink, which probably didn't help.

As if conscious of it, Stanley Porter apologised vaguely for the 'mess'.

'That's all right, sir,' Trudy said with a smile, to put him at his ease. 'I just wanted to ask you a few questions – about an ongoing case. First, can you please confirm that this is your daughter, Rebecca?'

She showed him the carefully folded photograph, and saw the man's face fall and pale. He swallowed rather audibly, and abruptly sat down on one of the kitchen chairs surrounding the square wooden table, as if his knees had given out on him.

'I knew it would come to this,' Stanley Porter said, looking sick. 'Ever since those bloody photos came in the post. I just *knew* it would come to this…'

Trudy, her heart suddenly fluttering wildly in her chest, remained standing, watching Stanley Porter closely. She hadn't expected to make a breakthrough so quickly, and she felt a little wrong-footed.

What was she supposed to do now? Call for assistance? But she didn't think that would be a good idea. By the time someone else had come from the station, her witness might have recovered his equilibrium and started to clam up.

No, she had to strike while the iron was hot! Getting out her notebook, she began to quickly take notes.

'You say photographs like these were sent to you through the post, sir?' she asked for confirmation, wishing now that she'd gone to Floyds Row to ask Dr Ryder if he'd like to come with her. Right now, he could be asking the questions while she listened and watched.

But at the time, back in the café when the waitress had finally come up with a name, she'd been too pleased with herself at having identified one of the girls to want to waste any time.

Now she sent a quick glance around the room, realising how quiet the place was. Clearly the lady of the house wasn't home, for she could hear none of the telltale sounds of the house being occupied.

Stanley Porter was the sort of man who looked as if he liked using his fists. Right now, he seemed docile enough and prepared to answer her questions, but if he became belligerent or angry…

But she had her police whistle, and her short truncheon, Trudy reminded herself stoutly. And she knew how to use the truncheon to its best advantage. It was one of the things her tutors at the police-training college had drummed into her.

Besides, she was probably worrying about nothing. Her witness didn't look as if he was contemplating violence.

Well, not yet, anyway.

'When was this, sir?' she asked quietly, determined to be thorough but to go gently and keep the man calm.

'Oh, months ago. Along with a letter demanding money.'

Trudy's heart rate ratcheted up another notch, and she forced herself to take a slow, careful breath. 'You were being blackmailed, sir?' she asked, pleased her tone came out so even and matter-of-fact.

Stanely Porter gave a sudden, bitter smile. 'Yeah. Not for much, like.' He shrugged his large shoulders. 'I don't have much to give, do I?' He looked around the tiny kitchen balefully. 'I ain't exactly Rockefeller, as you can see,' he said with a sardonic grunt. 'But every week, regular as clockwork, I'd post it off.'

'Where to, sir?'

'Oh, nowhere with a name and address, girlie,' Stanley Porter said with a weary smile. 'The bastard, whoever he was, was too wily for that. He probably knew that if I could have got my hands on him, I'd have wrung his bleeding neck for him.' He sighed heavily. 'No, it was one of them post-office numbers. In the city. I went there once, to see if I could see who picked it up, but it was useless. Didn't have the time to hang around all day, every day, to see. Had to be at work, didn't I? Besides, there was people in and out, in and out, all day, going to boxes and whatnot. And then, in the very next letter, the bastard charged me more. Said he'd seen me watching. I'd been naughty, he said, just like my Becky. So I'd have to pay a bit more. Sneering, cocky little bastard,' he grumbled savagely.

Uneasily, Trudy wondered if Stanley might have gone back

195

again – perhaps in a disguise of some sort. And, second time lucky, been successful in picking up Derek Chadworth's trail. Had he then... What? Gone to the picnic party and drowned Derek?

Hardly, Trudy thought, with an inner snort. This middle-aged, working-class man would have stood out like a sore thumb among the likes of Littlejohn and his Marquis Club.

'Can I speak to your daughter, sir?' Trudy asked instead. 'I need to...'

'Don't know where she is, Constable,' Stanley interrupted her wearily. 'She finally up and left for London like she always said she would.'

Trudy bit back a sigh. So it was true then – the gossip the waitresses had passed on about the daughter running away from home.

'Broke her mother's heart,' Stanley swept on. And then his face twisted into an odd sort of a smile. There was something sort of twisted and just *bad* about it that made a shiver run up Trudy's spine. 'Broke her brother's heart even more, I reckon. Always was daft on her, was our Reggie. Not natural the way that boy always pined after his little sister.'

He broke off suddenly and flushed an ugly colour as he shot a quick look at Trudy, and then away again. She noticed he was now looking across to a Welsh dresser where a family portrait was resting.

Trudy walked over to it and lifted the framed photograph and looked at it closely. Stanley she recognised at once. The middle-aged woman he had his arm around had to be his wife, she mused – a rather faded, strawberry-blonde woman. And the girl from the pornographic print stared out at them, looking the very picture of innocence. How old was she here? Thirteen maybe. Beside her stood a tall, very red-haired man – her big brother apparently.

A tall, red-haired man.

'Sir, where's your son now?' Trudy asked urgently.

'Reggie? At work, I dare say,' Stanley said indifferently. 'He works in a shop on the High.'

But his father was wrong.

Reggie Porter was not in his shop.

Right at that moment, Reggie Porter was lunging at Lord Jeremy Littlejohn in a deserted back alley, his hands reaching out for His Lordship's exposed throat.

Littlejohn saw the flash of sunlight on red hair, followed by a close-up of an ugly face, contorted in rage and coming right at him, like an image emerging from a nightmare. Hands outstretched and grasping, like a creature from a horror movie.

His Lordship didn't hesitate. He wasn't one of his old school's best batsmen for nothing.

Using his unwieldy suitcase as if it were a bat, Lord Jeremy swung it up and around and gave a grunt of satisfaction as it caught the other man right under his chin, lifting him up onto his toes and sending him staggering backwards in order to keep his balance.

Reggie Porter howled in pain as the force of the unexpected blow sent his teeth through his tongue, and his vision blurred as tears of pain poured from his eyes, to roll down his face and mingle with the blood already beginning to leak down his chin.

Weeks of pent-up rage and fear shot through Littlejohn as he saw his enemy at a disadvantage, and, with a wild and savage cry that was so far removed from his usual lethargic, sophisticated image as to be farcical, the man in white began to kick his opponent ferociously.

In his office, Clement Ryder reached for a letter opener – a Toledo blade in the form of an ornamental dagger that his wife had bought him one year for his Christmas present. He began slitting open his mail – a task he preferred to do himself, rather than delegating it to his secretary.

The first was an invitation to attend a talk in Cheltenham. It sounded boring, but he put it to one side to consider it further. The next was a letter from a former student, asking for a reference. The next was a notice from the Lord Mayor's office which he barely bothered to even skim.

The fourth was a handwritten letter, and began,

'Dear Sir,
   In reference to the notice you put in the Oxford Mail, asking for anyone who had been in or around Port Meadow on the morning of the death of the student Derek Chadworth to get in contact with you...'

Trudy had barely returned to the station when the call came in. In fact, she hadn't even got as far as going across the office floor and knocking on DI Jennings's door when she heard it on the radio behind her.

Rodney Broadstairs, out on his beat, had broken up a fight between two members of the public. He'd requested assistance, but what had instantly attracted Trudy's notice were the names of the two men involved.

Her heart racing, she turned to answer the call, only for Sergeant O'Grady to get there ahead of her. 'Yes? Right… anyone need an ambulance? All right, bring them both in. Yes, here to the station. We can get a doctor to look at them if it turns out they need it. What? No, leave that to Inspector Jennings. I'll go and inform him now. Right. See you in five minutes. Are they giving you any trouble? Good.'

Trudy, who'd been watching the Sergeant's face in fascination throughout this one-sided conversation, also watched as he stepped smartly towards the Inspector's office, tapped and was called in.

Barely a minute later they both stepped out again. 'Right, well, have them in my office, I think,' Jennings was saying. 'If we need to separate them and interview them individually later on, we can. Did Broadstairs give you any information on His Lordship's attacker?'

'Not much, except...'

'Sir...' Trudy could stand it no longer. Ignoring (but not without an inward qualm) the annoyed look on the Inspector's face as he turned to look at her, she blurted out quickly, 'Is he a tall man, with fiery red hair?'

She turned to look enquiringly at Sergeant O'Grady.

His face said it all. 'Yes, that fits Broadstairs' description of him all right,' he said, staring at her a shade suspiciously – a look, she noticed, that was mirrored on their superior officer's face also.

'WPC Loveday,' DI Jennings said with rather ominous and forced calm, 'just what do you know about all this?'

Trudy gulped.

Chapter 25

'Sir, I was just about to report in,' she began hastily, but was allowed to say no more in her defence.

Quickly, Jennings checked his watch, then sighed. 'In my office, now,' he snapped at her impatiently. 'O'Grady, put a call in to the police doctor and have him come down here at once. I know Broadstairs said neither of the men's injuries were serious, but we don't want the Duke breathing down our necks if it turns out his precious son needed medical attention after all and we didn't provide it.'

'Yes, sir,' the Sergeant said smartly, giving Trudy a brief scowl as he passed her by. Like most of the senior men in the station, he didn't altogether approve of the WPC being seconded to the cranky coroner, even if it did give her something to do and got her out from under their feet.

But, like Jennings, he hadn't really seen that there could be much harm in it.

Now he wasn't so sure. Especially since it seemed to be giving her ideas above that of a lowly probationary WPC.

'So, WPC Loveday,' Jennings began ominously as he ushered

her into his office, then moved around to sit behind his desk. 'This report you say you were about to give me? Let's have it, and make it quick.'

'Sir,' Trudy said, and launched into what she hoped was a concise but thorough account of her actions since she'd left him at Derek Chadworth's studio. She was careful to make no mention of the fact that Dr Clement Ryder had 'borrowed' four of the photographs but said instead that she'd taken a detailed description of some of the women who appeared in the photographs, in order to see if she could make an identification.

As she stumbled through this lie, she was very much aware that she was almost certainly blushing, and saw from the sceptical look on his face that her superior officer didn't believe her. Perhaps he knew the coroner better than she did and guessed what he had done. But, if so, he obviously decided it was better for him to overlook the matter, for he didn't interrupt her report.

No doubt, Trudy thought with rapidly growing cynicism, it would suit his book better to be able to deny any and all knowledge of stray photographs, should things start to get hot for him with his superiors later on. Deniability, she was fast learning, was often the name of the game.

'So I learned one of the girl's names was Rebecca Porter, sir, and traced her address...' She went on to describe her interview with Stanley Porter, who'd admitted receiving blackmail letters from someone – almost certainly the dead boy, Derek Chadworth – and thence to her observance of the family photograph.

'I remembered at once, from the coroner's witness reports, several people mentioning a red-haired man who was seen at the fatal picnic, sir. He was also mentioned as a person of interest by several of the students I cultivated while out of uniform. Which is why, when I heard about the recent attack on Lord Littlejohn...'

'Yes, yes,' Jennings said, standing up when he heard loud shouting beginning to seep through from the outer office. 'It sounds like they're here. And Loveday,' he added coldly, 'I don't

201

like the way you're linking the dead boy's activities with Lord Littlejohn. There is nothing to suggest that His Lordship even knew about the other lad's sideline. So let's have no more idle speculation, hmm? Just stick to facts and leave the thinking to me. Is that clear?'

Trudy blinked hard and swallowed the growing rage that rose inside her. Of course, she would do everything in her power to see the aristocrat got his comeuppance somehow, but it would be pointless – if not self-defeating – to let DI Jennings suspect this.

So she nodded smartly. 'Of course, sir. But, sir, perhaps I should be present at the interviews,' she heard herself saying, and then blinked in surprise at her own forwardness as the DI, who'd been striding towards the door, turned to look back at her angrily.

'Oh, you do, do you? Perhaps you want to conduct the interviews themselves, WPC Loveday?' he asked sarcastically.

Trudy flushed, but stuck to her guns. 'No, sir. It's just that, at the moment, I'm the one with the best overview of the case, and I'll be able to pick out any lies or misleading statements from either man more easily,' she pointed out with faultless logic.

Then, some little imp couldn't stop her adding with a sweet smile, 'Unless you'd prefer Dr Ryder to come here and listen in, sir?'

DI Jennings merely growled at that, then sighed heavily. 'Very well, Loveday,' he said, gritting his teeth. Then he pointed dramatically to one of the corners at the back of his office. 'But you will stand there, and you will listen, and you will not say a word – *not a single word, do you hear*? And take notes – you might as well be useful. After – get that, *after* – I've finished the interview, I will consult you, and if you've spotted anything that strikes you as significant, you will then fill me in on it, and I'll do a second interview if necessary. Is all that clear?'

'Yes, sir,' Trudy said happily, and went to stand in the corner, feeling rather ridiculously like a little schoolgirl being told to do so by an exasperated teacher.

But she didn't care! She was going to be in on things instead of being sidelined for once!

She looked eagerly towards the door as the DI opened it, and heard Lord Littlejohn's annoying, upper-class drawl say querulously, 'I do hope someone's called my legal man. I distinctly told this flatfoot the name of my father's solicitors.'

Trudy saw DI Jennings nod his head through the glass upper partition of the open door. 'Of course, Lord Littlejohn. Sergeant O'Grady, make sure His Lordship's solicitor is informed.'

'Tell him to come here at once,' the peer demanded arrogantly. 'He can jolly well pry himself away from London for once.'

'Bring the prisoner in here, Broadstairs,' Jennings said, standing in the doorway and holding the door open as Rodney manhandled a struggling, petulant-faced man into the room.

He was indeed tall and thin, with a head of very red hair and a pale, freckled face, much smeared with blood.

Trudy, rather meanly, hoped it was Lord Littlejohn's blood, but when that young man strolled in casually behind him, his face was disappointingly unmarked. His white clothes, however, looked distinctly disarranged, and patches of blood appeared on his blazer cuffs, and a few more on the front of his white shirt.

Rodney didn't see Trudy standing in the corner, but Littlejohn did, and he stared at her balefully for a moment. Luckily, he was then distracted by DI Jennings, who began speaking to him again.

'If you'd care to take a seat, my Lord, I'm sure we can sort this out quickly. Sergeant O'Grady, if you'll kindly take charge of… do we have a name for this gentleman, PC Broadstairs?'

'No, sir,' Rodney said stiffly. 'The gentleman refuses to give his name.' He placed his large hands on Reginald Porter's shoulders, thus forcing him to sit down on one of the chairs in front of the DI's desk.

The prisoner said something very filthy, making Lord Littlejohn smirk in appreciation.

'I see,' Jennings said mildly. 'You're dismissed, Constable.'

'Sir,' Rodney said, with obvious disappointment. It was only as he stepped away, letting O'Grady take his place behind the prisoner sitting on the chair, that he noticed Trudy standing in the corner.

Nonchalantly, she turned a page in her notebook and gave him a brief smile. She knew Rodney hadn't liked that she'd been allowed to go about in plain clothes 'as if she were a proper detective', for she'd heard him say as much to one of the other PCs in the office. And now, to see her standing in on the interview he was going to miss out on made his big blue eyes narrow ominously.

Trudy smiled sweetly at him.

Not daring to say a word in front of the Sergeant or Inspector, Broadstairs left, shutting the door behind him, and leaving Reginald Porter's heavy, angry breathing as the only sound in the room.

'Now then, let's get things straight, shall we?' the DI said, retaking his seat behind his desk. 'My Lord, perhaps you'd like to begin?'

'Certainly, er, Inspector... Sorry, I've forgotten your name.'

The Inspector smiled calmly. 'Jennings, my Lord.'

'Yes. Jennings. Well, I was walking back to my car – a nice little Morgan; I keep her parked in one of the little back alleys opposite my college, you know – when this chap just springs on me and attempts to assault me. Well, naturally, I'm not having that! So I hit him with my suitcase – rather as if I was playing at the wicket for the old cricket team. Then we had a bit of a set-to, and then your flatfoot came along and took charge. I agreed to come here to help get it sorted out, but really, you know, I had intended to be back in London in time for dinner.'

Here, His Lordship, who was sprawling rather indolently in a hard-backed chair, glanced casually at a gold watch on his wrist. 'So I do hope this won't take too much time.'

'I'll see what we can do, my Lord,' Jennings said, with such false amiability that Trudy, busy scribbling in her notebook, almost winced.

'Now then, sir...' Jennings turned to the truculent redhead. 'You are Mr Reginald Porter, I believe?' he said, making the other man's jaw drop. 'Oh, yes, we know all about you, Mr Porter,' Jennings said, rather stretching the truth somewhat. 'Care to give us your version of events?'

Reginald glowered at him silently.

'No? Then perhaps I can help you out,' Jennings said, with false bonhomie. 'I believe you have something of a grudge against His Lordship. A little matter to do with your younger sister, Rebecca Porter?'

'Oh, don't tell me all this trouble is over some little tart or other,' Littlejohn drawled, then swung out his foot to kick Reginald in the stomach as he tried to lurch out of his chair and attack him once more.

The kick wasn't landed, however, since, thanks to Sergeant O'Grady's big, meaty hands, Reggie Porter never make it out of his chair.

'Now then, settle down, both of you,' Jennings roared. 'I'm having none of that in my office.'

'Then tell him to keep his foul mouth off my sister!' Reggie roared.

'Perhaps it would be best if we could keep things civil, my Lord,' Jennings suggested mildly.

Lord Jeremy Littlejohn sighed elaborately and rolled his eyes. 'Very well, if you insist. But this little oik has been pestering me for months,' he said, studying his nails casually. 'At least, I assume it's been him and, with this latest assault on me, he's finally decided to come out of the woodwork and into the light of day at last.'

'In what way, my Lord?' Jennings asked, genuinely curious now.

'Oh, you know. The usual silly little things,' Littlejohn said, yawning ostentatiously. 'Death threats – anonymous, of course. You can't expect a gutless wonder like this sorry specimen to—'

He broke off as, once again, Reginald made to lunge at him, and was once again prevented.

Littlejohn sighed theatrically. 'Dead rats left in my locker. Oh, and the latest jaunt was to leave poisoned champagne outside my door. I mean, I ask you! As if I'd drink it!' the fair-haired man snorted. 'Really, does he think I'm a total idiot?'

'Poisoned?' Jennings said sharply. 'Are you sure about this, sir? I mean, my Lord?'

'Well, you'd have to have it analysed, of course, or whatever you do with such things,' Littlejohn said wearily. 'It's back in my room at college if you want it.'

'I'll have someone pick it up, my Lord, and get it checked out,' Jennings promised. Then he turned back to the other man, who was staring truculently at his feet.

'Well, Porter? Have you anything to say for yourself?'

'He deserved it!' Porter said savagely. 'Do you know what he and that friend of his were up to? Well, do you?' Reggie snarled, making the DI look uncomfortable for the first time.

Because, of course, thanks to that damned coroner and his own WPC, he knew exactly what they'd been up to. And wished he didn't!

'Oh, grow up!' It was Lord Littlejohn who saved him from having to answer the accusation. 'If some silly little tarts want to earn some money by taking their clothes off for the camera, so what?'

'So you admit it!' Reggie raged, once again trying to get his hands on the grinning aristocrat next to him, and once again being prevented by the burly sergeant.

'You should be careful what you say, my Lord,' Jennings felt obliged to put in, with a quick, nervous glance at Trudy, who was scrupulously getting it all down in her fast, meticulous shorthand.

'Oh, well, I'm only saying what I think,' Littlejohn backtracked somewhat. 'Derek sometimes boasted about his little sideline, but we never knew whether to believe him or not.' The Duke's son gave a careless shrug.

'We, my Lord?' Jennings asked mildly.

'My fellow members of the Marquis Club,' Lord Jeremy said, yawning yet again. 'We thought it a hoot. A bit grubby, mind you, but a hoot. But then Chadworth… well, let's just say he wasn't really one of us, was he? His father was some piddling little legal man up north. Hardly blueblood stock, and all that. So, really, what could you expect?' Lord Jeremy shrugged his shoulders elegantly, then glanced at his watch again. 'Speaking of legal men, I wonder where my own damned specimen has got to?'

'Just a few more questions, sir,' Jennings said. 'On the day Mr Chadworth drowned, did you notice Mr Porter here at the picnic? Or see him anywhere on Port Meadow?'

'Hmm? Him?' Littlejohn rolled his head around to fix a suddenly still and alert Reginald Porter with a jaundiced eye. 'Did I? You know, now you mention it, and I come to think of it, I might have done. Yes! I seem to remember a tall streak of wind with that freakish coloured hair arriving on the banks with the girls who had set up the food. I just assumed one of them had brought him.'

'Well, Mr Porter,' DI Jennings said quietly. 'Were you there that day?'

But Reginald Porter, it seemed, had suddenly run out of things to say. He simply stared at his feet in mutinous silence.

Littlejohn stared at him, fascinated. 'So it was you who did for poor old Derek!' he mused. 'Well, well, who'd have thought it. Took some revealing little poses of your sister, did he? The rogue.'

'My Lord, I don't think that's very helpful,' Jennings said. 'In fact, I think, Sergeant O'Grady, in view of the circumstances, you should take Mr Porter here to a holding cell. We'll be interviewing him more formally later.'

The Sergeant obligingly hauled the pale-faced man to his feet.

'Look here, I didn't kill that bloody pervert!' Reginald Porter suddenly shouted. 'And what's more, you can't prove it, nor make me say I did, now then!'

Lord Littlejohn gave him an impertinent finger wave as he was dragged to the door, making Reginald Porter struggle furiously in the Sergeant's grip.

'What about him!' Reginald spat. 'I'll bet *he* was the one who killed his friend! Scared he was getting in too deep, and wanted to shut Chadworth up! How about that?' Reginald was still shouting accusations and epithets in equal number as the Sergeant hauled him away.

'Now then, my Lord,' Jennings said, when the noise had finally died away. 'Shut the door, Constable,' he suddenly said to Trudy, who gave a little start, then went over to shut the door.

'Ah, yes, the lovely Loveday,' Lord Jeremy drawled, watching her with cold, thoughtful eyes. 'I was wondering what she was doing here, Inspector. I thought I'd made it clear in my phone call to you that I didn't want this woman harassing me any further?'

'Oh, WPC Loveday has her uses, my Lord,' Jennings said amiably. 'She and Dr Ryder, the coroner who sat at Mr Chadworth's inquest, have been very active in this case. In fact, most of the things we know about your attacker can be put down to her hard work.'

'Ah. So she's actually been my guardian angel all along then, you might say?' Littlejohn drawled hatefully, looking at her and then blowing her kiss. 'Thank you so much! If I'd known you were looking out for my best interests so assiduously all this time, we might have got on so much better.'

Trudy felt her fingers close around her pencil so hard she was surprised it didn't snap.

Mindful of the Inspector's warnings not to say a word, however, she managed to hold on to her temper – and her tongue – and remained silent. But it was a bitter pill to have to swallow.

'Now, about the day Mr Chadworth drowned,' Jennings said, making His Lordship sigh.

'Must we go over all that again? I've said I think that Porter creature was there. Ask some of the others, why don't you? I'm sure they can confirm it,' Lord Jeremy said, the epitome of boredom.

'Yes, my Lord. But if you'll just bear with me...'

Eventually, Lord Littlejohn's solicitor arrived on the premises, and, appalled at what he'd said so far, promptly brought the questioning to an end.

Trudy wondered cynically who was more relieved – the Duke's son or her DI. Clearly, he was unhappy to have such an eminent man in his office, making statements that might later come back and bite them both.

It was decided Lord Littlejohn would return to his rooms with a PC, hand over the bottle of champagne, and then stay the night at his college before going back to London in the morning. That way, if they needed to put any follow-up questions to him after their interview with Reginald Porter, he would remain available.

A few minutes later, when Trudy (again allowed to stand at the back of the interview room and take notes) first saw their prisoner, she could tell just by the set, mutinous look on his face that they would be getting very little out of him.

And so it proved.

Reginald Porter would admit to 'taking a walk' across Port Meadow on the day Derek Chadworth died, before returning to work, and that was all. And he openly defied them to find anyone who'd seen him in the river, or walking away from it with wet clothes, during the hours of the student picnic.

'Clearly, he's confident he wasn't seen,' DI Jennings said with disgust when they were back in his office. 'Or else, he had nothing to do with the boy drowning, and it was an accident after all,' he added sharply, giving her a gimlet glance.

'Yes, sir,' Trudy said. 'But Dr Ryder is sure it's murder.'

'Is he?' Jennings said flatly. 'Well, type up your notes, and then you can start talking to the students at that picnic again. How many of them saw a man of Porter's description, and what was he observed doing?'

'Sir,' Trudy said, in some dismay, 'most of them will have "gone down" by now and be scattered around the country.'

'Then get on the telephone, WPC Loveday,' he said grumpily. Then, relenting wearily, added gruffly, 'You can ask PC Broadstairs to help you, if you like.'

'Yes, sir,' Trudy said with a sigh, her lips twitching. Well, that would please the blue-eyed boy – being told he had to help *her* out on *her* investigation!

But she had barely sat down at her desk (let alone had time to give Rodney the good news!) when the telephone rang.

When she answered it, she recognised the coroner's voice at once.

'Trudy, can you come to my office right away? Something's come in the post that you need to see.'

'Yes, all right,' she agreed eagerly, conveniently forgetting her DI's orders. 'In fact, there are some things I need to tell you as well. You won't believe all that's happened…'

'Well, stop wasting time and get over here then,' Clement Ryder said abruptly and rang off.

Trudy stared at the buzzing telephone receiver in her hand, and grimaced. 'Yes, sir, Dr Ryder, sir,' she said.

But she was already grinning.

Outside, she grabbed a station-house bicycle and set off, pedalling furiously.

Things were coming to a head all right. She could just feel it!

And she was really looking forward to hearing just what it was that had put the excitement in the coroner's voice for once. For she was sure she'd be able to top it!

She turned into Floyds Row a little while later and left her bicycle leaning against a red-brick wall not far from the mortuary, then all but ran towards Dr Ryder's office.

His secretary didn't even leave her seat to show her through, so common a visitor was she becoming nowadays.

Clement looked up as she burst into his office, her cheeks flushed, her eyes shining. 'You'll never guess what's been happening!' she breathed, before he had a chance to speak.

Throwing herself into the chair in front of his desk, she began to brief him, her words tumbling out of her mouth so fast it was all she could do to be coherent.

Clement listened with a satisfying and absorbed attention, only interrupting her to put in a question or two where she hadn't been totally clear.

When she was finally finished, he nodded and smiled, all but rubbing his hands in glee. 'Yes, things are definitely progressing. Now, come and read this and tell me what you think,' he encouraged her.

And so, with a sense of anticlimax, Trudy got up and went to stand beside him, leaning in closely to read the letter lying on the blotter in front of him.

As she did, he breathed out, and a strong smell of mint hit her nose.

For a second, her heart stuttered. Breath mints! He'd been sucking breath mints – just before she'd come in, going by the strength of the peppermint aroma. All that old PC Swinburne had said about secret drinkers suddenly flooded back to her.

So did that mean the coroner had actually been drinking in his lunch hour? That wasn't normal, was it? Most people didn't drink in the middle of the day, at work. Not unless they had a problem with alcohol…

'You'll probably be struck at once by the same thing I was,' Clement said, snapping her painful thoughts back to the matter in hand.

Forcing herself to focus on the letter, she began to study it carefully. It was written on nice notepaper, and with a very fine, copperplate, flowing hand. The first sentence revealed it had been

211

written in response to the coroner's newspaper appeal for more witnesses.

With a sigh, and forcing her buzzing mind to stop whizzing around and concentrate, she began to read out loud.

'Dear Sir,

In reference to the notice you put in the Oxford Mail recently, asking for anyone who had been in or around Port Meadow on the morning of the death of the student Derek Chadworth to get in contact with you.

I live not far from Port Meadow and, in my leisure hours, have occasion to walk sometimes along the river. On the morning of the fatal drowning, I had such occasion. However, I must state at once that, although I noticed, and heard, the rather ebullient party of students in its early stages, I neither witnessed the collision of the punts, nor saw or heard anything that caused me concern.

However, since you have asked for details of any and all extraneous information, I feel obliged to write this letter and make clear what I did observe that day.

I was walking along the pavement opposite the meadow and was just approaching a patch of the road where cars are apt to park, when I noticed a fisherman climbing up from the meadow and making his way to a parked, dark-blue, old Riley.

I'm afraid, since I don't own a car myself, I have very little to add about this car (for instance, I had no reason to note the number plate).

I noticed the fisherman in particular, as he appeared to be burdened not only with his fishing rods and tackle, but also carried a folding canvas wheelchair – the kind you saw in use after the war. I assumed he used this apparatus either to sit upon when fishing, or else to help him lug about his equipment.

As to the person himself, I didn't take much note of him, except to say that he was wearing one of those soft-canvas-type hats full of colourful fishing flies, and was wearing sun-shade glasses. He was not young, but not old, and was fairly tall and well-built. But that is all I can say.

I walked past him, and a little later his car passed me, heading towards the top road – that is to say, where he could either turn on to the Woodstock Road, and thus into the city proper, or else turn the other way – perhaps heading towards Kidlington or Yarnton.

I have no idea if this is of any help to you and can only hope that I haven't wasted any of your valuable time.

Yours faithfully,

Clive M Horton, Esq

'A bit long-winded and pompous, isn't he?' Trudy mused, returning to her seat thoughtfully. She watched the coroner as he picked up the letter and read it again. Did he look drunk, she wondered worriedly?

After a few anxious seconds' perusal, she had to say that no, she was sure he didn't. But when next he spoke, she listened carefully to see if any of his words were slightly slurred, or if he was being particularly careful with his pronunciation.

'Yes, he's a pedantic sort, sure enough,' Clement agreed, in his usual speaking voice. 'But that's what makes him an expert witness. I can see him taking a lot of time and care over this missive of his, and only stating exactly and meticulously what he observed. Which is very interesting, don't you think?'

Trudy, suddenly detecting a certain emphasis in his words, stopped worrying about whether or not her mentor had been drinking, and paid more attention to what he was actually *saying*. She sat up a little straighter on her seat.

'Is it?' she said, after a little while. 'We already know from the

213

witness who was out walking his dog that there were fishermen on the river that day. Two, in fact.'

'Yes. You had no luck tracking them down, I suppose?' Clement put in.

'No, I'm afraid not,' Trudy admitted. And then had to silently add to herself that she hadn't really tried all that hard.

'Hmm. The closed season for fishing is March to mid-June,' the coroner mused. 'So it could be our fishermen had anticipated the open season by a few days, and thus aren't keen to come forward and admit to it – lest they get hit with a fine, or have the water bailiff after them. Or it could all have a much more sinister interpretation. Don't you think?'

Trudy was slowly but surely getting the uncomfortable feeling that she was missing something – and maybe something obvious. But whatever it was, Clement had *not* missed it.

'I'm sorry. What exactly are you saying?' she was forced to ask.

'Why do you suppose a fisherman, already having to carry rods and tackle and things, would also lug about a folding canvas wheelchair?' the coroner wondered aloud.

'To sit on? As our Mr Horton suggested?'

'You're obviously not an angler,' Clement grinned, 'or you'd know that most of us take, at most, a little foldaway canvas stool, or else we have a padded top on top of a hardwood fishing case, and sit on that. I've fished man and boy for over forty years, and I've never seen an able-bodied fisherman with a wheelchair.'

Trudy sighed. 'Perhaps he had a friend who wasn't able-bodied?' she said. 'Didn't our witnesses describe two fishermen on the river that morning?'

'So you're saying that our friend in the old blue Riley... what? Pinched his friend's wheelchair? And left him sitting on the river-bank without any way of getting home?' Clement proffered, smiling widely. 'Our letter-writing friend makes mention of seeing only one man get into the car, remember?'

Trudy scratched her chin thoughtfully. It did sound odd, put like that.

'And there is, of course, something else that immediately leaps out at you from this letter, isn't there?' Clement said carefully, watching her closely.

Trudy shifted uncomfortably in her chair. Again, she felt as if she was being tested and was coming up wanting. The trouble was, she so badly wanted the culprit to be Lord Littlejohn that that was all she could think about. But unless she was way off track, all this talk about mysterious fishermen and wheelchairs was dragging the investigation in a far different direction.

With an effort, she forced herself to stop feeling angry, elated, frustrated and hard done by (which pretty much covered her day so far!) and forced herself to think logically instead.

A fisherman. A wheelchair. What else had the letter told them? An old, dark-blue Riley...

'An old, dark-blue Riley,' Trudy said slowly. 'That rings a bell. We've seen one of those recently. Now where... oh.' Her face clouded as she made the connection.

Clement nodded. 'Yes. There was an old blue Riley parked outside Keith Morrison's house in Islip, when we went to talk to him.'

Trudy sat up even straighter in her chair. 'Yes. But there must be a lot of dark-blue Rileys about,' she felt compelled to point out. 'And Mr Clive Horton,' she added, pointing at the letter, 'didn't get a registration number.'

'Agreed. But think, Trudy,' the coroner said urgently, his eyes sharp and glinting. 'We know Mr Morrison's daughter had once been a girlfriend of Derek Chadworth. Which, given his proclivities, means the odds have to be very high that he used her, as he so obviously used a lot of girls, to pose for his filthy photographs, and make money from peddling them.' He paused for breath and sighed heavily. 'We know Jennifer Morrison committed suicide late last year. We know, from the Porters, that Derek

Chadworth, not content with making money from pornography, wasn't above a bit of blackmail on the side as well. And if he was touching up a working-class man like Porter for a few bob here and there, how much more likely is it that he would have been fleecing a man with more means. Such as Keith Morrison?'

Trudy opened her mouth to object, then realised there was no objection to be made.

Clement smiled wanly. 'I know you desperately want the killer to be Littlejohn,' he commiserated with her softly, 'but just think back to the very beginning. What was our – all right, *my* – main problem with the case? What got me interested in it in the first place?' he urged her.

'You didn't like the way the students gave their evidence. How they couldn't seem to be pinned down to saying whether or not Derek was on the punt when it overturned,' Trudy responded promptly.

'Right. Now, let's take a step back, and look at things from Littlejohn's perspective for a moment,' Clement swept on briskly. 'You say this redheaded chap, Porter, had been harassing him for some time? Threatening letters and such?'

'Yes, that's right,' Trudy agreed slowly.

'So, he already knew somebody had it in for him,' Clement went on. 'He might have suspected it had something to do with Derek's extracurricular activities. Or, who knows, he might even have suspected that Derek himself was behind it. I don't expect loyalty and friendship were high priorities between Marquis Club members,' he put in dryly. 'But then, all of a sudden, Derek's body is found floating in the river within hours of him holding a punt and picnic party. A party where there'd been an accidental collision between punts. Now, what's his first thought going to be?'

Trudy sighed, seeing now all too clearly where the coroner was going with this. 'He thought the author of the threatening letters might have killed Derek. Either as a really frightening warning to himself, or out of revenge.'

'Exactly. And with the death of Chadworth, His Lordship could be in no doubt that his tormentor had to be someone like a husband or other family relation to one of the girls they'd corrupted. So, if you're Littlejohn, what do you do?' Clement urged her to think like the beleaguered lord. 'You don't know what the killer intends to do now. What if he's trying to frame you for Derek's death? If you say Derek definitely *was* on the punt, you lay yourself open to all kinds of suspicion. After all, you were in an ideal position to drown him! But, on the other hand, what if this *isn't* an attempt at framing you for murder? What if the killer simply meant to kill Chadworth, and now it's all over? In that case, all you have to do is lie low and wait for things to calm down. You don't want to say Derek definitely *wasn't* on the punt either, because that might throw the "accidental" theory to the winds and focus not only the police attention back on to you, but the killer's attention too. Because if the killer's sitting pretty, thinking he's got away with murder, he's not going to be pleased with the man who rocks the boat – so to speak.'

Trudy nodded. She could see all that clearly enough – and the bind Littlejohn had been in. 'So you need to sit on the fence and see which way the wind's going to blow,' she said flatly. 'That way, you can either come down one way or the other, depending on which suits your interests best. In other words, he was hedging his bets,' she said bluntly. 'And getting all his lackeys to help him do it.'

'This explains why some students were a bit hazy in their testimony in my court,' Clement said, nodding. 'And, you'll notice, it was the students with the least to lose, like our Miss Maria DeMarco, who'll soon be living abroad, or who had something of a conscience, like our divinity student, Lionel Gulliver, who were most clear that Derek *wasn't* at the party.'

Trudy nodded. 'Yes. I see. So you're saying Lord Littlejohn is innocent,' she said glumly. 'And that poor Mr Morrison is the killer?'

Chapter 26

'But does it really stack up?' Trudy complained, after a moment or two thinking about things. 'It's a bit of a leap to say that owning an old blue Riley makes you a candidate for murder. For a start, I shudder to think what DI Jennings would say if that's all we could offer up by way of evidence.'

Clement smiled. 'So let's see what else we can find, shall we? You agree, at least, that Morrison's motive is a strong one?'

'*If* he found out about the photographs,' Trudy, always willing to play devil's advocate, quickly pointed out.

'I think we can assume that. In fact, I don't think it's a leap too far to suppose that, just like Mr Porter, Mr Morrison had received photographs and a blackmailing letter in the post – and had been paying out for some time.'

'OK,' Trudy said, going along with it. 'But then his daughter commits suicide – poor thing, she can't stand the shame. And Mr Morrison's attitude quickly changes. He becomes bitter and vengeful.'

'And he does what Mr Porter had also attempted to do – that is, try to find out who's behind it all. But being a more intelligent man perhaps, he actually succeeds in learning the identity of his blackmailer.' Clement took up the baton. 'Perhaps he even

218

hires a private enquiry agent to find out who owned the PO box.'

'So now he knows who Derek Chadworth is.' Trudy pushed the theory along. 'And what... just plans to kill him? Just like that?'

'Why not? Murders have been committed for far less, as we both have cause to know,' the coroner reminded her, a shade grimly. 'Derek Chadworth made the simple but fatal mistake of pushing a grieving and desperate man too far. And paid the price for it.'

'OK. Let's accept all that for now. But how does Keith Morrison actually go about it?' Trudy asked. 'Right at the beginning, you yourself pointed out that it was hard to drown someone in a river – and not be seen. The victim – a young, fit boy – could struggle away, or you could be seen by anyone walking their dog in the meadow. Or even driving along the road and looking out of their car window for that matter.'

'Yes. But he didn't drown Derek in the river in Port Meadow,' Clement said quietly.

'*What?*' Trudy yelped. 'No – wait a minute. He must have done! He couldn't have drowned him in a bathtub, or a rain butt or something. The medical evidence said he had *river* water in his lungs.'

'Yes. With a lot of sediment too,' Clement agreed. 'But think back to our interview with Keith Morrison, Trudy. Where were we standing?'

'In his garden... with the river at the back of it! The river runs through Islip! Of course – I never thought of that,' she added dejectedly.

Clement smiled a little at her downcast face. 'But what's to say he wouldn't have been seen by any passing village dog walker, if he'd drowned him in the river there?' he pointed out. 'The same argument holds true, whether it be Islip or Port Meadow.'

Trudy gazed back at the coroner in frustration. 'But... if he didn't drown him in the river at the back of his house, what's the point of mentioning the garden?' she demanded, beginning to feel a little aggrieved. She knew it was because she was feeling stupid. Dr Ryder had it all figured out, and she still felt clueless. Unless of course…

'What else…' Clement began, but by now Trudy was already there.

'The pond!' she almost squeaked with excitement. 'He'd had the pond dug out with a trench to the river, to let the river water fill the pond. So the water in the pond would comprise river water as well! And because it was a pond, it was a more confined space and so had a lot of sediment in it, because it hadn't had the chance to settle properly! And,' she rushed on, 'it would be easier for him to drown Derek in a smaller body of water – there was far less likelihood of him being able to wriggle away!'

'Exactly,' Clement said, proud of her for being so quick on the uptake. 'So, say he lures Derek to his home – perhaps with the promise of a big, one-off payment for all the photographs. Or perhaps he uses a threat – he's found out Derek's identity, and unless he's willing to renegotiate the blackmail terms, he'll go to the police.' Clement waved a hand vaguely in the air. 'Whatever. We can sort out the details later. He lures Derek to his home that morning. Drowns him. Now he has to get rid of the body. How?'

But Trudy was already nodding. 'He dresses him up as a fisherman – with the hat and sunglasses to disguise the fact that he's dead. Manhandles him into the car – and puts an old wheelchair, which he must already have had at hand, into the boot. Perhaps his old mother or somebody had needed one in the past and he'd held on to it? Or, if he'd planned it all out, bought one beforehand? Anyway, he drives to the meadow and, when nobody is about, puts Derek's dead body into the wheelchair, wheels him to the river, and sets up on the riverbank – himself on the top of the bank, and Derek's body a little further down. Jimmy Roper, our dog walker, saw them there when he walked past. He must have had the wheelchair folded down and lying out of sight in the grass beside him.'

'Exactly.' Clement took up the tale. 'Then all he had to do was wait for the picnic party to begin, take the hat and sunglasses off the "fisherman" and slip the body gently into the water. Being careful not to get wet himself, of course, in case he should be spotted by someone later. And then all he has to do is pack up his gear and go back to the car.'

'Where our letter-writing friend saw him...' Trudy concluded. 'But wait a minute,' she suddenly objected, seeing a snag. 'How did he know there was going to be a punting accident at all? To account for the fatality?'

'Maybe he didn't?' the coroner said. 'Maybe he just got lucky.'

Trudy frowned. 'That's a bit of a coincidence, isn't it?' she said uncertainly.

The coroner sighed. 'Coincidences are a fact of life. Otherwise we wouldn't have invented a word for them,' he said dryly. 'There are also always uncertainties and loose ends,' he added wearily. 'It's only in books or in the cinema that everything is neatly wrapped up at the end with a ribbon. The point is – it fits and makes sense of all the evidence. And even if the punting accident hadn't happened, we'd still have been looking at that student party as the most likely cause of the dead body turning up down-river,' he pointed out reasonably. 'After all, if you find a dead student in the water, and then learn a party of drunken students had been mucking about swimming in the river only hours beforehand... Well, you'd assume the boy had most likely been part of the revelry and had got into difficulties and nobody had noticed. In the end, the punting accident was actually superfluous and was just one of those things that can sometimes come along and confuse the issue.'

Trudy nodded cautiously but didn't look totally convinced.

Clement smiled. 'Life, real life, has a way of being unpredictable and messy. And part of your job as a police officer is going to be

221

learning to sort the wheat from the chaff. What's important and needs to be followed up, and what isn't relevant and can be sidelined. Just keep your eye on the evidence and take nothing for granted.'

She knew Dr Ryder had vastly more experience of life than she did, so she was quite happy to listen to his advice.

'I think the Inspector is going to want His Lordship's role in all of this to be swept under the carpet,' she suddenly said, with a bitter cynicism that made the older man look momentarily sad. Clearly this case had shattered quite a few of her youthful ideals about her job, and her superiors in particular. But then, Clement thought sadly, that was almost inevitable, given the circumstances. Trudy Loveday was growing up fast – and learning even faster. She'd need to get tougher still if she wanted to make something of herself and her chosen career.

'And you'd far rather it wasn't,' Clement said with a grin. 'Me too. So I suggest we split up,' he said briskly, giving her no time to brood. 'I'll tackle Mr Morrison – see what he has to say for himself and test the waters. You need to go back to Lord Littlejohn and warn him he may still be in danger.'

'What!' Trudy yelped. Then, 'Oh, do I *have* to?' she wailed. 'There's nothing to say Mr Morrison – if he is the killer – even knows Lord Littlejohn exists. Let alone intends to make him his second victim.'

The coroner looked at her thoughtfully, head cocked to one side. 'I know you have issues with our fair-haired Adonis, but do you really think you'd feel better if you allowed Keith Morrison to murder him?'

Trudy went slightly pale. Then sighed. Then got up. 'His Lordship went back to his college. I daresay there's a good chance he's still there – in his rooms.'

But she spoke without much enthusiasm, and wondered, a little while later, as she watched the coroner driving off to confront their potential murder suspect, whether or not she was doing the right thing in letting him go alone.

Chapter 27

Lord Jeremy Littlejohn was indeed in his room. He'd handed over the bottle of champagne to the forces of law and order and, now he was once again alone, busy celebrating his troubles finally being at an end by steadily consuming a half-bottle of very fine cognac.

Thus, he was feeling distinctly and pleasantly squiffy when he heard a knock at his door. Taking another swig of spirit from a very fine, bulbous glass that was nearly two hundred years old, he walked unsteadily to the door and threw it open.

Clement Ryder made good time to Islip. But Keith Morrison wasn't there. At this time of day, his wife informed him, he was at his office. However, she willingly gave him the address.

Cursing himself for not thinking of that, and saving himself both a trip and some time, Clement got back in his car and set off back towards the city.

Trudy Loveday pedalled determinedly towards Littlejohn's college with a hard and set look on her face. No matter what happens, she told herself resolutely, I will *not* let him get under my skin. I will *not* lose my temper. It was a mantra she repeated to herself all the way to the lodge gates.

Luckily, the porter remembered her from her previous visit and, since she was now back in uniform, was happy to remind her of Littlejohn's room number and the location of it. She thanked him politely, crossed the quad, stomping along with a grumpiness that was almost comical, and sprinted up the narrow, stone, spiral staircase.

At the top of a small landing she was rather surprised to see His Lordship's door standing a little ajar. She pushed it open quietly, and then froze for a second as she heard an odd sound. It was a sort of scuffling, scraping noise that was now and then interrupted by an even odder, almost gargling sound.

For a rather hysterical second, she wondered if she might be catching the Duke's son during a session of gargling with mouth-wash. She almost smiled at the thought of the outrage on his face if she should catch him out doing something so plebeian (she'd looked the word up) as brushing his teeth! She could well imagine that he guarded his public persona avidly. He didn't dress so ostentatiously in white all the time, and maintain those striking fair locks of his, without knowing the impact they made. And as for that boneless, irritating, nonchalant way he went about things, and all the time with that smug, superior look on his face…

To catch him out actually spitting into a sink would be too good to be true!

All amusement fled, however, as she stepped through the doorway, past the coat rack that stood to one side of the entrance, and turned into the room proper.

For a moment, it felt as if time stood still, allowing her to make sense of the tableau confronting her. The first thing her stunned brained noticed was Lord Jeremy Littlejohn's face – mostly because it was such a startling shade of puce, beginning to turn slightly purple. His eyes were bulging and bugged out, and his mouth was gaping open in a wide O. He looked so ugly, and so unlike his usual handsome self, that she almost didn't recognise him.

While her brain was looking for an explanation for this oddity, the second thing she noticed was the broad back and shoulders of the second man in the room, who faced away from her.

The third thing she noticed was his large hands, wrapped around the younger man's throat.

It must have taken her less than a second to process it all, but it felt like much longer. But even as Trudy felt herself lunge forward, her brain was racing ahead of her, summoning up all her memories of her police training and what she needed to do in a situation such as this.

She wasn't aware of her limbs moving, but they were.

Get out your truncheon. Make sure you have a firm grip on the handle.

Lift it.

Remember to choose the best contact point – go for the arms! The arms!

It's imperative you break the man's grip and allow the victim to breathe.

Bring the truncheon smartly down directly across the lower forearm – it doesn't matter if you break the ulna.

It was almost as if Trudy could actually hear her trainer's voice in her head – a calm, beefy, retired sergeant who'd been the veteran of many a quelled riot in his time.

Once contact between victim and attacker is established, remember to go for the 'put down' blow.

Trudy wasn't really aware of moving or of obeying the set of instructions she could hear in her head. She was vaguely aware her heart was racing, and she was sweating as adrenaline raced into her bloodstream. She thought she might even be panting a little. But all of that seemed irrelevant.

And when the bigger man bellowed with pain, half-crouched, and began to turn around to face her, she was already reversing her truncheon in her hand, so that the rounded end was now pointing outwards. So that when Keith Morrison – *of course it was Keith Morrison, Trudy thought fatalistically* – turned to direct the force of his attack on to her, she simply chose her spot and thrust the truncheon, rounded head first, right into his solar plexus.

From giving out a painful bellow as the truncheon had slashed across his arm, his breath now went out of him in a noisy whoosh, and he collapsed onto his hands and knees, retching and whooping for breath.

He swayed a bit, then slowly toppled over onto his side, his knees tucked up protectively around his stomach.

He was trying to breathe, but finding it hard.

Knowing the immediate danger was now past, Trudy turned next to look at the victim. Littlejohn, too, had fallen to the floor and was finding it hard to breathe – but already, although still red-faced, that distressing blue-purple look was fading, and she could see, with relief, that he was getting air into his lungs.

But a person who'd been manually strangled could still die if their bruised airway started to swell, she remembered. So she needed to act fast!

As the threat receded, so too did the preternatural calm she'd been feeling, and she began to feel herself begin to shake in reaction. Grimly, she fought it off. She needed to stay in control.

She looked around quickly for a telephone, knowing a man of His Lordship's status was bound to have had one installed. Not for him the indignity of having to go down into the communal hall and have any passer-by listening in on his conversation. She saw it at once, on a small table beside the window, went to it and immediately rang for an ambulance.

It was only then, and beginning to feel distinctly shaky and weak in the knees now, that she sat down abruptly in a chair, and began to laugh.

She didn't laugh for long, of course. She recognised it for what it was – a sign of shock – and, as such, something that had to be warded off.

She took several deep breaths and forced herself to think, all the while keeping a wary eye on Keith Morrison, who was still lying on his side and hugging his knees to his chest and gasping on the floor.

There had to be something she should be doing. What was it... what... of course!

With a hand that still trembled slightly, she drew the telephone to her once again, and rang the station.

DI Jennings listened in stunned silence as she gave her report, ordered her to do nothing and touch nothing until he arrived with reinforcements, and hung up.

Over in his corner on the floor, Lord Jeremy Littlejohn began to be spectacularly sick.

Trudy watched this disgusting spectacle with a great deal of satisfaction.

Then she watched nervously as Keith Morrison put out a hand underneath him and rose slightly higher onto one side. He looked over at her.

'I'm sorry,' he said, wheezing painfully. 'I never meant to frighten you. You're the same age as my daughter would have been...' He shook his head sorrowfully. 'I didn't hurt you, did I?' he asked contritely.

Trudy found herself shaking her head.

'I'm glad. Men who raise a hand to a woman should be shot,' he said simply, between painful breaths. It was clear, after the blow to his stomach, that he was having trouble breathing without pain.

For a second she felt absurdly guilty for having hurt him. Then, realising she had to get her act together and act like a proper police officer with her duty to do, she said carefully, 'Mr Morrison, tell me what happened that day. You did kill Mr Chadworth, didn't you?' she added encouragingly, almost holding her breath now, in case she frightened him out of talking.

But she needn't have worried. All the fight had obviously gone out of him now.

'Oh, yes,' he admitted simply enough. 'I killed him all right. I don't regret it, even now.'

'Because of what he'd done to your daughter,' she said softly.

'Yes. I found out who he was, you see. I'd been paying blackmail money for some time over photographs that had arrived in the post with an anonymous demand for payment. But after my daughter killed herself because of… well, you know… she couldn't live with the shame… well, then I had to get revenge. Whoever had lured her into posing for those vile photographs had as good as murdered her! So I hired a detective to watch the post-office box drop where I sent the money.'

'And so you got the name of your blackmailer,' Trudy said, nodding. 'And once you knew who it was, you began to make your plans?' She egged him on gently and very unobtrusively, writing it all down in her notebook.

She was glad that Keith Morrison was now staring blankly down at the carpet in front of him, and didn't see what she was doing. Clearly, he was going back over things in his mind, lost in another time and place.

'Yes. It must have given him a nasty shock to find out I knew his identity! But I lured him to my place on the promise of giving him one final massive payment. I knew the greedy devil wouldn't be able to resist that,' he mumbled bitterly. 'I told him we'd meet in the open, in my garden – that way he'd feel safe. He knew he could always outrun me if I cut up rough – he was younger and faster than me by a long shot. And he was so cocky – thought he was invincible. But I was way ahead of him. I'd had the pond built special, you see – in advance. Getting him anywhere near the river would have been too risky – we might have been seen by a villager walking his dog or what have you. And Chadworth might have been too leery to go near a large body of water. But a little garden pond? He never gave it a thought. I could see he didn't,' he added, disgust lacing his tone now. 'So all I needed was to gradually get close enough to him to make a grab for him and then...' Morrison's face twisted savagely. 'Believe me, once I'd got my hands on him I had no compunction about drowning him like you would a rat in a rain barrel.'

Over in his corner, Lord Jeremy Littlejohn had fallen into an appalled silence as he listened to this confession. No doubt it was coming as a salutary lesson to the spoilt, blueblooded youth. Life wasn't one long party after all.

'I'd always planned to dump the body in the river somewhere far away from Islip, and had bought a second-hand wheelchair the previous week,' Keith Morrison continued, then suddenly, shockingly, gave a harsh bark of laughter. 'And can you believe it, when we met, out there by the pond, the dirty little bastard actually told me he couldn't stay long because he was going to a student picnic in Port Meadow?'

He looked up at her in amazement, as if inviting her to share in his incredulity, and she quickly stopped writing in her notebook to look back at him. 'That must have made you really angry,' she said softly. And not without genuine sympanthy.

'Oh, it did. The thought of him quaffing champagne and living the high life while my poor girl was cold in her grave...' Keith shook his head. 'But in the end, it almost felt as if providence was giving me a nudge. You know – as if it was meant to be. For suddenly I saw how ideal it all was. I could dump his body further downriver from Port Meadow and everyone would assume he'd simply drunk too much or got pulled under by some weeds or something. It just felt so right, as if it was...' He grappled for words, but couldn't seem to find them.

'Poetic justice?' Trudy offered helpfully.

'Yes. Just that. Exactly that!' he agreed eagerly. 'Anyway...' He turned now to lie fully on his back and stared up at the ceiling, and Trudy quickly began to scribble his confession down again. 'I reached into my pocket as if to bring out the money, and of course Chadworth stepped closer to look, eager to get his hands on it, I suppose. And I just reached out suddenly and grabbed him and that was that. He let out a yell, but I quickly put my hand over his mouth, and then I dragged him kicking and screaming to the pond and held his head under. He might have been quicker and faster than me, but I have more heft and muscle. The murdering, dirty little swine couldn't wriggle free of me.'

Trudy swallowed, feeling faintly sick now. Over in his corner, Lord Littlejohn began to retch anew too.

'When I lifted his head up to see if he was dead, the dirty little rat begged for his life, and confessed to it all,' Keith carried on, sounding exhausted now – as if he wanted nothing more than to roll over and go to sleep. 'He also tried to divert some of the blame in order to save himself. That's when he told me all about how his high-up friends posed in his dirty pictures too, and encouraged him to find more girls to corrupt. He was really anxious to tell me it wasn't his idea, and that the real moving power in their dirty games had always been this blueblooded parasite here.' At this point, he lifted his head far enough to glance up and across to the still-prone figure of Lord Jeremy Littlejohn, who froze and stared back at him, white-faced and aghast.

'And so His Lordship became your secondary target.' Trudy nodded. 'Yes, I can see how he would,' she added, trying to keep her voice calm, but shooting the blond-haired man a hard, dark look.

If possible, Lord Littlejohn went even whiter.

'Yes,' Keith agreed with a heavy sigh. 'When you and the coroner came asking questions, I realised you might know more than I'd thought and that I might not have as much time as I'd hoped to plan a second, proper murder. So I decided to take a chance and do it quickly instead. I waited until the porter had stepped out of the lodge, and then I came here, to Littlejohn's room. I planned to stay here all day after doing the deed, and make sure I hadn't left any fingerprints or clues behind, then sneak out after dark. From what Derek Chadworth said before dying, I knew His Lordship was rotten through and through, and that the chances had to be good that there would be a fair few people with a motive for killing him.'

Keith sighed heavily and rubbed a hand tiredly across his eyes.

Trudy, still holding Lord Littlejohn's appalled eyes, gave a slow, bitter smile. 'I'm sure you're right, sir,' she said flatly. 'Had we found His Lordship's body, I'm sure we'd have had an embarrassment of suspects, all with any number of reasons for wanting him dead. And so you hoped the true motive would never be traced back to you?'

In reply, Keith Morrison turned his back on her and began to cry quietly.

And Trudy was very glad, at that moment, to hear the police sirens approaching the entrance to the college. Finally, reinforcements had arrived.

Chapter 28

'So, did we get it right?' Dr Clement Ryder asked her, about an hour later. 'Our reconstruction of the crime?' They were in the station house, standing outside the main office in a small corridor, where it was quieter and less manic.

'Yes,' Trudy said wearily, leaning one shoulder against a wall. And told him all about it.

Now it was all over and Morrison was being processed, she just wanted to go home to her mum and dad and cuddle up to the cat. Which was impossible, of course. She had her notes to type up and the Inspector was bound to want to debrief her.

She only hoped she had enough energy left to do it all.

Clement looked at her with some concern. She looked so very washed-out. But he knew better than to suggest she go home and get some rest.

She wasn't the sort to appreciate being mollycoddled, he thought, feeling proud of her.

Trudy yawned hugely, then looked suddenly pensive. 'He's going to hang, isn't he?' she said, a shade forlornly. 'Mr Morrison? It seems so sad. He loses his daughter and now he's going to die as well. His poor wife! What she'll go through!'

The thought of Mrs Morrison's pain reminded her of the pain of another wife she'd met recently – the wife of the hit-and-run victim lying in a coma at the hospital. Two women – two such very different tragedies. 'Life really isn't fair, is it?' she said sadly.

'I shouldn't be so quick to assume the worst, if I were you,' Clement warned her quietly, casting a quick look over his shoulder to make sure they couldn't be overheard. 'Between you, me and the gatepost, I wouldn't be at all surprised if some sort of deal wasn't done about all this.'

'A deal? What do you mean?' Trudy demanded, feeling suddenly alarmed.

'The Duke is a powerful man,' the coroner said simply. 'He's not going to want it to come out that his son was consorting with a known pornographer and blackmailer. I can see him, the legal powers that be and your DI Jennings and his superiors all getting together and offering Morrison a deal. Maybe offer him an insanity plea, perhaps? You keep quiet about your motive, and we'll make sure you avoid the noose. Something along those lines, anyway.'

'Do you think he'd take it?' Trudy asked, not sure whether to be appalled or glad.

'Wouldn't you? If you were in his shoes?' Clement asked pragmatically.

'Can they get away with that?' Trudy asked, aghast.

'Why not? The only people who might protest about it and kick up a fuss would be Derek's parents. I don't suppose they'll be happy to see their son's killer only get a life sentence. But on the other hand, do you suppose they'll want the true story of their son's actions coming out in court for all the world to hear – and the newspapers to gloat over? If you were them, would you rather have your son avenged – and be revealed as a heartless, grubby little pornographer and blackmailer? Or would you rather let him rest in peace, with his reputation intact?'

Trudy sighed. It was all so complicated and muddled. And she felt so tired! 'On the one hand, I feel so sorry for Mr Morrison and his wife. They've been through so much. And part of me persists in feeling that, somehow, Derek Chadworth was such a bad person that...'

'He deserved what he got?' Clement finished for her bluntly. And was heartily glad when she instantly shook her head.

'No. No, I wasn't going to say that... but... I don't know. I don't *want* to be responsible for what happens to Mr Morrison either. The thought that he might hang because of me is awful!'

The coroner looked at her sadly. She looked all done in. He wanted to pat her on the back and tell her everything would be all right. But he couldn't. Nor could he protect her from the harsh realities of life as a police officer either. For the simple truth was that, if she did her job properly, people would go to prison because of her. They might even hang too.

'Poor Trudy,' he murmured. 'This has been a tough case for you, hasn't it? You're learning your superiors have feet of clay, and justice, truth and "right" aren't as clear-cut as you once thought. Is it making you re-evaluate your choice of career?' he asked softly.

Tired, shocked and dispirited as she was, her chin came up instantly.

'No,' she said emphatically. And then, with great dignity, 'I'm not a child, Dr Ryder. I know life isn't black and white. I just...'

'Don't like the grey areas much.' He grinned back at her. 'Not many of us do, Constable Loveday. And talking of grey areas—' he became rather more solemn '—I take it DI Jennings *is* going to try and trace Reginald Porter's missing sister? I know everyone's been saying she ran off to London, but now we know a bit more about Derek, her disappearance might turn out to be rather more sinister...'

'Oh, no, that's all right,' Trudy reassured him quickly, glad to have some good news for once. 'The Inspector did get on to

London a little while ago, but they quickly traced her. Apparently, she was given a warning just recently for soliciting, so she was already on their books,' she added, a little sadly. 'It seems her dream of becoming a star of the stage hasn't worked out like she hoped. I only hope her brother doesn't find out what she's been up to.'

'Who's going to tell him?' the coroner asked dryly.

'Nobody, I hope. It seems she's going to come back home for a bit,' Trudy said with a grin. 'I think, from what the London police said, she was quite relieved to be found and have an excuse to give up on the London dream for a while. You know, her mum needs reassuring and wants to have her home for a bit, and all that. But I wouldn't be at all surprised if Becky doesn't stay home for good. At least her brother will be pleased!'

'So,' he added briskly, straightening up and beginning to put his hat neatly back on top of his head, 'can I take it that, the next time I feel the need for a police liaison, you'll still want the job?'

'Oh, yes,' Trudy said eagerly, not even having to stop and think about it. For the truth was, working with the coroner, no matter what problems or compromises it involved, was still a hundred – no, a *thousand* – times better than doing the unimportant 'make-do' jobs DI Jennings always assigned her.

But then her face fell. 'But I think, after all this mess… the dirty pictures, the potential scandal and whatnot… I can't see DI Jennings assigning me to you again,' she admitted forlornly.

But Clement Ryder grinned broadly. 'Oh, I wouldn't be so sure of that if I were you,' he said, eyes twinkling. 'After all, you now have a duke in your corner who owes you the odd favour or two. You did save his son's life, remember?'

'Oh,' Trudy said, a bit blankly. 'But I don't think…'

'And once I've had a quiet word in the Chief Constable's ear, you might even see a police medal for bravery winging its way towards a certain probationary WPC who tackled a dangerous criminal all on her own.'

Trudy blinked. 'But I wasn't at all brave,' she protested.

'I don't think many people would agree with you on that,' Clement objected. 'And if any honours or commendations *do* come your way,' the old man advised her sagely, pushing on quickly before she could interrupt with more protestations, 'you'd do well to just accept them and say "thank you very much". After all, you're going to need all the advantages you can get if you're going to make Detective Inspector yourself one day,' he added with a grin.

Trudy blinked. Was it possible that she could rise that high?

Clement, seeing the sparkle come back to her eyes, doffed his hat at her, grinned and walked away.

A minute or so later, DI Jennings came out of the interview room and saw her lurking in the corridor.

'Loveday!' he bellowed. 'What are you still doing here? Get yourself back to hospital duty at the Radcliffe Hospital. That hit-and-run victim looks like he's going to make it after all, and is about to regain consciousness. When he does, I want you right by his side, taking notes.'

That would keep her out from under his feet while he and his superiors sorted out this whole Morrison/Chadworth/Littlejohn mess. And one thing was for certain, Jennings fumed – if WPC Loveday thought she'd be allowed any access to the rest of the case, just because she was the one who'd broken it wide open, she was sorely mistaken.

He glowered at her, just waiting for her to object to the assignment, and looking forward to giving her the good tongue-lashing he was already rehearsing in his head.

'Oh! Oh, sir, I'm so glad!' Trudy gasped instead, beaming at him. 'That's wonderful news! I felt so sorry for his wife. I'll get right over there now, sir,' she promised happily, dashing into the office for her satchel and accoutrements, and then racing back out for her bicycle.

This – helping people who had been hurt, and catching the

people who did the hurting – this was what she'd joined the force for!

Jennings, struck speechless by her joy, could only watch her in bemusement as she bolted through the door.

Acknowledgements

I'd like to thank all those who were willing to share with me their memories of the 1960s and Oxford.

Keep reading for an excerpt from *A Fatal Flaw*...

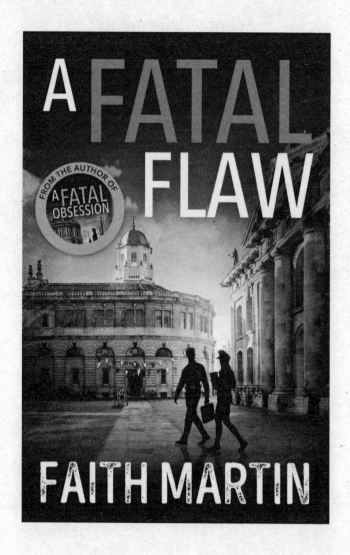

Oxford, England, 1960

PROLOGUE

The fine September morning had dawned that day with a very welcome and concealing mist. Even so, as a figure slipped cautiously into one of the many churchyards that were scattered about the city, it looked around quickly.

The clock in the bell tower was yet to chime six. Unsurprisingly, there was no one else out and about so early, save for the stray milkman or conscientious dog-walker. Yet the figure – who was dressed in a rather disconcertingly ghostly-looking pale-grey mackintosh – nevertheless made sure that the attached hood was up and pulled well forward, thus concealing their face.

A lone blackbird perched on a gravestone gave its familiar chinking alarm but the figure in grey ignored it, making quickly but carefully towards the oldest part of the graveyard. Here the stones were made illegible by lichen and time, and an ancient yew tree survived in defiant and baccate splendour.

The only living inhabitant of the graveyard looked anxiously around, making sure that their next action would remain unseen and forever secret, before reaching out and plucking several choice, wax-like red berries.

These precious berries were quickly picked and thrust into a small brown paper bag, which was then hidden out of sight in one of the mackintosh's large side pockets.

The anonymous figure in grey paused at the churchyard gate and peered carefully down the deserted small side street in either direction. As expected, nobody else stirred the early morning mist.

A clock in the city of dreaming spires chimed the hour, and the gatherer of berries paused to count them and smiled whimsically. Oxford. Here, in the hallowed halls of academe, the knowledge of the ages could be found. From the most obscure fact about a minor metaphysical poet, to the latest breakthrough in nuclear fusion. In this world-famous university city, with just a little time and effort, you could discover whatever you wanted to know, about any subject under the sun.

Like the properties of poison, for instance.

The figure slipped out of the churchyard gate and moved silently along the slick and damp pavement.

How many people knew that yew berries were poisonous? And of those that did, how many of them ever gave it a single passing thought that they could be so significant?

People were so complacent; so ignorant and oblivious to the ugliness in the world. So long as they were all right, and their own small personal universes were running smoothly, they cared little for anything or anybody else.

But as the person in the mackintosh headed quickly but cautiously for home now that the precious cargo had been safely harvested, they began to smile and nod. For soon the whole city would be made aware of just what the fruit of the humble yew could do. Oh yes. There would be a fuss made then, all right.

People always sat up and took notice when the young and the beautiful began to die.

CHAPTER ONE

Grace Farley paused outside the garden gate of her old friend, Trudy Loveday, and took a deep breath. At just turned 22, she was a few years older than Trudy, whom she'd first met at their local primary school. But it had been a few years now since she'd last seen her, and she needed a moment or two to compose herself.

She was not at all sure that what she was about to do was the right thing. What if it all backfired on her? A worried frown creased her pretty, freckled face as she debated whether or not to just turn around and go back home.

Part of her was sorely tempted to do just that. After all, so much could go awry, yet things were getting increasingly desperate, and there was no doubt in her mind that she needed help. Everyone knew that Trudy had joined the police and was doing really well. Grace's Auntie May had heard from the hairdresser that Trudy had helped solved two murders. Mind you, everybody believed it was really one of the city's coroners who had been the true force behind the cases. But even so.

Grace, a pleasingly plump girl, with short, curly reddish-brown hair that lent itself nicely to the poodle cut she favoured, glanced around, knowing that she couldn't stand hovering outside the Lovedays' garden gate all day long. People would begin to notice and wonder, and that was the very last thing she needed. Drawing attention to herself could be disastrous. Besides, it was getting on for six o'clock, and would soon start getting dark, so she needed to get back to her mum. She'd promised to help give her a bath, and…

Realising that she was still putting the moment off, she determinedly pushed open the gate, marched up to the front door and before she could stop herself, firmly rapped the knocker three times.

She realised then that her hands were trembling visibly, and quickly thrust them into her coat pocket. In her head on the way over here, she'd rehearsed time and time again what she would say, but most of it was swept away when the door opened, and there stood Mr Loveday, Trudy's father. She knew he drove the buses, though not the one she took into work each day.

She forced a bright smile onto her face, and said, somewhat breathlessly, 'Hello, Mr Loveday. Is Trudy in?'

Frank Loveday looked down at the worried face of the girl looking up at him, her big grey-green eyes open wide and unblinking, and gave her a friendly smile in return.

'Grace! Long time, no see. Of course our Trudy's in. Come on in, Barbara's just put the kettle on.'

'Oh, I don't want to put you to any bother,' Grace said quickly, stepping into the small hallway, and then following him down the little corridor to the back, where the kitchen was. Her own council house, when she'd lived in this area just a few streets away, had the exact same layout, as did their house once they'd moved to the other side of the city for her dad's job.

'Look who's come to pay a visit,' Frank Loveday said, ushering a suddenly shy and obviously nervous Grace into the kitchen. Cheerful yellow was the dominating colour, and the tiny space was filled with the appetising aroma of the shepherd's pie that the family had just consumed for their tea. Grace smiled uncertainly at Barbara Loveday, who was at the sink washing up. Quickly drying her hands on a towel, Trudy's mother bustled forward to give her a quick hug.

'Grace Farley! My, but you've grown into a pretty girl. Hasn't she, Frank?' Barbara demanded of her husband.

'She certainly has,' Frank agreed, taking his seat back at the kitchen table, where a copy of the local paper lay spread out at the sports section.

'How's your mother doing, Gracie?' Barbara asked, lowering her voice a few notches. 'Is she feeling any better?'

Her eyes sharpened in concern when the girl paled slightly, but Grace nodded bravely.

'Oh, well, you know, the doctors are doing all they can,' she said, with forced briskness. Then her eyes moved over the older woman's shoulder and met those of a tall, dark-haired girl with large pansy-dark eyes and a wide smile. 'Hello, Trudy.'

'Grace!' Trudy, who'd been drying the dishes as her mother passed them to her, put down her own towel, and correctly reading the appeal in her old friend's eyes said, 'I've had my bedroom redecorated since you moved away. Want to come and see it?'

'Oh, I'd love to,' Grace lied with a bright smile. 'I bet it's green. That's your favourite colour, right?'

'One of them.' Trudy laughed, and leaving her parents to listen to Tony Hancock on the wireless, she led her old school friend to the hall then up the narrow flight of stairs to her small bedroom at the back of the house.

Little more than a box room really, it had enough room for a single bed, a wardrobe and a small dressing table. As they had done when they were still both in pigtails, Grace and Trudy sat side by side on the bed without thinking, the years dropping away.

Although Trudy was glad to see her, her mind was nevertheless working overtime. The Farleys had left this area of town some four years ago now, and although she'd heard the odd bits and pieces of news about them from various sources, she had no idea what could have brought Grace back to her door.

She knew that her old school friend had a good job working as a secretary or book-keeper or something for some shop or business in the 'posh' end of town. She'd also heard, sadly, that Grace's mother was now rather seriously ill.

As if sensing her curiosity, Grace suddenly gave a wry smile, and began to nervously pleat and re-pleat the folds of the skirt she was wearing. It was a habit she'd had ever since she was little, and Trudy frowned, knowing that she only ever did it when she was upset or nervous.

'I suppose you're wondering why I'm here,' Grace said abruptly. 'I'm not sure, really, if I should have come at all. But I didn't know who else I could talk to. I mean, with you being in the police and everything.'

Trudy blinked in surprise. Whatever she'd expected Grace to say, it hadn't been that. For what on earth could someone like Grace want with the police? A more law-abiding, respectable family than the Farleys was hard to imagine.

'Blimey, Grace, that sounds ominous,' Trudy said, trying to force a touch of lightness into her voice. 'What's up?'

Uneasily, she wondered if it was possible that one of her family was in trouble with the law, and Grace was expecting her to help pull some strings? But if one of her relatives had been caught in some minor unlawful practice, there was really nothing Trudy could do about it. She was a mere humble probationary WPC – and as such, had no power or clout whatsoever. Even if she was inclined to do anything, which she wasn't, particularly. In her opinion, people who deliberately broke the law should take the consequences.

'It's about my friend, Abigail. Abigail Trent. The girl that died,' Grace said abruptly, the words shooting out of her mouth so fast and hard, that it was clear she'd been holding her breath without realising it.

For a second, Trudy was flummoxed. Died? It was nothing petty then, Trudy thought with dismay. Nothing to do with an unpaid fine, or a car tax 'misunderstanding' or...

And then Trudy suddenly remembered. 'Oh! The girl who died from drinking poison,' she said, somewhat belatedly putting two and two together. She'd read all about the case over the past few days in the Oxford papers, of course. A girl aged around 20 or so had drunk orange juice laced with some kind of poison and had sadly died because of it. The inquest was due to open any day now. 'Wasn't it something to do with a poisonous plant. Berries or something?' she said.

'Yes.' Grace nodded miserably. 'Yew.'

'That's right. And she was a friend of yours?' Trudy mused quietly. 'Oh, Gracie, I'm so sorry. It must have been awful. Did you know her well?'

'Sort of. I mean, not that well, but...' Grace sighed and took a deep breath. 'The thing is, Trudy, everyone's saying that she committed suicide. At work, in the neighbourhood, people you overhear chatting in the café or on the bus... You know how people gossip.'

Trudy nodded. 'Yes. These things tend to get around. Everyone seems to know everyone else's business. They're saying she was depressed and moody, I expect?'

'Well, see, that's just it,' Grace said flatly. 'I don't think she *did* commit suicide. To begin with, I don't think Abby knew anything about poisons, let alone which berries were poisonous or how to turn them into something that could kill. I mean' – the older girl twisted a little around on the bed, the better to look at her friend – 'I don't know anything about that stuff either, I'm not a chemist or what-have-you. I didn't even do science at school, and what's more neither did Abby! But don't you have to distil stuff like that, or put it through some sort of process before it becomes really lethal? Surely it can't be something as simple as just... I don't know, pouring some hot water over some berries and then drinking it. Can it?'

Trudy looked at Grace's big grey-green eyes and saw how troubled she looked, and shrugged helplessly. 'I don't know either.

But maybe it is? I'm sorry. But didn't she drink the stuff with orange juice to help mask the taste? That's what the papers said, anyway.'

Grace shrugged and sighed heavily. 'I think so. But I just know that Abby wouldn't have killed herself,' she insisted stubbornly.

'All right.' Trudy nodded amicably, not willing to argue. Clearly, her old friend believed she was right. But now that she was remembering more details, things didn't seem to quite bear out what Grace was saying.

Tentatively, she said, 'But didn't the people who were closest to her say that she was... well, rather moody? That she could be depressed sometimes? I think even her own mother was reported as saying that she could be a bit... intense?'

Grace again sighed heavily. 'Oh, that was just her way. She was only 19 after all, and yes, she could be a bit up and down. A row at work would get blown up out of all proportion, or a present from her boyfriend would have her walking on air. It was just her way. But that doesn't mean that she was suicidal!' Grace argued. 'Abby had great plans for her life. She talked about them often. And she enjoyed herself far too much to seriously want to die! For a start, she was looking forward to the beauty contest too much!'

Trudy blinked. She knew that a beauty pageant was being staged, of course, from the notices she'd seen around town, but it hadn't really registered with her much. 'Oh, she was in that, was she?'

Grace nodded, and with her hands restlessly folding and unfolding her skirt, began to speak rapidly.

'I work for Mr Dunbar, who owns Dunbar's Jams, Honey and Marmalade. You know, the factory up past Summertown?'

'Oh right,' Trudy said. 'You're his secretary or something?'

Grace gave a rueful smile. 'Hardly! I'm not that high up! I do the odd bit of book-keeping – petty cash mostly, and fetch the coffee, do the filing and some bits of typing that the other secretaries don't like doing... all tabs and... never mind that.' Grace suddenly waved a hand in the air. 'It's not important. What *is* important, is that last year Mr Dunbar came up with a plan to help promote his honey. He wanted to put Dunbar Honey up there with the famous Oxford Marmalade brand.' She paused to smile whimsically at this bit of obvious folly, and shrugged. 'So he came up with this idea of holding an annual Miss Oxford Honey beauty pageant.'

Trudy couldn't help but smile. Her friend, catching her look, laughed suddenly.

'I know – it's hardly Miss World!' Grace said, rolling her eyes a bit. 'But actually, it's quite a clever idea. All the papers will cover it, and Mr Dunbar knows someone who owns that old theatre just off Walton Street who's letting him hold rehearsals there for free. He's also agreed to host the beauty contest for the public one Saturday night next month. Tickets are already nearly sold out. That's one of the reasons why they decided not to cancel the event after Abby died. Everybody was so excited about it, it seemed a shame to call it all off. Not only that, he's got local shop owners putting up big prizes and acting as judges, so it's hardly costing him a penny.'

'He's obviously quite a businessman, your boss,' Trudy said, somewhat sceptically.

'Actually, he probably is,' Grace said flatly. 'But that's not really the point. I was asked to help out on the organising side of things, since I wasn't exactly indispensable in the office,' Grace laughed. 'And Mrs Dunbar...' For a moment the name seemed to catch in her throat, and then she smiled ruefully. 'Well, let's just say that Mrs Dunbar was adamant that her husband shouldn't spend time on the beauty contest or let it get in the way of the business of making honey!'

'Ah, I get it,' Trudy said with a wicked smile. 'She didn't want her husband spending too much time hanging around with pretty girls.'

Grace dragged in a large breath, but was obviously far too discreet to either confirm or deny her friend's interpretation of how she'd come to be the hands-on manager of the contest. 'So, anyway, a few weeks ago Mrs Dunbar drafted a piece for the newspapers, asking girls who lived in the city or within a twenty-mile radius, and who wanted to take part, to get in touch and sign up for the auditions. Obviously, they had to be over 18, but under 30 and well, er, they had to be, er…'

'Pretty and with good figures?' Trudy put in helpfully, when her friend seemed to struggle for a diplomatic way to phrase things.

Grace suddenly giggled. 'Well, you'd have thought that went without saying, wouldn't you? But some of the women and girls who turned up…' She rolled her eyes with yet another giggle. 'Well… let's just say that me and Mrs Dunbar and Mrs Merriweather – she's the old lady who's a Friend-of-the-Old-Swan-Theatre, and is helping us run the show – anyway, we had a bit of a job persuading some of them that they weren't… er… quite suitable for what we had in mind.'

Trudy shook her head. 'The tact and diplomacy must have been quite something!'

Again, Grace giggled. Then her face suddenly fell, as she remembered why she was there.

'Yes. Well… anyway, Abigail and her friend Vicky were one of the first ones to apply, and we signed them both up straightaway. Over the next week, we whittled the applicants down to about twenty or so. Actually, the process is still ongoing but, again, that's not what matters. The point is I got to know Abby, and… well, to put it in a nutshell, she was fairly confident that she had a good chance of winning. She was so looking forward to the competition night. She had stars in her eyes! What's more, she was so upbeat about her "talent" spot and she just loved trying on the evening gowns and… Trudy, there was just no way that girl killed herself,' Grace finished forcefully.

Her eyes were now open so wide, and were fixed on Trudy with such a glare, as if she thought she could make Trudy believe her by sheer force of will. 'And I don't know what to do about it. If they bring in a verdict of suicide, as everyone seems to think they will... it just won't be right!'

Her hands were shaking again, and Trudy reached out and held them firmly. 'Gracie, it's all right – just calm down a bit. But I don't quite know what you think I can do about it,' she told her gently. 'I'm just a probationary constable. And I didn't know this girl, or anything about the circumstances surrounding her death.'

'No, but you know this Dr Ryder man, don't you? He's a coroner, isn't he? Can't you ask him to help?' Grace asked quickly.

For a second or two, Trudy stared at her friend aghast. How could she possibly explain to her friend, who knew nothing about the police force and how its hierarchy actually worked, why her request was so impossible. For a start, if her boss, DI Jennings, ever found out that she'd gone behind his back about a case, he'd skin her alive! Especially since the Inspector was hardly a fan of the coroner.

But as if sensing what was coming, Grace got in first. 'Please, Trudy, can't you just speak to him? At least ask him to call me as a witness or something? I can testify to her state of mind, at least, can't I? Won't the inquest want to know that Abby wasn't feeling suicidal at all?'

'But, Grace, how can you be so sure?' Trudy asked helplessly. 'None of us know, not really, how someone else is feeling.'

Slowly, Grace's shoulders slumped. 'So you won't help?' she asked flatly, her gaze so accusatory that Trudy almost winced.

'It's not that I won't. It's that I can't,' Trudy tried to explain. 'I'm not even one of the officers assigned to the case,' she pointed out. 'And believe you me, my superiors... well, let's just say, they won't be in any hurry to listen to what I might have to say,' she added, a shade bitterly. The thought of the look that would cross her DI's face if she came to him with this tale was enough to make her shudder.

Seeing what she was up against, Grace decided that if she was in for a penny, she might as well be in for a pound, and took a deep, deep breath.

'It's not only this thing with Abby,' Grace said, sounding almost defiant all of a sudden. 'It's other things as well. At the theatre…' She paused, closed her eyes for a second, and then took the plunge. 'Things have been happening.'

'What do you mean?' Trudy asked sharply.

Grace shrugged, her eyes suddenly darting around the room so that they wouldn't have to meet Trudy's. 'Oh, just things,' she said, rather unhelpfully. 'Stupid things. Nasty little tricks… For instance, someone tied a string over the bottom step in the stairs that leads up to the stage, so that one of the girls took a tumble. Oh, she wasn't hurt – but she did have to rest her ankle for a few days, so she lost rehearsal time for her dance routine. And then something must have been added to one of the girls' jars of face cream which brought her skin out in a rash… It faded after a few days, but she pulled out of the competition anyway. Just silly little pranks like that.'

Trudy frowned. 'But isn't that likely to be a simple case of rivalry between the contestants? It sounds like the sort of mean tricks that some girl who wants to scare others into withdrawing from the contest might use.'

'Yes. That's what everyone seems to think,' Grace admitted reluctantly. 'But, Trudy, I'm not so sure. I have a bad feeling about it all. I think… Oh, I just wish you'd talk to your coroner friend about Abby! Perhaps you could come down to the theatre sometime, during rehearsals or something, and just take a look around? See if anything strikes you as… odd. But you mustn't tell anyone that you know me, or that I've been talking to you, because then I could lose my job,' Grace added hastily, suddenly clutching her arm and holding it in a tight grip. 'Mr Dunbar wouldn't like it if he thought that I'd been speaking out of turn. He's dead scared as it is that the papers will get to know about our little problems and give us bad publicity. So you mustn't come in uniform or anything… I know!' She suddenly beamed brightly. 'You could pretend to be thinking of applying to be a contestant or something. It would give you the perfect excuse for being there and having a look around. Oh, Trudy, please?'

Trudy, unable to resist the appeal in her friend's eyes, suddenly gave in. What could it really hurt, just to put her mind at rest? DI Jennings need never know about it. Besides, she was intrigued.

'OK. I'll go and see Dr Ryder and tell him what you've said. If nothing else, he can at least give us some advice. But I'm not promising anything mind!'

'Oh, Trudy! Thanks ever so much!' Grace leaned across and gave her a hug. 'Now, I've really got to get back to Mum,' she said. 'I don't like leaving her in the house for long with just Dad to look after her,' she admitted, and Trudy gave her a quick, fierce hug back.

'Of course!' she said, her voice suddenly thick with emotion. 'And I do hope your mother gets better soon,' she said. She simply couldn't imagine what she'd do, or how she'd feel or cope, if her own mother suddenly got so ill. The thought made Trudy feel quite sick.

She jumped up and ushered her friend downstairs. And with a quick 'goodbye' called out to the older Lovedays who were still in the kitchen, Grace was gone.

But as Grace Farley walked to the end of the street and caught the bus across town, she sat in her seat, swaying slightly and looking out at the darkening city with a growing sense of panic.

Had she done the right thing? What if it all backfired? What if Trudy didn't come through for her? Or worse yet, what if she did, but didn't get the results that she, Grace, so desperately needed her to get? And what if her old friend was really good at her job, and learned far more than was good for her?

Grace shifted on the seat, fighting back a growing sense of unease. What if she'd miscalculated, and it all went wrong?

For a long moment, Grace Farley felt chilled to the bone.

She could actually end up in prison.

Or worse yet! What would her tormentor do to her if it came out that she, Grace, had brought the police sniffing around the theatre?

And yet… And yet, the risk *had* to be worth it.

She simply had to get something on her persecutor, before… well, before things got totally out of control.

Trudy Loveday was the only one she knew who might be able to find such ammunition. But she'd have to watch her old friend closely.

Chapter 2

Dr Clement Ryder watched his hand, which was lying flat on the tabletop, and scowled as it began to twitch slightly. Grimly, he used his other hand to massage the palm, and after a while, the twitching slowly abated. But he knew it would be back.

He'd self-diagnosed himself as suffering from Parkinson's disease whilst still a surgeon in London, which had led to him resigning from his medical career and embarking on his new life as a coroner in Oxford.

Although, so far, he'd managed to keep his condition a secret from everyone – his friends, family, and work colleagues alike – he was well aware that he faced an uphill struggle in the years ahead to keep the secret safe, as the disease inevitably progressed and worsened. And the symptoms became more and more obvious.

But at least, being a widower and living alone now that both of his grown children were off living lives of their own, his domestic situation put him in a good position to keep his private demons strictly private.

Which was why he scowled somewhat ferociously as he heard the doorbell ring. Visitors were seldom welcome. He glanced outside, saw that it was nearly fully dark, and wondered who could be calling at this time in the evening.

Although he was a man of influence and power, and often socialised with Oxford's movers and shakers, his real friends were few and far between, and all of them knew that he wasn't the kind of man that you simply 'dropped in on' to have a chat and a nightcap with.

He got up somewhat reluctantly from his chair, a tall man at just over six feet in height, with a shock of thick silvery-white hair. He was a few years off his sixtieth birthday, but looked comfortably closer to 50. As he walked out into the hall, he watched his feet carefully. The stumbling uneven gait of a man in his condition was a dead giveaway to well-informed eyes, and he was glad to notice that, so far, he was walking as well as he'd ever done.

Perhaps, in the future, he might have to feign some sort of leg injury to cover up any falls or mishaps? Or a touch of fictional arthritis might fit the bill? It would certainly give him an excuse to use a walking cane. He'd have to give it some thought.

He opened his front door with a peremptory sweep, and then blinked in surprise as he saw the young, tall, brunette woman standing anxiously on his step.

Trudy Loveday had never called at the coroner's home before. On the previous two occasions that they'd worked murder cases, she'd always gone to his office to make her reports or to meet up with him.

She'd found his name and address in the phone book and hadn't been at all surprised to have to find her way to the prestigious area near South Parks Road, where he lived in a terrace of large, Victorian houses, in a leafy street not far from Keble College.

'Hello, Dr Ryder,' she said now, launching nervously into speech. 'I hope you don't mind me calling on you like this… If you've got company, I can always come back…' She half-turned, almost wishing he'd say that he had, so that she could go away again.

For now that she was here, she was feeling distinctly uneasy. It was one thing to be assigned as this important man's police liaison by her boss, but that was a whole world away from coming to his private residence, out of uniform, and begging for a favour. It smacked of presumptuousness, and as such, was enough to send her face flooding with colour.

Which was why she'd come over barely ten minutes after Grace Farley had left, as she'd felt that the sooner she got it over with, the less fraught her nerves would become.

'No, no, I'm alone,' he reassured her pleasantly. 'Come on in, Constable Loveday,' Clement said, using her title rather than her name, since he'd instantly picked up on her anxiety.

Trudy forced a smile and stepped inside a small but – to her eyes at least – still rather grand hall, with black and white tiles on the floor, and a large oval ornately-framed mirror set over a narrow console table. She noted the private telephone that rested on it and was once again reminded of the differences in their status.

If the Lovedays ever needed to make a telephone call, they used the phone box at the end of their street, like everyone else.

'Come on through to the study,' he said, indicating the door that stood open to their left. 'I was just about to make some cocoa,' he lied. 'Would you like some?'

'Oh, no thank you,' Trudy said instantly. 'I won't stay long, and I don't want to take up your time,' she insisted. But even as she spoke, she wondered if it was true that the coroner had been about to drink so innocent a beverage.

Once or twice in the past, she'd wondered if he drank too much. Occasionally she'd noticed one or two signs that might indicate intoxication. But she watched him now as he led her into a pleasant, book-lined room with large sash windows over-looking the tree-lined street beyond, and he seemed to be alert and sober.

'Take a seat,' he offered, indicating one of the green leather button-back chairs that sat in front of a walnut desk. He took his own seat behind it as Trudy, still feeling very much the supplicant, lowered herself into the chair.

'The reason I've come,' she began, launching into her story before she could give herself time to chicken out, 'is that I've just had a visit from an old friend of mine. And what she had to say… I thought you should know about it.'

'Oh?' Clement asked, clearly puzzled but also intrigued. Which was, Trudy hoped, a good sign.

'Yes. It's about the girl who died recently from ingesting poison – the yew berry case, and she—'

Clement Ryder quickly held up his hand. 'Before you go any further, let me stop you just a moment. That's one of my cases – I'm holding the inquest the day after tomorrow.'

'Oh. I rather hoped it might be one of yours,' Trudy admitted. 'It makes things so much easier.'

Clement smiled wryly at her. He'd come to know Trudy Loveday quite well during the past year, and had come to respect her ambition and intelligence, but she could still be heart-breakingly young and naive sometimes.

'It might, or it might not,' he said firmly. 'But it's not really the done thing to discuss details of an inquest before it's even started. And if you're here to ask questions about the case, I'm afraid I simply can't discuss it with you. Even if you've been assigned the case in your official police capacity…?' He paused delicately, one eyebrow raised, and Trudy quickly shook her head.

'Oh no, I'm not,' she confirmed. And didn't need to say any more. Both of them knew that her boss wouldn't have assigned her to work on such an important case since DI Jennings preferred her to do office work, make the tea, and hold the hands of female victims of handbag-snatchings or lost cats.

Letting her work on a case that involved actual police work wasn't something that would have occurred to him!

'No,' Clement agreed, a shade heavily and with an ironic glint in his eye. 'But even if you had been working the case—'

This time it was Trudy's turn to interrupt him, which she did, aware that she was blushing slightly.

'It's all right, Dr Ryder, I haven't come here to try and find things out. I'd never presume on our…' She found herself wanting to say the word 'friendship' and managed to alter her tongue just in time. 'Acquaintance. Actually, it's just the opposite. I've come here to tell you something that you might find relevant. Or not. I'm not really sure,' she said, suddenly feeling confused and not at all as confident as she had been that that this important man would be interested in Grace's opinion at all.

Suddenly, sitting here in this posh house and in this rather imposing room, Trudy began to wonder what she could have been thinking.

Had she been horribly stupid? When she'd set out, she'd been sure that, because he liked her and they'd got on well in the past, he would be glad to see her and interested in what she had to say. Now, she felt far less sanguine.

'Well, I won't know until I hear it, Trudy,' Clement said casually, amused by her sudden lack of coherence, and determined to put her at ease. She reminded him a little of a cat set down in an unfamiliar environment, and he was glad when she began to relax. 'So, tell me what it's all about then,' he advised her amiably.

Thus encouraged, it didn't take her long to recount the substance of Grace Farley's visit, and when she'd finished, she waited expectantly to see what he had to say.

Clement took only a few moments to process the information, and briefly consulted his memory – which, mercifully, was still functioning perfectly. 'The files on the case are all back at my office, of course, but I'm pretty sure Grace Farly isn't one of the witnesses on my list,' he finally admitted.

'Does that mean you can't call her as a character witness then?' Trudy asked, disappointed, and making Clement laugh softly.

'It's not a criminal trial you know,' he reminded her gently. 'I'll be calling the person who found her – which was her mother, I believe – along with medical experts and such like. And her best friend, I believe, who, presumably, will be saying much the same as your visitor?'

Trudy shrugged. 'I don't know if she will or if she won't. But Grace was really adamant that Abigail wasn't suicidal. I just thought you should know. And I promised Grace I would tell you, so…' She shrugged graphically.

Clement nodded. 'So now the ball's in my court, as they say. Both literally and figuratively speaking.'

She grinned, then looked wistful. 'I wish I could attend the inquest. I'm sort of interested now. But I don't think the Sergeant will let me have the time off! Not even if I make the case that it's all good experience for me.'

'Never mind. If you come round to my office when it's over, I'll fill you in,' he promised.

'Will you? Thanks so much,' Trudy said, already rising. He politely walked her to the door and was still smiling slightly as he shut it behind her.

Her youthful enthusiasm, as always, had lifted his spirits a little and helped lighten his mood. She might not have realised it, but the coroner was glad she'd come.

It wasn't until after she'd thanked him and was on her way back home, that Trudy wondered what he'd made of Grace's other concerns about the tricks being played at the theatre.

Had he been interested in that anyway? The rather catty goings-on of a bunch of would-be beauty queens couldn't have concerned him much.

In any case, it couldn't hurt to pop by the theatre herself one afternoon during rehearsals, just to satisfy her own curiosity. She knew from what Grace had said that the theatre's owner was happy for them to use the building during daylight, as long as they vacated the premises long before the evening performances began. Presumably the place didn't do matinees.

It sounded fun, in a way. She'd never seen a beauty contest being held before, and it had a certain appeal. All those pretty dresses and things. Mind you, she couldn't imagine stepping out in front of people just dressed in a swimming costume! The thought made her shudder.

But just to have a look around and put Grace's mind at rest – well, where was the harm in that? When Trudy had first started school, it had been a daunting time and the slighter older girl had been kind enough to take her under her wing. She'd even intervened once, when a playground bully had tried to push her into the sandpit. So far, she'd never been in a position to repay the debt, but now, finally, she could.

It never once occurred to her that by doing so, she might be putting her own life at risk.

Why would it?

Dear Reader,

We hope you enjoyed reading this book. If you did, we'd be so appreciative if you left a review. It really helps us and the author to bring more books like this to you.

Here at HQ Digital we are dedicated to publishing fiction that will keep you turning the pages into the early hours. Don't want to miss a thing? To find out more about our books, promotions, discover exclusive content and enter competitions you can keep in touch in the following ways:

JOIN OUR COMMUNITY:

Sign up to our new email newsletter:
http://smarturl.it/SignUpHQ

Read our new blog www.hqstories.co.uk

🐦 https://twitter.com/HQStories

🅕 www.facebook.com/HQStories

BUDDING WRITER?

We're also looking for authors to join the HQ Digital family!
Find out more here:

https://www.hqstories.co.uk/want-to-write-for-us/

Thanks for reading, from the HQ Digital team